I0723731

LUCK OF THE DEMON

STACIA STARK

CHAPTER ONE

Danica

"You should eat something," Vas said.

I didn't bother taking my eyes off the man lying in the bed in front of me.

"I'm not hungry." Even the thought of food made me nauseous.

Vas heaved a sigh from where he stood behind me. "If he were here, he wouldn't tolerate you wasting away like this."

"He *is* here."

Silence.

I reached out and stroked Samael's cheek. With his extremities slowly turning to ash, it was one of the few places I could touch without risking pieces of his body crumbling beneath my hand. But his cheek was cold. Cold and lifeless.

Vas was right. If Samael were awake… if my demon wasn't dying…

He'd likely be forcing food down my throat at this point.

The corner of my mouth lifted. Overbearing jackass.

"Fine," I said. "Let's eat."

Vas stepped forward. He must've arranged for the kitchens to make comfort food, because one of the servers wheeled in a cart loaded with chicken soup and what smelled like bread fresh from the oven.

I ignored the pitying look she sent my way.

I didn't need pity. I needed actionable advice and intelligent suggestions.

Vas handed me a tray and my stomach rumbled. The first mouthful almost made me throw up. The second made my hands shake with a sudden ravenous hunger. I dunked the bread and kept my gaze on Samael.

I needed to leave him soon. There was work to be done. Samael wasn't going to survive if I just sat here with my busted leg raised up on a chair while I felt sorry for myself.

My hands fisted at the thought of how we'd ended up here.

Two days ago, I was betrayed.

Cara turned on me. As far as Ben, Bruce, and Wes were concerned, I'd never expected anything other than duplicity from them. But Cara's betrayal had hit me like a fist to the face.

Of course, I'd also taken more than a few of *those* that night.

All four of them had worked together. They'd taken orders from one of Lucifer's demons, who'd promised them all kinds of things if they could just get me through the portal to the underworld.

Since– according to a prophecy– I was the only one alive who had a chance of killing dear old granddad, I would've likely been dead moments after I was pushed through the portal.

I'd held my own, considering how beat up I'd been. Rose killed Cara, Mella killed Bruce—I didn't think I'd ever get the image of her eating his heart out of my head—and I pushed Wes through the portal.

But the part I'd never seen coming—and I should've—was the Spell of Three performed on those who were working for the demons. Performed by none other than Gloria herself—Samael's black witch. She changed sides, and by now, she was likely up to no good in the underworld, if she hadn't already been killed.

If she *was* still alive, I'd make her beg for mercy before I killed her myself.

The Spell of Three was one of the nastier spells in existence. Entirely illegal, it involved the sacrifice of a sentient being—Gloria had used a gnome—and the spell itself was completely invisible. That meant that the person who got caught in it wouldn't know what had happened—until their power was reflected back at them… times three.

Samael had arrived just in time to find me wrapped in Naud chains with broken ribs, a dislocated kneecap, and a mage with a gun pointed at me. I couldn't blame my demon for going a little crazy.

All of the blame lay with me. I'd had all of the clues right in front of me, and I hadn't put them together.

Samael turned Ben to ash.

And the Spell of Three reflected back at him.

Even now, I don't know exactly what happened next. When I remember that moment, all I get are flashes.

Mostly, I see Samael's face, and the sick realization in his silver eyes as the spell hit him. That expression hadn't been sadness at his own fate. Even then I'd known it was because he was leaving me.

Those eyes met mine, and the last thing he said was my name.

At that moment, someone freed me from the Naud chains. I suspect I couldn't have achieved what I did next without the sudden flood of power that broke through the last of the suppression spell placed on me as a child.

I *reached* for his soul and tied us together, intertwining our fates. If Samael died, so did I. But most importantly, I bought us time. How much of it, we didn't know. Bael seemed to think I had a week or two, if we were lucky.

I placed my empty bowl back on the tray and studied Samael's forearm. Beneath the chalky black, an intricate gold mark proclaimed that he was mine. Just as I was his.

And we weren't going out like this.

Lia let out a low purr. She was curled up within a few inches of Samael's hand, but she seemed to know not to touch him.

"Danica?"

I blinked. I was staring into space. Vas held out his hand and took my empty tray.

"You should get some rest," he said.

I shrugged, shifting uncomfortably on my chair. I'd had surgery to relocate my kneecap, and Eldan had continued healing it every few hours so I could get back on my feet. But for now, I had to keep it elevated.

My voice felt croaky with disuse. "What's happening with the wand?"

We'd found a bone wand while we were looking for Riona, and I'd asked Samael's people to check it for prints and then attempt to trace who it belonged to. But by the time we knew it was Gloria's, she was long gone.

"They're using every known tracking spell on it. Your witch friend has also offered to help—Selina."

I attempted a smile. "Maybe she'll find something."

I wasn't hopeful. Gloria was either dead or in the underworld. Either way, finding her wouldn't help me save Samael.

"We need a plan," I said.

I felt a presence behind me and glanced over my shoulder. Kyla.

She attempted a smile, but it disappeared as soon as her gaze landed on Samael.

"I'm sorry, Danica."

"I'm going to fix it."

"*We're* going to fix it."

I smiled. "Thanks."

"There is no fixing it," a deep voice said, and I didn't bother looking at him. Agaliarept may be ready to give up on Samael, but I never would.

I could practically hear him grinding his teeth as I ignored him. He stepped further into the room, circling the bed, Bael trailing after him. Both of them avoided looking at Samael, as if it were too difficult.

Agaliarept leveled what he likely thought was an intimidating stare on me. I ignored him some more, returning my gaze to Samael's face.

The last conversation Ag and I had, he'd told me that by accepting the bond between Samael and me, I'd become the co-ruler of the demons in his territory. And with Samael out of action, I was now in charge.

Oh, and he'd been sure to mention that I was the only hope for his people, which meant they were all doomed.

"You need to address the demons," Ag said. I ignored that. What the hell was I supposed to tell them? I'd fucked up, and within a week or two—at most—Samael and I would likely both be gone?

My voice sounded far away when I forced myself to speak. "Explain to me how I'm keeping him alive."

I needed to understand it fully, so I had the best chance of bringing Samael back to me.

Ag looked at Samael, and it was only because I was watching him that I caught it. Pure, unadulterated grief flashed through his eyes. When he glanced back at me, those eyes were blank, his face carefully neutral.

"It was half luck, half sheer stupidity," he said.

Vas cleared his throat and Ag ignored him, keeping his gaze on my face.

"Samael had a bond with Scylla," he said.

His dragon.

I narrowed my eyes at Ag. "Keep talking about Samael in the past tense and I'll kill you."

Silence claimed the room. Kyla took a step closer to me, likely ready to go furry at a moment's notice. Ag just gave me a look that told me I was welcome to try.

"When you cemented the bond between you and Samael, you created a three-way bond. You, Samael, and Scylla. The simplest explanation is that Scylla holds his body, and you hold his soul."

His tone made it clear that I wouldn't understand the complicated explanation. With Samael out of action, the cold war between Ag and me was heating up.

"Both can only be held for a limited time," Ag said. "Eventually, you'll become weaker, have difficulty accessing your power. The drain will kill the dragon, and then it will kill you."

So whatever I did, I needed to do it soon. I didn't have time to sit here feeling sorry for myself.

"There must be some way to counter a Spell of Three."

There were very few spells in existence with no way out. It was the nature of magic—especially witch and fae magic—to have some kind of loophole.

Bael shifted. "There are rumors—" he started, and Ag shook his head.

"This spell has been in existence for centuries. Do you not think if there was a solution, we would know about it?"

I ignored that, my gaze on Vas. Ag strode toward the door.

"I will address your people," he said. "Since you are obviously not in the right frame of mind."

The 'your people' was an effort to piss me off. He knew just how I felt about the idea of being in charge, even in the short term.

"You do that." I sent him a sweet smile and he stalked out of the room.

I didn't blame him for refusing to hope. I couldn't imagine all of the loss he'd seen over the centuries, and since I was directly responsible for this situation, he likely couldn't entertain the idea that I could fix it.

That was fine. I didn't need his belief.

"Tell me," I ordered Bael.

Now that Ag had left the room, some of the tension dissipated. Kyla plopped into the seat next to me, Vas leaned against the wall, and Bael took the chair on the other side of Samael's bed.

"Like I said, they're only rumors," he warned. "It's been said over the centuries that the seelie king has access to something that counteracts a Spell of Three. No one knows what it is, or if the rumors are true, but the king has ruthlessly shut down any suggestion that he has such a thing over the years."

I thought about that. If he didn't have it, the rumors that he did only made him appear more powerful, since no one else had access to it. If he *did* have it, and he wanted to keep that knowledge to himself because he had a limited supply, it made sense for him to quash those rumors.

Kyla shifted in her seat beside me, and it was clear from the intent expression on her face that she'd come to the same conclusion.

Bael shook his head at us. "The light fae king is at war with Finvarra. Samael is allied with Finvarra. There's no way the seelie will help you with anything that could save Samael's life."

Oh yes he fucking would. I merely shrugged, my mind racing.

Bael sighed and finally looked at Samael, his gaze landing on the brand new gold mark on his forearm. Then his eyes met mine.

"I'm going to keep the faith," he said. "Because if anyone can bring him back, you can."

Aw. I attempted a smile, but I was pretty sure it looked more like a grimace. Bael got to his feet and, with a final look at Samael, wandered from the room.

"Can I ask you a question?" Kyla said, as Vas took

Bael's empty chair.

"Yeah."

"Um. Where's Evie?"

I sighed and reached into my jeans pocket, handing her the letter my sister had left for me. I'd memorized it by now.

Dani

I don't know if I ever properly said it, but congratulations on your new office. I know you're going to do incredible things here. I'm SO proud of you for everything you've done since you left the Council. They were stupid to let you go, but I'm glad they did, because you were never supposed to spend your life bounty hunting for them.

Instead, you're going to be a badass who runs her own business.

I know you're going to hate this, and I'm sorry. But I can't sit around and wait for you to save me all the time.

I never told you, but Mom tried to call me a few times over the years.

I refused to talk to her. I blamed her. I tried to hate her. And she was doing everything she could to save my life.

I talked to your demon. He told me a few things about Lucifer. About how he's obsessed with breeding for power. How he loves the new and unexpected. Mom knew his people would've been looking for you. And if they found you, they would've found me.

And unlike you, I don't have a kick-ass prophecy attached to me.

I've been doing some research since we found the lab.

And I've located the dark fae guy who hung around when we were kids. I'm pretty sure he's related to me in some way, and I know where to find him.

I'm the reason Mom is dead. I know it, deep down in my bones. But even from beyond the grave, she's still saving me.

It's my turn now. I'm going to help you find out who killed her. And we'll make them pay. Together.

For now, the next part is up to me.

Thank you for being the best big sister, and I'm sorry for leaving without warning.

I love you,

Evie

If my sister had learned what had happened to Samael—and what was happening to me—she'd be right here brainstorming with us. But she'd gone searching for an unseelie man she believed could help lead us to our mother's killers.

Kyla scanned the letter. "Wow. Probably a good thing she's not here, to be honest. Especially if you're going to take the big slide."

I stared at her. And then I threw my head back and laughed. Some of the tension left Vas's face and he smiled at me. Okay, so I'd been more than a little grim since Samael began dying. But that was enough of that.

I took a deep breath and surveyed Samael, so still in his bed. It was time to pull myself together and find a way to save both of our lives.

So I better get moving.

CHAPTER TWO

Danica

As soon as Vas disappeared with my note, I changed from sweats and into my usual uniform of jeans and a t-shirt.

Then Kyla and I headed to Mariam's. Of course, she wasn't downtown at the fae representative's offices. Instead, the pixies waiting in her office informed me that she was working from home this morning. They obviously weren't invited to the monstrosity Mariam called a house.

I wasn't either.

"Wow," Kyla said as we drove up the long drive.

I surveyed the sprawling, four-storied McMansion.

"Yeah. Neither power nor money can buy taste."

Kyla let out a choked sound as she took in the marble columns and the huge fountain they'd recently had built in the middle of the driveway.

"That's new," I said, surveying the naked fairies, which appeared to be either killing or seducing the minotaur below them, while water spewed from the minotaur's mouth.

"Are they–?"

I shrugged. "No idea."

I was surprised the light fae guards had let us this far. As I had the thought, a slender male rushed out the front door toward us. He'd tucked his long blonde hair in a braid, displaying his pointed ears, and he wrung his hands as he took us in.

I parked, turned off the engine, and opened my door.

"Ms. Amana," he chewed on his lower lip. I had no idea who he was, but the same obviously wasn't true for him. He attempted a smile. "My name is Drostan…. I'm Mariam's new executive assistant. She doesn't have any meetings scheduled with you today."

"I know." I got out of the car. On the other side, Kyla did the same.

It was noon. Mariam was probably eating lunch. I was prepared to wait.

Drostan wrung his hands some more and I caught on. A few months ago, I'd helped the light fae locate some missing artifacts that had been stolen by humans. The reasons they'd been stolen were mostly due to fae arrogance, and the entire situation could have been even more embarrassing if I hadn't located them before the hate group who'd stolen them did even more damage.

Clearly, I was considered important enough that Mariam's people would no longer turn me away at the gate. Go me.

"I can wait until she's free, but I *will* talk to her."

He hesitated, and I took one step closer to him. Then I let him feel a hint of power.

Thanks to the removal of the Naud Chains–and the sudden influx of my power–the suppression spell that had once kept me almost powerless was no longer an issue. My power surrounded me like a dark tornado, stretching toward the fae until he shivered like he was about to piss his pants.

Kyla gaped at me and I shrugged. If there was one thing I no longer had, it was time to waste.

And patience. I guess I didn't have that either.

"Danica," a voice snapped, and I slowly pulled my power back into me. It no longer hurt to stop using it.

Mariam stood in the entrance, her hands on her hips. Her blonde hair had been left free around her shoulders, dangly earrings hung from her pointed ears, and her blue eyes were currently narrowed in annoyance.

"I need to talk to you," I said, stalking past Drostan.

"I gathered," she bit out.

The fae began stuttering apologies behind me and she merely held up a hand. "It's fine, Drostan. Ms. Amana doesn't believe in manners."

Kyla stepped up beside me and slid me a grin as Mariam turned, her heels tapping on the floor as she stalked into a small sitting room. She held the door open and shut it behind her as we walked in.

"Kyla, Mariam. Mariam, Kyla."

They nodded at each other. Kyla and I sat down on the sofa while Mariam perched on the arm of the armchair across from us.

"I heard about what happened to Samael," she said before I could say anything. "I'm sorry for your loss."

I ground my teeth. "Don't count your demons before

they're ash," I advised her. "He's not dead yet."

I was getting used to the pitying looks people sent me when they learned I still held out hope, so I ignored Mariam's.

"Before I get started… has there been any new information in Harriette's case?"

Harriette was my mom's closest friend. The seelie woman had been close-mouthed, but she certainly hadn't deserved to be viciously murdered.

"The investigation is ongoing," was all Mariam said, and I nodded.

"I need your help."

Mariam surveyed me, finally letting out a sigh and waving her hand for me to spit it out.

"I need you to set up a meeting with the light fae king."

Another huge sigh as she pinched the bridge of her nose. "You've asked for this before, and I'm going to give you the same answer as last time."

I'd been pretty sure she'd say that. So I had something to sweeten the deal. I glanced at Kyla.

"Can you call Nathaniel? Put him on speaker."

She raised her eyebrow at me but reached for her phone. While the werewolf Alpha likely wouldn't hesitate to send me to voicemail, I knew damn well he'd answer for one of his wolves.

"Kyla? What's wrong?"

From the concern in Nathaniel's voice, I had a feeling she didn't call her Alpha often.

"It's Danica."

If he was surprised, he didn't let on. "What can I do

for you, Danica?"

"You owe me a debt from taking Kyla on." I slid her an apologetic look. If anything, I owed Nathaniel for giving me Kyla. She shrugged.

Something rustled on Nathaniel's end. "You want to call in that debt now?"

Mariam's eyes were lit with curiosity, and I met them as I asked my question.

"Would you allow me to transfer that debt to the light fae representative?"

Silence. Nathaniel was thinking it over. "The debt would remain equal to the favor you did me by giving Kyla a chance."

"Agreed."

For a fae who was centuries old, Mariam didn't have much of a poker face. The avaricious gleam in her eyes told me I had her.

"I'll get back to you," I said to Nathaniel and hung up.

Kyla burst out laughing and I frowned at her. "People don't hang up on Nathaniel," she clarified.

I shrugged and glanced at Mariam. "Well?"

We both knew that a favor from the werewolf Alpha was a big deal. It was unlikely she'd ever have this chance again, since Nathaniel wasn't the kind of guy who was in the habit of being indebted to the fae.

If I survived the next couple of weeks, I might feel bad about that.

"I need twenty-four hours," Mariam said. I stared at her and she raised one eyebrow. "While I can imagine you're impatient, given the circumstances, it will take me time to talk to my king. I will contact you as soon as I have an answer."

I'd have to accept that. We got to our feet. Mariam nodded at me.

"Good luck," she said. Surprise flashed through me. The fae seemed to actually mean it.

"Thanks."

Danica

Our next stop was in the same neighborhood, just a few streets away.

Aubrey was a fae I'd met while working the case Mariam had hired me for. His sword had been stolen, and I'd managed to recover it before he ended up on his king's shit list.

"He's a flirt," I warned Kyla. "But he's a good guy. He even gave me an ancient weapon."

Incredulous silence.

I smiled as we pulled up to the gated entrance. The gates slid open. Like Mariam, Aubrey had instructed his guards to allow me to visit without an appointment. Nice.

"You're going to have to fill me in," Kyla said.

"It's a khopesh. It was once a *cursed* khopesh, and it was entombed with King Tut." Now it hung on the wall in my living room.

"I meant the fae," Kyla smirked.

"He's a weapon's collector. And he may be my best lead when it comes to negotiating with his king."

I turned off the engine and stepped out of the car. Aubrey had a fountain as well. But it had been here last time I visited, and it wasn't anywhere close to the ostentatious display Mariam's was.

Aubrey stood in the entrance of his home, the door open behind him. He smiled at us as we approached.

"Danica. I assume you're not here for that history lesson about ancient weapons."

"Unfortunately not. I *am* hoping for some of your time, though."

"Of course. And who's this?"

"Kyla."

Aubrey stared at her. "Werewolf?"

She nodded, and his mouth dropped open. Aubrey gaped at her for long enough that it got a little awkward as we waited him out. Kyla peered at her nails, likely well used to this reaction.

The chances of anyone having the specific biology required for them to turn into a werewolf when bitten? Low. The chances of a *female* turning? Approximately one in a million amongst the werewolf population.

Aubrey's silver hair was half-up today, the style highlighting the sharp cheekbones that encouraged a woman to trail her fingers along his cheek. He needed a shave, but the scruff tempered his other-worldly beauty enough to make him approachable.

Violet eyes twinkled at me. "And how did you end up with a werewolf sidekick?"

"She could be *my* sidekick," Kyla muttered sulkily. Aubrey laughed and stepped back, gesturing for us to step in. Kyla immediately sneezed.

Aubrey sent her an apologetic look. "Your nose should become accustomed within a few minutes."

Whatever powers Aubrey had, they clearly stemmed from plants and flowers. Entering his house was like entering a greenhouse, but without the heat and humidity. The heady fragrance climbed up my nostrils and stayed there, while Kyla itched her nose.

Last time, Aubrey had taken me upstairs to his weapon's room. Today, he led us through the entranceway, down a short hall, and into his kitchen.

"I was just making a latte," he said. "You'll have one with me."

We both nodded and took a seat at his counter. Aubrey went to work at his espresso machine, which gleamed like a new car.

A human woman stepped into the room and shook her head at him. "You have guests. Go sit in the parlor and I'll bring the coffee to you."

"You know I enjoy doing it myself." Aubrey waved her away. She rolled her eyes at us and I couldn't help but grin.

"There are fresh blueberry muffins in the pantry," she told him. "I'll be in the laundry room if you need me."

I'd never known the fae to be so informal with their staff, but it somehow didn't surprise me that Aubrey wouldn't tolerate bowing and scraping.

Within a few minutes, Aubrey was setting a plate of muffins in front of us, and I was sipping a—frankly, incredible—latte.

"I usually prefer black," I murmured as I took another sip. "What did you do to make this so good?"

"Magic," Aubrey said. Kyla narrowed her eyes, and he grinned. "Just kidding." The smile slid from his face and he leaned against the counter, raising the cup to his lips. "Now why don't you tell me what's wrong?"

"You haven't heard about Samael?"

He shook his head. "I've been in the seelie realm on business. I returned last night."

I put my cup down, took a deep breath, and filled him in. My voice broke when I got to the part where Samael was lying in his bed, slowly turning to ash. Kyla squeezed my hand and took over.

Aubrey's eyes gleamed with what appeared to be genuine sympathy, and he reached across the counter and took my other hand. "That's awful. I've never met Samael, but I hope he pulls through."

Kyla delicately cleared her throat. "It's not just Samael who's in danger," she said. "If he dies, Danica dies with him."

Aubrey froze. It took him a moment, and then he shot me a furious look.

"You bonded to him? Are you out of your mind?"

"I'm going to fix it," I gritted out.

He merely stared at me, and I rolled my shoulders. "I'm here to ask you for help."

"Of course. I will help in any way I can."

"Tell me what you know about the sword that killed Grendel's mother."

Whatever he'd expected me to say, it wasn't that. His mouth dropped open, and I freed my hand, taking another sip of my latte.

"I don't understand... ah. If you think to use it as

bargaining power, I can assure you it won't work."

"And why is that?"

"The seelie king has been looking for the blade for centuries. He even used Hrunting to attempt to locate it—as you correctly guessed when you were helping us find that sword."

"Why didn't it work?"

Aubrey's lush mouth twisted. "It was, as you would say, a 'long shot.' The swords are not actually related in any way. My king was hoping that Hrunting would have some memory of the golden sword's imprint."

"The golden sword?"

He shrugged. "The sword is technically nameless. But we know for sure that it has a golden hilt. According to legend, it is engraved with markings that speak of the first wars in all the worlds. They also provide a record of those for whom the sword was first made."

"Sounds sweet," Kyla said.

The corner of Aubrey's mouth kicked up. "Indeed. Many people have hunted this sword over the centuries. None more so than Taraghlan—the seelie king."

The implication was that I didn't have a hope in hell of finding it. But I'd bet there was no one else as motivated as I currently was.

"Why does he want it so bad?"

Aubrey circled the counter and pulled out one of the chairs, sitting next to us. "The legend of the blade does not match the reality. According to witnesses, the blade melted after it was used."

Kyla held up a hand. "Can you start at the beginning? Who exactly was Grendel and why did this guy want to kill his mom?"

Aubrey grinned. "Let's start with Beowulf himself. The man was fae-touched. This was during a time when many of the fae—both seelie and unseelie—were taking humans to boost their numbers. Occasionally, human children who grew up in the fae realms would grow into certain powers. Beowulf was taken as a changeling and a young goblin left in his place—glamoured to appear as a human child.

"But the seelie king at the time—Taraghlan's father—had a seer who insisted this child be returned. She foretold a fate for him that would change the future for seelie and unseelie. The child—a toddler by this stage— was returned to his parents with them none the wiser. But his time in the seelie realm had given him certain gifts. He was both faster and stronger than an ordinary human."

My mind was officially blown. "The portals were closed. How were they getting across?"

Aubrey gave me a look as if I was a fool. "Just as your demons were able to lend power to those without enough to cross from the underworld, the fae are able to do the same for mortals, allowing them to travel to our realms. Of course, most of those mortals will never have enough power to return to their homeland."

"Gross," Kyla muttered.

Offense flashed across Aubrey's face for a moment, and then he shrugged it off.

"Our focus then turns to Hrothgar," he announced, and I had a feeling he was enjoying himself. "This was approximately the sixth century of the common era in your time. He was the king of the Danes and, from all accounts, a good one. However, one of the seelie king's courtiers had decided it would be amusing to turn a couple of giants loose. He wanted to see how much carnage both Grendel and his mother would cause in this world without magic."

Kyla shot me a disgusted look, and I shrugged. Sounded on-brand when it came to the fae.

"Grendel attacked Hrothgar's mead hall, killing Hrothgar's best friend. By this time, Beowulf was grown, and he fatally wounded the giant, who crawled back to his mother. The giantess attempted vengeance, but Beowulf followed her back to her cave at the bottom of the lake."

Kyla frowned. "Hold up. How did he get to the bottom of the lake without drowning?"

Aubrey smiled. "He convinced a selkie to loan him her pelt. That allowed him to breathe underwater as long as he had it in his possession. Grendel had been tormenting the selkie's people."

My mind flashed to Mella's face and the sight of her sharp teeth as she'd taken a bite of Bruce's heart. I shuddered.

"Anyway," Aubrey said, "once Beowulf found his way into the cave, he attempted to kill Grendel's mother with Hrunting, which proved useless. However, during the fight, he spotted a fierce-looking sword hanging on the wall, and he used it to behead the giantess. The sword's blade melted, and Beowulf gave it to Hrothgar." Aubrey scowled. "He should have known better. The blade regrew," he said as I frowned. "Hrothgar kept it hidden away, well aware of how dangerous such a sword could be. We have few records of what happened to it next."

"Okay. So the golden sword exists, and its blade is intact. Why does the light fae king want it?"

"The same seer who predicted Beowulf must be returned, also prophesied that the golden sword could be used to kill the unseelie king."

"Fuck."

Audrey nodded. "Indeed."

The unseelie king would not be pleased if the weapon prophesied to be able to kill him ended up in his enemy's hands. And he'd be even less pleased if *I* was the one to make that happen.

I swallowed. Finvarra was a scary bastard. Sure, I had no doubt that even with the sword in Taraghlan's hands, he could more than look after himself. That didn't mean he wouldn't be *pissed* if he learned I was the reason his life was suddenly much more complicated.

I pushed that thought away. There was no limit to the things I would do—to the lines I would cross—if it meant saving Samael's life.

"You said the seelie king had been looking for the sword. Who did he think had it?"

This time, Aubrey's eyes were full of pity. He opened his mouth and I held up one hand, cutting him off.

"I know the chances are minimal. I have to try."

He sighed. "You must talk to the Dearg Due."

That name meant nothing to me, and I gave him a blank look.

Aubrey shook his head. "Convince Taraghlan to deal with you, and I will tell you everything you need to know."

CHAPTER THREE

Danica

I knew I was dreaming the moment the dream began. A choked sob ripped from my throat as I stared at Samael.

There was no ash, no chalky black skin, no crumpled wings. He stood in front of me completely whole.

"I'm dreaming."

"Yes," he said as he moved toward me. "But we've established that I can cross into your dreams. I've waited for you to sleep, my love."

Confusion clouded my mind and he smiled. "Without the benefit of sleeping aids or painkillers."

Tears were streaming down my face. "Is this real? Or am I making this up?"

He leaned down and took my mouth with his, and I ran my hands up his chest. Warm and solid and whole.

I pulled away long enough to gaze up at his face. He pushed a lock of my hair behind my ear and I caught his hand, gazing at the gold mark I'd left on him, no longer warring with black ash.

"Yes," he said, no longer sounding pleased.

"That. What the hell were you thinking?"

Ah. It definitely wasn't just *my* dream. The demon wouldn't lecture me in my dreams. He'd be too busy stripping my clothes off.

"You're welcome."

He took my shoulders, giving me a shake. "You'll die with me, little witch."

"You're not going to die, so it's a moot point."

"I need you to break your end of the bond."

I gaped at him. "Wow. Someone's changed their tune."

"This is not a joke," he growled. Silver eyes glittered, and his hands tightened on my shoulders. This was not the conversation I'd imagined we'd have if I got to talk to him again.

"I had no choice."

"You would have survived my death with only half the bond, Danica. Now, you'll die with me unless you can break it."

"I know."

He nodded as if I was finally being reasonable. "Talk to Ag. There are rumors that his mother broke a bond with his father."

"I'm not breaking the bond, Samael."

He cursed, released my shoulders and turned, pacing away from me. His wings were visible here, and I ached at how lush and real they looked. In reality, feathers were strewn amongst his sheets, his wings turning to ash with the rest of his body.

"I break it, and you die sooner," I attempted to keep my voice reasonable, although my throat tightened at the thought. "At least now we have more time."

He sent me a vicious look over his shoulder and opened his mouth. I narrowed my eyes at him. "If you think you can make me break the bond by being a complete and utter asshole, think again, mister. I'll just deface your body so all your demons see you with a penis drawn on your forehead or something."

His lips twitched, and a fraction of the frustration drained from his expression.

I sighed. "You once said the ferryman owed you a favor," I reminded him, and he shook his head.

"The ferryman is powerful enough to choose not to take a mortal, but even he cannot ignore the compulsion to take *me* to my final resting place." He stalked back to me and pulled me into his arms once more. "I love you," he said. "But I need your word."

I attempted to push back from him and his hands tightened.

"Your power will be keeping me alive. Yours and Scylla's. I need your promise that if you're too drained to function, if it looks hopeless, you will find a way to break the bond."

My chest was so tight I couldn't take a full breath. Samael's expression turned tender, and he pressed a kiss to my forehead.

"Everything dies eventually," he murmured. "I'm thankful I got to experience the pain, and fury, and elation that comes with loving you before it was my time to go."

"Now I *know* you must be dying," I said sulkily. He laughed.

"Promise me, witchling."

I looked up into his beautiful face.

"I promise," I lied.

Samael

Danica was fearless.

No, not entirely fearless. She was smart enough to fear Lucifer and what he represented, even if she mostly dreaded what he would do to those she loved.

She was made of courage. Her will was unshakeable, her bravery astounding.

Often, in my quieter moments, I'd wish she didn't need that courage. Wish I was just a man, and she was just a woman, and we could have years of peace together.

I didn't think either of us would know what to do with peace, but it might be a nice change.

Of course, all my moments were quiet now. I'd heard of this place, from those of my kind who experienced near-death. Some called it purgatory. Most called the loneliness Hell. If not for the fact that I could communicate with my little witch, I would call it the same.

I would have to save my strength. Because while communicating with Danica took a fraction of my power, the talk I would need to have with Ag would drain some of that much-needed life force.

I knew my witchling, and she would never give up on me. She wasn't built that way.

And so, if I was unable to do it myself, and if my stubborn little witch refused, I would involve Ag. He would put my plans into motion, ensuring Lucifer would pay for what he had done. And he would find a way to break the bond.

I hoped that one day, when I was long gone, Danica would forgive me. But it would be enough if she had a life to live. Even if she cursed my name for every moment of it.

Danica

"This is horseshit," Kyla snarled, poking at the jewels decorating the bodice of her dress. I tried my best not to laugh, but I couldn't help the snort that escaped me at her expression.

Mariam had managed to get us an audience with the seelie king, but unfortunately he was at court. That meant we needed to travel to the light fae realm. To say I wasn't excited about it was an understatement, but the entire experience was worsened by the formal gowns we were expected to wear.

The fae enjoyed pageantry, and both of us were wearing the kind of gowns that would apparently allow us to fit in at court. Aubrey had managed to convince his tailor to help fit the gowns Mariam had unexpectedly provided, and we were both standing in one of his guest rooms, staring into the mirror.

"You're not wrong," I said. "But at least you suit yours."

Kyla showed me her teeth and I grinned back at her.

Mariam had put her in pink. Thankfully, it wasn't Pepto-Bismol pink, but more a soft blush. Her dress fell off her shoulders, the ombre effect darker at the top and lightening to a pink so light it was almost white near the bottom.

Jeweled vines wound up the bodice, highlighting Kyla's tiny waist and sparkling in the light. The flowers themselves were white, and the back of the dress tied up corset-style.

The tone worked perfectly with her light-brown skin. Her fine bones made her look almost fragile in the dress, but I could see her point. She definitely didn't look like she could kick some ass.

Enslie, one of Aubrey's maids, had pulled Kyla's light brown hair back into a complicated braid, leaving a few tendrils free to frame her face. She blew one of them out of her eyes and glowered at her reflection.

"You know, if your ears were pointed, you'd–"

"Don't make me hurt you," she said mildly, and I grinned.

Neither of us suited pastels, but apparently, that was what most of the light fae court wore. My dress was a light blue that washed out my pale skin. The seelie tailor had tutted over my shoulders and biceps, proclaiming them far too muscled. In the end, she'd added tulle across the shoulders and upper arms in an attempt to 'soften' my appearance.

I wasn't offended. I worked out so I didn't die when I fought creatures much bigger and stronger than me.

My dress was also adorned with flowers, only they were made from various types of fabric. They covered most of the material, overlapping on the bodice and spilling down the rest of the gown in a gaudy hodgepodge.

They'd left my hair loose, curling it to fall over my shoulders and back. Likely another attempt to 'soften' me up. I had a hair tie around my wrist just in case I needed to pull my hair up and out of the way of anyone who might grab it in a fight.

I glanced at Kyla. "Look on the bright side. If the shit hits the fan, all you need to do is use your claws and you can have that thing off you in a few seconds."

The frown disappeared. "That's true." She glanced at me. "I can cut yours off too."

"True friendship right there." Both of us wore pants and boots beneath our dresses and we'd strapped our weapons in all kinds of interesting places.

I grinned as I took in my dress. "This is what you call putting lipstick on a pig."

"Nonsense," Aubrey said behind me. "You both look delightful."

We both turned, finding him leaning against the doorway. He was wearing cream, with light-brown riding boots and actual flowers in his hair. If I didn't know him, I'd imagine he was exactly what he looked like—an empty-headed fashion plate.

"It's important to fit in at court," Aubrey murmured, nodding at whatever he saw in my expression. "As you well know, it's much better to be underestimated. I can sense the Mistilteinn dagger on you, Danica. If you bring it into the seelie court, they will strip it from you."

I ground my teeth but pulled my dress up. Aubrey sighed as I revealed my jeans and boots, but he made no comment as I unstrapped Misty from my thigh sheath. I replaced it with my Nim Cub, since the dress left no room for my lanyard and knife sheath. I'd manage to fit the rowan arrow and it was tucked beneath the bodice. At this point, I considered the invisible weapon almost like a good luck charm.

"Okay. We're ready."

"Excellent. My driver will take us to the portal."

Of course, Aubrey traveled by limousine, and he offered us drinks from the fridge on the way. I declined, although Kyla took a glass of champagne.

"It'll be out of my system by the time we get there," she promised me. "Werewolf metabolism."

"Now remember," Aubrey said, "don't eat anything in the seelie realm. Don't speak to anyone you don't know. Make no bargains with the fae, except potentially with Taraghlan, and pay careful attention to your every word. Do not—"

"I've dealt with the fae before," I reminded him, and he gave me a wry smile.

"You've dealt with fae who are used to this world. Many of them have softened. The fae who stick to *my* realm have no need to cater to mortal ideals."

I nodded. "Warning noted."

I hadn't had any idea where the closest portal to the light fae realm was, and I frowned as we filed out of the car.

A faint smile danced around Aubrey's mouth. "Not what we would have picked, but, like every other faction, we have no control over the location of the portals in your world."

We were standing in what had once been Cates Landing—a luxury human housing development in Hillsborough. I took in the abandoned homes on either side of the street. I was guessing the appearance of the portal had made house prices plummet, and the locals had gotten out of here, likely at the beginning of the Decade of Despair.

I glanced at Kyla and it suddenly hit me. Werewolf. "Can you cross?"

She rolled her eyes at me. "Yup. Nathaniel makes all his wolves try. Our natural power is attached to dominance and most wolves keep trying over the years, until they've worked their way up the pack. I managed to make it first try."

"Excellent," Aubrey said. He held out his arms. "Take my hands."

I slid my hand into his. On his other side, Kyla did the same, and we stepped into the portal.

CHAPTER FOUR

Danica

There were horses and a carriage waiting for us on the other side of the portal.

I winced, and Aubrey laughed at me. "These things must be done," he said. "Appearances matter."

The horses spooked as Kyla approached. They weren't fooled by her ridiculous dress. They knew damn well she was a predator.

A seelie male sat at the front of the carriage, and he attempted to calm the horses. Finally, when one of them bucked as Kyla got within a few feet of the carriage, the driver shook his head at Aubrey.

Aubrey sighed.

"I can wait here," Kyla said hopefully.

I sent her a dark scowl. "You just want to ditch the dress." Truthfully, I wanted Kyla with me. She had good instincts, and her nose had saved the day more than once. Werewolves could also see when the fae were using their powers.

I trusted Aubrey up to a point, but his allegiance was to his king.

Aubrey's expression was mournful as the

driver took off.

"Jumpy idiots," Kyla said as the carriage moved past us. One of the horses flattened its ears at her and she showed it her teeth.

I'd shoved a werewolf into an uncomfortable dress and dragged her into the seelie realm. I should've expected this.

"If you ladies can wait in this field, I'll be right back," Aubrey announced. He turned and strode through the portal, leaving us standing on the seelie side.

We stepped aside, moving further into the grassy field, and I swept my gaze over the landscape in front of us. To our left, the portal swirled in shades of green— from the emerald at the edges to the mint green in the center. To our right, a dense forest waited, somehow invitingly. Wildflowers were scattered at the forest's edge, as if waiting for a weary traveler to sit and pick them. Or to lie down and nestle their head in soft grass—

"What are you doing?"

I stiffened. Kyla's hand was clamped around my upper arm. I'd started walking toward the forest without even realizing I was moving.

"Shit."

"Yeah. Don't—"

"Trust anything in fairy. I remember." I managed to pull my gaze from the forest and examined the lush meadow in front of us. It stretched into the distance, only interrupted by the wide, dirt path down which the driver had driven the horse and carriage.

The rumble of an engine sounded and I froze. He wouldn't—

If someone had asked me if a car could be transported through a portal, I would've assumed they'd been drinking. I knew the rumors and myths around the fae and iron weren't true—otherwise they wouldn't have flooded into our world—but the idea of a fae driving a car in the seelie realm seemed impossible.

Aubrey wound his window down. "Well, get in," he grinned at us. "It's not quite the arrival I was hoping for, but it'll have to do."

The driver obviously had no problem crossing the portal. He got out of the limo, and opened the door for us so we could climb in.

"Are you out of your mind?" I asked Aubrey seriously. "I thought the whole plan was to try to fit in. Hence this monstrosity," I plucked at my dress.

"Yes, well that was before I realized our other mode of transportation wouldn't work." He slid Kyla a look and she rolled her eyes.

"How was I supposed to know you'd be expecting me to travel by horse and carriage?"

"You have a point," he smiled. I was beginning to learn that very little upset Aubrey. The angriest I'd ever seen him was when he realized someone had stolen Hrunting from his office.

That didn't mean he wasn't dangerous. Only that he didn't get particularly angry before he struck. That was a fae thing. They weren't exactly known for displays of emotion. Maybe that was why I enjoyed needling Mariam so much.

I blocked out their good-humored bickering and turned to stare out the window. The forest still beckoned on the edge of the field, but then we rounded a bend and I gasped.

"Whoa," Kyla murmured. "It's like something out of a fairytale."

"Yeah. Probably means something will try to kill us soon."

Aubrey sent me an amused look, and I let out a tiny laugh. Even I had to admit that the castle was beautiful.

It glowed like the sheen of a pearl. It was as if someone had taken my every expectation of a fairy palace and made it *more*.

It was all turrets and towers, with a moat that encircled the castle, accessible only via a bridge across that moat. I had a sudden longing to see the sunset here. To watch the reds and purples and pinks reflect off the pearlescent glow of the castle.

I half expected to see unicorns frolicking in the courtyard.

We stopped at the gate in front of the moat. A group of guards surrounded our car. One of them held up his hand, and the engine shut off. Aubrey rolled down his window and smiled at them.

"My friends have a meeting with the king."

While he arranged for us to be allowed into the castle, I studied the guards.

They were dressed in white, which was a terrible choice for people who would be expected to spill blood in defense of the castle, but it wasn't exactly surprising in this place. They moved as a team, well-trained, but the one who'd used his power to stop our car was clearly in charge.

"The vehicle stays here," he said, and we climbed out.

The water in the moat was so clear, I could see the varying colors of the stones that lay on the bottom. My mouth twitched and Kyla glanced at me.

"What is it?"

"Just comparing this delightful experience to the castles over human history. That water would likely have been filled with human excrement and occasionally cleaned by the peasants."

She wrinkled her nose and Aubrey shot me a warning look. I shrugged.

More guards stood on either side of the main entrance, all of them watching carefully. Surprisingly, they didn't ask to check us for weapons. Maybe with our dresses, we looked like we didn't know how to use a weapon. Or perhaps they knew neither of us had a chance if the seelie king decided we'd offended him in some way.

My own power flickered at the thought.

"I can't go in with you," Aubrey said as we crossed the courtyard. It was creepily quiet, and my neck itched at the eyes on us. A guard bowed, opened the door to the castle itself, and we stepped inside.

"If you wish to negotiate on your terms, you must do so alone," Aubrey continued. "I'll have to wait outside the throne room." A hint of regret flashed through his eyes and I nodded.

"Thank you for getting us this far."

My feet sank into the lush white rug beneath my feet, and we all moved silently down the entrance hall.

My eyes scanned over the gold panels of the walls and

up to the painted ceiling above us. I'd once seen pictures of the Sistine Chapel before the Decade of Despair, and my heart had ached for the ruination of all that beauty. This looked entirely too familiar.

Aubrey smiled at me when I met his eyes.

"Our king was quite impressed with the talents of the mortal responsible for such beauty."

Bitterness warred with relief in my gut. On the one hand, it was nice to know that some of Michelangelo's genius had survived. On the other hand, it was so like the fae to allow beauty to be destroyed in our world, but to keep it for their own.

One of the guards held up a hand, gesturing for us to stop in front of two gold doors.

"The king will see you now."

The doors swung open and I swallowed, my mouth suddenly bone dry as all eyes turned toward us. I'd thought we'd look ridiculous in our dresses, but Enslie and Aubrey had been right—we would've stood out a lot more in jeans and sweaters.

Courtiers lounged in chairs near the back of the room, their outfits making ours look sedate. One woman's neckline plunged almost to her bellybutton, and around her neck hung a chain connected to a tiny cage. The cage held a single bird which attempted to stretch its wings, only for them to press up against the gold bars.

The sight made me claustrophobic. Next to me, Kyla let out a growl so low it was almost soundless, but the hair on the back of my neck stood up.

"Keep your shit together," I hissed, and the growl cut off suddenly as she took a deep breath and nodded.

There were probably five or six hundred people in the room, and they quieted as we walked down the long aisle. Halfway down, my eyes met the gaze of seelie guy I'd seen around Meredith's bar a few times. "I know you," he purred, his gaze falling to my arm. "The bondmate of Samael himself."

The rest of the room went silent at that, and I ground my teeth.

But the reminder helped. I could get through this. I *would* get through this, and I'd be a step closer to making sure Samael woke up.

Aubrey had instructed us to keep our gazes down, and it went against all of my instincts as we made it to the throne, both of us dropping into deep curtsies.

It had seemed ridiculous when Enslie had instructed us to practice, and we'd broken into howls of laughter as we learned.

Neither of us was laughing now. The room was silent, and we waited, stuck with our legs bent as the king took us in.

He didn't say a word, letting us stay in the subservient position. If he thought this would be enough to make us uncomfortable, he'd miscalculated. The werewolf next to me could likely stay in the awkward almost-squat all day, and I worked out enough that I probably had a couple of hours in me.

"Rise," he ordered.

I lifted my head and stared at the seelie king.

I'd never seen him before. Unlike Finvarra—the unseelie king—who seemed to have plenty of his own plans in our world, Taraghlan kept to himself.

His hair was the color of moonlight. There was no other way to describe it. It wasn't the white-blonde of Mariam's, or the silver of Aubrey's. It was a color so unique that I couldn't help but stare as it seemed to glow in the sunlight pouring through the windows to our right.

His eyes were so light they seemed almost pearl-colored themselves, and I shivered at the look in them as his gaze swept over Kyla, finally finding my face, where it stayed.

He wore a long white robe embellished with silver and gold, and the crown on his head looked like it was made entirely of crystal—or diamond. Likely, it was a gem unique to the seelie realm. The king leaned back on his throne and watched us coolly.

"Danica Amana," he said. The silence in the room was so thick I could have hacked at it with my Nim Cub. "And who is your friend?"

"Kyla Hill, Your Majesty."

Taraghlan gave no indication that he'd even heard her, his eerie eyes still on my face. Distantly, a warning siren sounded up in my mind. He was powerful enough to keep us here as hostages if he wanted. Samael couldn't do anything about it, and I doubted Ag would march the demons through the portal, ready to wage war against the seelie.

"What is it that you want?" he asked, his body so still he could have been made of ice.

I took a deep, steadying breath. "By now you know what has happened to Samael."

Silence.

I continued anyway. "I'm aware of the rumors that

you have a counter spell for the Spell of Three."

The tiniest hint of a smile curled one corner of his mouth. "I'm afraid I'm not sure what you're referring to," he said.

Oh, you bastard.

Next to me, Kyla stiffened. We'd already discussed what would happen if this all turned to shit. She'd shift into her wolf form and run like hell. I needed her to get back to the demons, tell them what had happened, and find another way to save Samael.

Fine. While I'd hoped the king would at least admit he had the cure, I wasn't surprised he was refusing to negotiate with me. I was just the half-demon sleeping with Samael.

So I gave him my sweetest smile. "I heard you've been searching for a particular sword," I murmured.

"Leave," he said.

I frowned, but movement behind me made me turn. His court was silently filing out of the room, without a single word spoken. Taraghlan's eyes lingered on someone behind us. "Cellen, you stay."

A single male wandered over to us, positioning himself next to the king's throne. He studied me out of cold eyes, and I studied him right back, noting the sword at his hip and the smooth way he'd moved.

The king waited until only the four of us remained, and then he shifted, leaning forward slightly. That simple movement warned me to tread carefully.

"What, exactly, are you referring to?"

I took a deep breath. "I know you want the sword that killed Grendel's mother."

"You've been speaking with Aubrey," he murmured, and it was my turn to freeze. I needed to make it clear that Aubrey hadn't been gossiping.

"As you're aware, I was tasked with locating several fae artifacts a few months ago. The sword in question came up during the course of my investigation."

Some of the fury left the king's eyes, but he still looked *pissed*.

"Your point?"

I shrugged. "I have no point unless you have access to the counter spell to the Spell of Three."

He stared at me and I stared back. I was playing a dangerous game.

Finally, he gave a languid shrug. "If I did own such a thing, it would be hidden away for a time when it would most benefit my people."

Cellen tensed. "Your Majesty–"

I cut him off. "From what I've heard, that sword would benefit your people." And potentially doom the unseelie, but I'd deal with that once Samael was no longer knocking on death's door. "I'll make you a deal. I get you the sword, and you give me the cure."

His lips curved, and for a second I had a glimpse of the man beneath the king. But the smile was so cold, I couldn't help but shiver.

"The arrogance of youth," he murmured. "You truly believe you can find a sword I have hunted for centuries."

"Desperation is the mother of invention," I said, and it seemed to amuse him, because he leaned back on his throne and regarded me once more.

"Look," I said, "there's no downside for you. We

find the sword, you give us what we need. We don't find the sword, Samael dies."

Just saying the words made my chest clench, made my hands shake. I buried them in the folds of my dress and waited.

He waved his hand through the air. "If, in the unlikely event that you find the golden sword, I will give you what you seek."

"The counter spell that will save Samael's life," I clarified. The fae were tricky.

His eyes lightened. I'd amused him. "The counter spell that will save his life," he agreed. "However, it requires more than just the spell itself for it to work."

I stared at him. "What do you mean?"

"In order for the counter spell to work, you must have the cooperation of all factions. Witch, seelie, mage, unseelie, wolf, and demon."

I swallowed. Next to me, Kyla elbowed me lightly. Yeah, we would cross that bridge when we came to it. I sent her a shaky smile and then turned back to the seelie king.

"It's a deal."

He slowly unraveled himself from the throne and walked down the two steps until he was merely inches away. Cellen watched Kyla and me as if we were annoying, yet poisonous creatures his king had chosen to play with.

The king held out his hand. I gave him the hand without Samael's golden mark and he smiled. And then the back of my hand began to burn.

I attempted to pull free as the burn spread. It was as if acid was dripping over the back of my hand, melting into my skin. His hand tightened around mine, and Kyla let out a low growl. He spared her a single glance and then pressed one finger to the back of my hand.

He released me, and I stared down at the white slash that had appeared on my skin.

"Our deal," he said. I nodded. As much as I loathed wearing his mark, it was a good thing, since even the most powerful fae couldn't get out of a deal once it came with a mark on the skin.

He smiled, revealing sharp white teeth. "I wish you luck with this task, Danica Amana," he said formally.

"Thank you."

He turned, the movement an obvious dismissal, and I glanced at Kyla. She launched into motion, stalking down the aisle of the throne room. The guards obviously took too long for her liking, because she pushed the huge doors open herself.

Aubrey was leaning against the wall and he went still as we approached.

"How did it go?"

I rolled my shoulders and held up my hand. "I find the sword, and he'll give me what I need," I murmured.

He nodded, offering us both his arms as we walked back through the castle.

"Who is that Cellen guy?" Kyla asked.

Aubrey sighed. "Cellen was lucky enough to be born with a very specific type of power. One that had been thought to be a myth."

His voice trailed off and I rolled my eyes. "Don't leave us hanging."

Aubrey gave me a faint smile. "He is able to bend

time and space, opening his own portals between worlds."

I stopped walking and stared at him. "He creates his own portals? Are you serious?"

"Yes. His Majesty keeps him close—usually within a few feet. He is more valuable than any number of guards, with his ability to remove the king from danger." He met my eyes. "Be very careful with him. His sister was recently gaining favor with His Majesty, and she disappeared a week ago under suspicious circumstances."

No wonder I'd gotten a bad vibe from him. I shook it off. "I'm going to need you to fill me in about the Dearg Due," I murmured as we finally walked past the guards standing at attention on the front steps.

"I will," Aubrey said. "But you may wish I hadn't before all this is over."

With that warning ringing in my ears, we got into the limo and drove back toward the portal.

Danica

Samael stood in front of me, his eyes drinking me in. My eyes did the same, and my throat tightened.

I'd waited all day for this moment, hoping that when I slept I'd see him again.

"I miss you," I told him.

He smiled at me, his eyes lighting up as I walked toward him. Did he look tired? Was the spell having an effect on him, even here? My chest ached at the thought, but then his arms were around me, and his mouth was on mine, and all thought disappeared from my mind.

"It's difficult," he murmured against my mouth. "Being here, aware but unable to act. Knowing you are fighting for me, alone. Even while you are scheming your schemes."

The next moment we were in his bed. Or at least the dream version of his bed. My demon leaned over me, and I luxuriated in the feel of his naked body against mine.

He pushed the hair off my face and I smiled up at him. "I'm not alone. But Samael… you may not forgive me for the things I'm doing. We should probably talk about it."

I explained my plans so far. Displeasure gleamed in Samael's eyes as he lifted my hand, taking in the seelie king's mark. But he nodded.

"You make an excellent ruler, little witch." He gave me a wicked smirk. "Perhaps my demons will prefer you to me, if I live through this."

"Believe me, we're in no danger of that happening. But we need to talk about that, mister. Since when am I in charge if you're out of commission?"

His gaze dropped to my mouth and he leaned down to nibble on my lower lip. "Since you chose to bond me fully, witchling. That is just one of the consequences of your decision."

He raised his head and the expression on his face made it clear he was getting ready to give me another lecture. So I slipped my hand between us and wrapped it around him.

He jolted as if I'd given him an electric shock, and I grinned up at him.

"We can talk about that," I purred. "Or, we can use this time in a much more… enjoyable way."

I wouldn't think about the fact that each time I saw him in these dreams could be the last time. Flat-out refused to think that this could be the final time he touched me.

"I need you," I told him. His expression softened, and he lowered his mouth to mine.

His tongue swept in, claiming my mouth. I slid my tongue against his, claiming him right back, and his low growl made me shiver.

We kissed for so long, my head spun. Time was no longer a concept as we drifted in the lazy pleasure of having each other close. And my eyes burned at what Samael's slow movements told me.

Even now, when each time we found each other could be the last, he refused to be rushed. Refused to *not* take his time. Refused to give in to the rage and the terror that made my breath catch in my throat whenever I thought of it.

He slowly took his mouth from mine, his eyes lit with a primal, savage lust. Then he bent, his mouth dropping to my breasts, where he pressed kisses to every inch of them, until I groaned and he laughed, his tongue finding my nipple.

He gently—so gently—used the edge of his teeth, and I shuddered against him, my core clenching in need.

"Now," I ordered, tired of waiting. "Now, now, oh God."

He'd guided himself into me, and his hips rolled as he thrust, filling me up. I wrapped my legs around his waist and lifted to meet him, urging him on.

His eyes found mine, and we stared at each other, moving in sync, reaching for our mutual pleasure. I knew what he was doing, because I was doing the same— memorizing his face, imprinting this moment to my very soul. I choked out a sob and his eyes softened, his mouth gentle, achingly tender as he brushed kisses over my face, instantly removing any hint of tears.

I gasped as he circled his hips, and then he ground against me, his pelvic bone pressing against my clit as he caressed my g-spot.

Pleasure engulfed me, and I stared at my demon as I trembled, making him a silent promise.

Whatever it took.

I'd do whatever it took to make sure he lived.

CHAPTER FIVE

Danica

I woke after my dream with Samael. Then I tossed and turned, itching to go directly to the Dearg Due.

Aubrey had said he'd fill me in, but I didn't want to wait. I got up, collected my books, and headed into my office. Then I researched everything I could find about the creature I needed to convince to help me.

Once I'd made my notes–including a list of questions for Aubrey just as soon as it was an acceptable time to call–I showered in Samael's huge shower, missing him like a limb as I lathered myself in his soap. And then I curled up on the other side of the bed from him, where I wouldn't risk touching him if I did fall back asleep. Just a simple brush of my hand could make more of his body crumble, and I couldn't bear to watch it happen.

By dawn, I was up and dressed, gulping down a cup of coffee. Kyla met me in the office Samael had set up for me. I still hadn't had a chance to unpack the office I was renting from Keigan, but it wasn't exactly high priority right now.

Since Ag had insisted I was in charge of the demons, the first thing I'd done was give Kyla access to Samael's rooms so we could make our plans and strategies here, without me needing to go too far from my demon. I was relatively sure Ag was fuming about it, but I couldn't find it in me to care.

I handed Kyla a cup of coffee and she sipped with a pleased hum. "So, you want to tell me about the Dearg Due?"

I nodded, gulping my own coffee. "There are seven Dearg Due. The original was a part of the light fae court. Five of the others were turned over the past few centuries. I messaged Aubrey this morning, and he confirmed that we need to talk to the second Dearg Due created, who–unfortunately for the original–is the most infamous.

"Anyway, I'd heard of *this* Dearg Due before, but only as part of an Irish legend. A young, incredibly beautiful woman grew up in a place called Waterford. She fell in love with a local boy who was kind, good, and, of course, penniless. Her father was an asshole who arranged a marriage between his daughter and a cruel chieftain from an area close by."

"Uh-oh."

"Yeah. The chieftain was a sadist and regularly beat the crap out of her. Some of the locals said he liked to see her bleed. He locked her away, where she waited, hoping for someone to rescue her. Eventually, she realized no one was coming. Her love turned to hate, and she began starving herself to death, hiding away the food the servants bought her.

"According to Aubrey, she'd made a bargain with

one of the light fae. Her mother's ancestors had traces of fae blood, which had been passed down. While she was dying, she renounced her god and turned to the seelie instead. The portals in Ireland were never as tightly locked as those elsewhere, and she got her answer. She made a deal with the original Dearg Due, who obviously liked the idea of having a partner in crime. The woman would be allowed to temporarily 'die' so she could see who would mourn–and if either her father or husband would turn from their wicked ways."

Kyla winced. "Even then she was… naïve. But the girl had stones. Starving is a bad way to go."

"Yeah. You need commitment to turn down food, but this woman had plenty of that. Anyway, the locals had their superstitions about the dead, and it was tradition to cover new graves in rocks to prevent them from rising up. Either people felt sorry for the woman, or they remembered how kind she'd been before her husband ruined her, and they didn't leave a single rock. So she rose up and transformed into what the locals assumed was a vampire. Spoiler alert, neither her husband nor her father had suddenly turned over a new leaf."

Kyla shook her head. "Shocking."

"The Dearg Due hit up her father first, draining his blood. And then she took revenge on her husband, who'd already found a new wife."

"Cold." Kyla took a seat at the chair in front of my desk, stretching out her legs. But her eyes were intent.

"Yup, she thought so too. Anyway, she devolved into bloodlust and roamed southeast Ireland, focusing her rage and hunger on men. Then she disappeared. That's where it gets interesting. According to Aubrey, the seelie king got wind of the attention she was drawing to his people. Taraghlan ordered for her to be brought back to his realm, and she retaliated. She vowed that she would find what he wanted the most and ensure he never got it."

"Something tells me that's the sword."

"Yup," I popped the P. "That's where we come in. But here's the thing. She takes blood from men, but that's not what she takes from women—"

A crash sounded from elsewhere in the penthouse. I paused, shrugging when there were no other sounds.

Kyla angled her head, likely hearing something I couldn't. Then she turned her attention back to me. "Why hasn't the seelie king dealt with her by now?"

"The Dearg Due is powerful enough that Taraghlan can't compel her to tell him about the sword. He can kill her, but then he'll never know if she had something important, and the Dearg Due are impervious to torture." I shrugged. "Something about how they suffered enough during their mortal lives. So he sends his people to visit her every few months, in an effort to convince her to help him. So far, it hasn't worked."

"Sounds like she's got the light fae over a barrel. I can respect that."

I perched my butt on the edge of my desk. "I know, right?

We both jolted as my office door slammed open. I cursed as coffee sloshed over the side of my cup, and Kyla reached for the box of tissues on my desk, passing me a handful.

I'd seen Ag angry before, but he typically went with

cold disdain. This wasn't cold. He stalked toward me, and a breeze swept my hair back from my face. His wings were extended.

His voice was low, tone frigid. "What, exactly, do you think you're doing?"

I slid off the edge of my desk and planted my feet. "I'm not sure what you're referring to."

A muscle jumped in Ag's jaw. "Finvarra would have heard you were in the seelie realm the moment you went through that portal. He has spies everywhere."

"I know." I shivered. It was as if the temperature in the room had dropped several degrees.

"You will go to the unseelie king. And you will get down on your knees. Then you will beg. *Beg* him not to see this act as an act of war. You will convince him that you temporarily lost your mind, but you recognize the importance of the alliance between our people. And you will do whatever it takes to demonstrate your regret and commitment to that alliance."

"The alliance can be fixed when Samael wakes up," I snapped. "We have a more immediate problem we need to handle."

"Are you stupid, or do you just not care about your people?"

My power curled around me at the disdain in his voice. Kyla shifted until she was standing next to me, but she stayed silent.

I threw my hands in the air. "I'm trying to save him, you stubborn ass."

Ag merely bared his teeth at me. "You believe Samael will awaken? Think very carefully about the circumstances you want him to wake to. And maybe spare a thought for the world you will leave behind if you both die and you have burned through all of our alliances."

He turned and stalked out. I took a deep, shuddering breath and forced my power back behind my shields.

Kyla glanced at me. "You okay?"

"Yeah. I deserved that."

She frowned, but I shook my head.

"I've already contacted the unseelie king." I reached into my pocket for the letter I'd had Vas send to him. The king had returned it with his reply, and I handed it to Kyla.

She let out a choked sound and read it aloud.

Hey Fin,

Been meaning to catch up with you. Mind if we stop by on Tuesday?

She slowly raised her gaze and I shrugged. He'd answered in the same letter, below my note. One word.

10am.

"Do you have a death wish?" Kyla asked conversationally. "It's okay if you do, but it's probably something a partner should know."

I rolled my eyes. "Look, I don't know Finvarra well, but I do know one thing. These ancient creatures are bored. They crave the new and unusual. My only hope of keeping the alliance alive is to amuse or entertain him in some way."

Kyla sighed. "I can be entertaining."

Despite the anxiety making my stomach twist, I grinned. "I bet you can." My grin fell and I raked my hand through my hair. "Honestly, I don't know what I'll do if Finvarra chooses to kill the alliance. Ag's right, I could be doing more damage than we can take. Lucifer's spies are everywhere. If they find out the alliance is dead, while Samael is out of action, they could choose that moment to strike."

Kyla was silent for a long moment. Finally, she frowned. "You know when someone gets critically wounded, and the doctors or healers triage them?"

I nodded and she reached for her coffee, which she'd set on my desk. "Samael is the demons' heart. You have to resuscitate that heart before you can focus on the bleeding and fractures."

"I know," I said softly. "But I'm terrified that if he wakes up, he won't even be able to look at me after everything I'll need to do to save him."

Kyla smiled. "Somehow, I don't think you'll ever have that problem with Samael." She glanced at the clock. "Our meeting with the unseelie king is in an hour. Where are we going?"

I sighed. "He's making us go into his realm. It's a statement. We traveled to the seelie king, so even if Finvarra would usually be available in our realm, he'd still make us go through the portal and meet him on his turf."

Kyla rolled her eyes. "Sounds like a hell of a guy. Just tell me I don't have to wear a dress."

I laughed. "Nope. I don't think Finvarra gives a shit. Now I just have to sweet talk Vas into telling us where the hell the portal is."

"Vas already knows what you're up to," the demon announced, leaning against my doorway. I rolled my eyes, and he grinned at me, but it quickly fell from his face.

"My uncle is pissed," he said.

"Yeah, I caught that."

"I'll help you any way I can. I just hope you know what you're doing."

"Yeah. Me too."

Danica

Thankfully, Vas had been to the unseelie realm before. Had even traveled to Finvarra's main home as part of Samael's entourage, when they were in negotiations back before I was born.

The closest unseelie portal was deep in the Duke Gardens, next to a small pond almost completely covered in lily pads. Instead of handing the botanical gardens over to the unseelie when the portal had appeared, the humans in charge had simply erected a twelve-foot fence surrounding the portal. Vas landed us inside the fence, and I took one moment to examine the portal—shades of pink—before we stepped through.

"You're in luck," Vas told us. "We're close to Finvarra's main base."

A cobblestone path led us away from the portal.

"If the shit hits the fan, we'll distract the king," I told Vas. "You need to escape and get back to the demons."

Vas didn't look pleased by this plan, but he clearly knew better than to argue, because he nodded, his expression hard.

We rounded a bend, and Finvarra's home came

into view. My mouth dropped open. While the seelie king's castle had shot into the sky, the turrets gleaming like trapped moonlight, Finvarra had taken a different approach.

His home had been built into the side of a mountain, preventing any attack from that side. This wasn't a castle, it was a keep, a… *fortress*, with each level rising into the sky. And it sprawled over what had to be hundreds of thousands of square feet.

It was designed for war. For outlasting magical attacks. From the slightly blurred air that shimmered for several feet around every inch of the huge building, it was continually shielded from any such assaults.

It wasn't gray. It wasn't black. It was somewhere in between, and it stood as if waiting for someone stupid enough to attempt to take it from the unseelie.

I shivered. "It's freezing," I muttered.

Next to me, Kyla looked unconcerned. I scowled. "You're not cold?"

She grinned at me. "If I get really cold, it'll interfere with my shift, but it would have to be much, much colder than this."

Vas didn't seem concerned either. I shrugged and jiggled a little in an attempt to warm up.

Four guards were marching toward us, in step. Their uniforms were the same color as the keep, with burnished gold buttons. Their boots had been polished to a dull gleam.

The unseelie king obviously ran a tight ship around here. The guards halted, and one of them stepped forward.

"State your business."

Vas cleared his throat. "Do you not recognize Samael's bondmate?"

The guard's gaze dropped to the gold swirls on my arm and his eyes widened.

"I need to speak with the king." I didn't have Samael's threatening undertone, but the guard nodded anyway.

"Certainly."

He didn't ask us to remove our weapons. He'd obviously determined we were no threat to the king, but it was a dumb move. Samael's demons would've stripped us of anything sharp and pointy before we got within twenty feet of the place.

If this conversation went badly, Finvarra could declare war. And he would be alone in a room with three people who were highly motivated to make sure that wouldn't happen.

Of course, we'd be dead soon after, but desperate people did stupid things.

We approached the steps leading to the entrance of the keep. One of the guards waiting for us was one I'd seen before at Samael's tower. He nodded at us.

"Follow me," he said, and we trailed after him.

I didn't know if there was a throne room in this place, but if there was, Finvarra had chosen not to use it.

He was waiting for us in a library so large, it almost gave me goosebumps. Next to me, Kyla inhaled sharply, her eyes wide with wonder as she scanned the long walls packed with books. Above us, a mezzanine was packed with more books, and I gave it a quick scan for signs of movement before returning my attention to Finvarra.

The unseelie king wore unrelenting black, with an

obsidian crown glinting with jewels. This may not have been a throne room, but he sat on the huge, wing-backed chair as if it were a throne, watching as we approached.

His ears were as sharply pointed as my blades, his gold eyes glittered with ire, and he radiated pure, lethal threat.

Gone was the man who had pretended to be charming. Who had told me to call him 'Fin.' In his place was a man who made me wonder just how long it would take him to kill us if this turned bad.

True fear took up residence deep in my chest. My instincts knew damn well that this ancient being was the scariest predator in the room.

Vas was a silent shadow behind us. Despite my orders, Vas would fight to the death to give us enough time to run.

Next to me, Kyla was so still she could have been stone. Finvarra's gaze slid to her.

"A female wolf," he murmured. "Myth given life."

"That's me," Kyla sent him a shit-eating grin, and I could barely see the strain in it. "I'm mythical alright."

I shot her a look and she winked at me. Obviously, she'd taken that whole 'entertainment' thing seriously. Behind us, Vas shifted on his feet, clearly unhappy with this whole plan.

Finvarra didn't bother offering us a seat. He merely scanned both of us, lingering on Kyla for a long moment before his cold, burnished gold eyes met mine.

"You have been meeting with my enemy, Ms. Amana."

"Please," I said. "Call me Danica."

He merely stared at me, as if he was a jungle cat watching his prey.

"I had no choice," I began, and he held up one hand.

"There is always a choice. You chose to end my alliance with the demons without informing me of your decision to do so."

I raised one eyebrow. "I was unaware that the alliance would need to end."

He smiled at that. It wasn't a very nice smile.

"I find it difficult to believe Samael would have lost his head—and his heart—to a fool. But that's what you must be if you truly think I will allow those who were once my allies to collude with my greatest enemy without consequences."

I needed to step very, very carefully.

"I hadn't imagined you would be especially worried about the sword falling into Taraghlan's hands," I murmured. "My information was that you were unafraid of him. I apologize if this information was incorrect."

Finvarra tensed. Then he slowly got to his feet, his huge body uncoiling in a way that made all the spit in my mouth dry up.

He took a single step toward me, and Kyla lowered her head. A vicious growl ripped from her throat. Behind me, Vas let out a string of whispered curses.

Finvarra spared her a single glance, and something like amusement flashed through his eyes.

"You forget yourself, wolf."

She lifted her lip, revealing long, deadly fangs. What the hell was going on with her?

I shook my head. "You're not the only one who has

a bone to pick, Your Majesty. Your people have also been meeting with our enemies," I said softly. I was watching closely, so I caught the surprise that flickered in his eyes.

"I'm unsure what you're referring to."

"Two of your inner circle were seen speaking to Lucifer's right hand not long ago. I find it suspicious that this happened just days before the Spell of Three was used to weaken Samael."

"Unlike you, I do not break my alliances," he said. "What proof do you have that it was my people?"

I'd come ready for this. I pulled the photos out of my jeans pocket and handed them to him. Finvarra went still. Someone was likely to die horribly just as soon as we left.

He didn't bother mentioning that he'd had no idea about this little meeting. We both knew paranormal rulers were responsible for everything their people did.

"So you will use this as an excuse to break our alliance?" he'd recovered quickly, but a cold fury burned deep within his eyes.

I gave him an achingly sweet smile. "Of course not. I understand that sometimes alliances are weakened through outside forces."

He smiled back, and a hint of real humor danced in his eyes. "For a young human, you have taken to wielding your power well. One day, if you survive long enough, you will be a force to be reckoned with."

"Why thank you."

Kyla cleared her throat. "Look," she said carefully. "There's no guarantee that we'll even find the sword. So there's no point talking about broken alliances just yet, right?"

Finvarra waved that off. Clearly, he thought we'd find it. That made one person in all the realms, other than me and Kyla.

He sat back in his chair and frowned at both of us, clearly deep in thought.

"It's in my best interest for Samael to live. However, it certainly is not in any way helpful for my greatest enemy to have a weapon fated to kill me."

He gave us both a dark look, but there was no real heat behind it. That scared me more, since it meant he had come to a decision. And I had a feeling I wasn't going to like that decision.

"You may complete the bargain you have struck," he said finally. His gaze found Kyla's face—and stayed there. "But you will then complete a new bargain. You will take the sword back and bring it to me."

I was right. I didn't like this at all.

"You want us to steal it from the seelie palace? How the hell are we supposed to do that?"

Finvarra shook his head at me. "You misunderstand. This bargain does not involve you in any way."

"Excuse me?"

"If Samael's bondmate is caught stealing from the seelie, it will start a war. A war that would prevent Samael from taking back his throne, and impact my own plans. No, this bargain is for the wolf."

I glowered at him. "And you think Nathaniel won't be a threat if Kyla ends up dead?"

He shrugged. "The werewolf Alpha will have to accept that one of his wolves chose to operate without his permission."

"That could get Kyla killed." I didn't think Nathaniel would kill her, but we all knew many Alphas would at least maim a wolf who made a deal with an enemy faction.

Finvarra sent me a look. "We both know the Alpha would never kill such a rare, female wolf," he purred, his eyes returning to Kyla's face.

Shit.

I'd told Kyla to be interesting, but all she'd needed to do was walk in here to draw Finvarra's attention.

Kyla gave the unseelie king a cool look. "How long do I have to collect the sword once it's in Taraghlan's possession?"

"Three months. However, if Taraghlan strikes at me with the sword before this time, and you do not prevent it, I will consider our bargain to be broken. Three months from now, if the sword is not in my possession, I will consider—"

"Our bargain to be broken," Kyla finished with a roll of her eyes.

I let out a breath I hadn't realized I was holding. It was longer than I'd thought we'd have. Once again, I'd underestimated how differently time passed for the fae.

Kyla's face was carefully blank. "And if I fail?"

"You will leave your pack and join my people."

We all stared at the king in shocked silence. Vas stepped closer to us, and I felt the fine tremble of fury that rolled through his body.

I managed to speak through my suddenly dry mouth. "You'd risk war with the wolves?"

"One pack is no threat to me or mine."

This was spiraling out of control. Bringing Kyla here

was a mistake. Finvarra had obviously decided that taking a wolf from one of the most powerful Alphas in our world would be a nice little power move.

Finvarra and Kyla were staring at each other, animosity thick in the air.

"Fine," Kyla said. I jolted.

"Hold on."

Finvarra shot me a look that was so saturated in amused arrogance, my hand itched for my blades. Then he turned his attention back to Kyla.

I elbowed her. "We'll negotiate," I started, and she shook her head.

"Everyone in this room knows we don't have time," she said, narrowing her eyes at Finvarra. Panic fluttered in my chest. There was no way Kyla could break into the seelie king's palace. Period.

"Twelve months," Kyla said, and Finvarra gave her a slow smile.

"Six. And that is my final offer. But keep in mind, that you will need to watch the seelie king carefully. If he strikes at me before this time, our agreement is null and void."

"Fine."

"Wait," I said, feeling the world spinning out of my control. Finvarra ignored me and held out his hand. Kyla squared her shoulders and stepped forward. I grabbed her arm and stopped her.

"You're not doing this."

"I'm not going to be responsible for starting a paranormal war, Danica."

"You're not. I am. And they'll probably go to war

anyway! They're ancient and they have nothing better to do."

Finvarra sent me an amused look beneath his brows, and I resisted the urge to flip him off. He looked entirely too pleased with himself, and I had a feeling we'd played right into his hands.

One of Finvarra's people walked in with a contract, the ink still fresh. Obviously, there were unseelie stationed in the mezzanine above us, ready to jump into action.

Kyla shrugged me off, stepped forward, and scanned the contract. She tensed at something she read and then lifted her head, giving Finvarra a narrow-eyed stare. He merely raised one eyebrow as they had a silent conversation. Kyla rolled her shoulders, and I stepped forward in an attempt to read the contract.

Too late. She signed it and held out her arm. Finvarra's huge hand encircled her wrist, and I glanced behind me at Vas, hoping he had an idea that would help.

His face was pale, his eyes burning with vengeance, but he shook his head.

And then it was done. Within a few seconds, Kyla dropped to her knees, a scream ripping from her throat. To Finvarra's credit, he didn't look like he enjoyed her agony, but he didn't exactly look remorseful either. Bile burned up my throat as the long bronze mark appeared on the back of Kyla's right hand.

I'd fucked up. And I'd gotten my friend trapped in a deal she couldn't win. Kyla had only just started to accept Nathaniel's pack as family, and now she was going to lose that pack and be alone with the unseelie—

"Danica." Kyla's voice was gentle and I jolted,

realizing I was hyperventilating. Finvarra had left the room at some point, and I hadn't even noticed.

"It's my own fault," she said. "You told me he was bored, and I provided far too much entertainment. I don't know what happened. Something about him just made my fur stand up."

My lips were numb. "You shouldn't have done that."

"It's going to be okay."

No, it wasn't. I closed my eyes and took a deep breath. "I'm sorry I got you into this position. But when you're ready to go after the sword, you won't do it alone."

Kyla's face was pale, her eyes slightly glassy, but her lips firmed as she handed me the contract.

"You can't," she said. "If you do, it's an act of war."

He'd written it into the contract. I felt the blood drain from my face and Vas laid his hand on my shoulder, reading the contract with me.

"I swear," I said in a low voice, "I'll do everything I can to help."

"I know."

CHAPTER SIX

Samael

I paced back and forth for hours upon hours. I needed even less sleep than usual in this place, which made the time crawl by even slower.

This was a special kind of hell. Knowing Danica was roaming the realms, likely in constant danger, while I waited with no true ability to help…

My instincts roared in fury until my mind felt as if it would break in two.

My one comfort was that if we ran out of time… if we both fell, I would go first. I wouldn't have to witness the sole bright spark in my long life being extinguished.

I would wait for her on the other side. Our story wouldn't finish here. And if I found myself no longer by her side, if the fates judged my dark soul and found it wanting, I would cut them down until I made my way to her. I would carve out a space in the next world solely for us, and I'd never let her go. My little witch.

Something like panic roared within me, shaking my limbs. Danica had a long life ahead of her before she met me. She would have lived a full, rewarding life.

If I had anything to do with it, she still would.

Danica would be furious when she found out what I was about to do, likely aware of how much it would cost me. But I would make my wishes clear to the man who had stood by me when I was little more than an untested child.

Agaliarept wasn't asleep. But the oath he swore also bonded him to me, which meant I could silently urge him to take a nap.

It seemed to take an eternity. I reached for the bond between us, so much thinner and lighter than the bond I shared with Danica. I poked and prodded at it until an echo of surprise reverberated down the bond, followed immediately by determination.

I paced some more. Finally, when I was ready to give up, he appeared.

Agaliarept looked more exhausted than I'd ever seen him—even after he'd given up much of his power to bring Vas through the underworld's portal. But some of the tension around his eyes smoothed away as he stepped forward and slapped me on the shoulder.

"I apologize," he said as he drew back. "It took me some time to fall asleep."

"I understand. I don't have long. Already, I am weakening."

Concern flashed through Ag's eyes, but he nodded. "I'm listening."

"I need to ask you for a favor. I heard rumors, long ago, that your mother broke her bond with your father."

A muscle ticked in his jaw, but he nodded once more.

"It is not as simple as you are likely imagining, and there were severe consequences–"

"But she lived."

He sighed. "Yes. But she would likely have preferred that she did not."

My little witch was stronger than that. And she was surrounded by people who loved her. "If it seems all is lost… if you believe I am about to fall, I need you to break the bond. Danica will never attempt to do such a thing herself, and she *needs* to live."

From the acknowledgement in Agaliarept's eyes, he agreed, if not for the reasons I did. I needed Danica to live because the thought of being her downfall, of the world going on without her in it… it tore into me. But Ag knew that her devastation would eventually be tempered by vengeance, and she would find a way to kill Lucifer and save our people.

"I will begin researching," he said. "There is a demon in our realm who knew my mother, and I will speak with her." His expression tightened and I reached out, squeezing his shoulder. Ag would lose much by helping me with this.

Vassago would likely remain one of Danica's closest support systems. And he would be unlikely to forgive what he would see as a betrayal of his queen by his own uncle.

I was weakening faster than I had imagined, our connection fading. Ag flickered back and forth in front of me.

"Don't give up hope yet," he said. "If anyone can save you, it is your witch."

Danica

We didn't bother going back to the tower. As soon as we left the unseelie realm, we drove back toward the portal to the seelie realm.

I was mentally picking apart every word in the document. I couldn't help Kyla personally, but Finvarra had said nothing about using my resources. I had friends in different factions throughout Durham. Kyla wouldn't be alone.

"It's going to be okay," she said.

I shook my head. "I'm sorry. This is all my fault." I'd known she was a werewolf, relatively dominant, who didn't back down from a challenge. I'd also known she had impulse control issues, and I'd taken her with me anyway.

She let out a frustrated growl. "Enough, Danica. It's my life. I'm going to steal the sword and give it to him, and it'll be done. I'll prevent the seelie king from slaughtering him and creating a huge power vacuum, and I'll show Finvarra why he shouldn't have fucked with me."

I opened my mouth and then clamped it shut. I wouldn't have wanted someone picking apart my decision when I'd made my deal with Samael. I'd been kicking myself enough.

We left the car on a street near the seelie portal. While Aubrey had wanted us to make an entrance last time, this time, we wanted to keep our visit on the down-low.

"Do you know where the Dearg Due is?" Kyla asked as soon as we'd crossed the portal.

"Aubrey told me where he saw her last. But that doesn't mean she's still there." I flicked my gaze toward the creepy forest and Kyla froze.

"Oh hell no."

I gave her a toothy grin. "It's not too late to turn back and find a safer job."

She rolled her eyes. "Sure, and who will give me a reference if I leave you alone and you get eaten by a seelie forest?"

"Fair call." I blew out a breath and glanced at my phone. Of course, there was no service here, but I'd made detailed notes based on my discussion with Aubrey.

"Apparently, once we step inside, we'll see a path. I'm under strict instructions to stay on that path."

"Noted."

We gingerly advanced until we were at the edge of the forest. Then we peered at it in silence. It seemed like a welcoming, non-threatening kind of place.

I didn't buy it. From the expression on Kyla's face, she didn't either.

A small, gray rabbit hopped out of the forest in front of us, whiskers twitching. Kyla showed it her teeth and I nudged her with my elbow.

"Hungry?"

"Hilarious. It smells like death."

Awesome. "No point putting it off."

I took a single step into the forest. When nothing jumped out at me, Kyla did the same. We both took a few more steps, and–as Aubrey had promised–a narrow dirt path appeared.

"Seems suspicious," Kyla muttered. I shrugged. She wasn't wrong. While the unseelie realm gave the impression that monsters were hiding around every corner, the seelie realm attempted to trick visitors into thinking they were safe when they were anything but.

The trees–oaks or something similar–towered over us, providing just enough opportunity for the sunlight to stab through the branches. The forest itself was eerily still. Still and quiet. There was no breeze. No birds singing or animals rustling in the undergrowth. My skin prickled with awareness.

Kyla had her claws out. I'd drawn my Nim Cub at some point without realizing it.

It was nothing like the forest in werewolf territory. In Nathaniel's forest, I knew there were hidden predators continually watching me, all of them with incredibly sharp teeth.

Here, it was as if the trees themselves were watching us.

We continued down the path, both of us tense, scanning the forest as we walked. Wildflowers unraveled on either side of the path, encircling tree trunks and disappearing deeper into the forest. The trees themselves had thick branches made for climbing, but something told me they wouldn't take kindly to us using them to avoid whatever predators were in this forest.

"Where are we going?" Kyla asked, her voice so low it was almost a whisper.

I glanced down at my phone again. The screen was

flickering oddly, so I memorized the details as I read them aloud.

"Straight down this path until we hit a fork. Take the right, follow it to the next fork, take another right, and we should see her lair."

Kyla nodded, and we walked in silence for what had to be half an hour. The further into the forest we walked, the more sunlight disappeared above us as the massive trees crowded together, creating a dense canopy of branches and leaves. The fork seemed to appear out of nowhere, just as the dirt path had, and we turned, following it until it forked once more.

"You think that's it?" I asked.

Kyla shrugged as we both examined a huge tree. I'd never seen a tree that large in our world—even in pictures of the giant sequoias in our national parks.

The trunk shimmered, and we both tensed as a hidden door opened within the tree.

I swallowed. Next to me, Kyla's eyes sharpened as she examined the opening. It could be a trap. If we entered the tree, there was no guarantee we'd be able to get out again.

"I'm going to shift," Kyla said.

I nodded. She didn't need to be able to talk, and her fangs and claws could dissuade anything that wasn't fazed by my weapons. Plus, her nose was better in wolf form.

A few minutes later, Kyla had hidden the bundle of her clothes behind a bush. She scanned the forest and let out a low, warning growl, likely in an attempt to make sure her clothes were still there when we returned.

I slid my Nim Cub back into the sheath connected to

my lanyard and switched to my Mark II. It was a better choice for cramped quarters. I bumped Kyla aside with my hip, stepping in front of her and through the door before she could do the same. Her snarl told me she was unimpressed, but I ignored her. If something grabbed me, she'd at least have a few seconds of warning.

Carved steps. We were heading underground. I clenched my teeth, but followed the smooth wooden steps down as they spiraled below the earth. Within a few minutes, we were in some kind of underground cave. Aubrey had warned me to let go of any preconceived notions about physics and logic when traveling through this realm, but my mind still struggled to make sense of it.

Eventually, the steps ended, opening up to a larger cave.

I gave myself a brief moment to take in the dry, empty space around us. We were standing on a dirt floor that looked recently swept. The rough walls of the cave were interrupted by crude doorways. Kyla glanced at me, letting me know with a look that she'd be keeping an eye on those multiple exit and entry points.

And there she was.

The Dearg Due stood in the center of the cave. She hadn't been there when I'd glanced that way a moment ago, but now she stood as if she'd been waiting for us, and her lips curled into a terrible smile as we approached.

"What interesting guests," she purred.

My hand tightened around my knife and her smile widened, revealing delicate fangs. I'd seen corpses with more color to their faces, but her lips remained the vivid hue of venous blood. Her hair was long, black, and tangled, but her body remained curved in all the right places, ready to lure men into complacency when she needed to feed.

"Do you know why we're here?" I asked.

She took a single step closer, and Kyla lowered into a crouch, her body trembling in readiness.

"Of course. You wish to know where the sword is. The sword the seelie king has hunted for eons." Her face was now expressionless, but something dark shifted in her eyes.

"Yes. I need it to–"

"To save the man you *love*," she let out a sound that might have been a laugh, if I'd never heard real amusement before.

I needed her cooperation, so I merely nodded. "That's correct."

"A shame. If the underking takes everything from you, you may join us, you know. My sisters would love to welcome one with such an endless well of rage."

"Thank you for the offer, but I have no plans to let the underking win." I studied her. "You dislike the seelie king."

Her hands fisted, and black blood dripped to the cave floor as her sharp claws tore at her palms. "Taraghlan ordered me to remain in this realm as if I answer to *him*. And you believe I should help you find his sword?" She let out another of her almost-laughs.

I planted my feet. "If Samael dies, Lucifer won't be content with remaining king of the underworld. He'll no longer be stuck in his realm, and you bet your ass he'll ally with your king and wage war against the unseelie. Then the wolves. Then the witches. The males will *win*."

She watched me out of her black eyes. "And you believe handing the seelie king the sword he needs to kill his enemy is any better? I have gone this long without giving in to Taraghlan's demands. He even sent his little princeling friend to attempt to sway me. His blood tasted like sunshine and growing things."

Aubrey was a prince? He'd never let that slip. I took a deep breath. "We may have agreed to find the sword for the seelie king, but we never agreed to let him keep it." I glanced at Kyla and she nodded.

Interest flickered in those dark eyes. "You will double-cross the seelie king."

I knew she'd like that. "You want me to make him pay for curbing your freedom? Done."

"And why would you make the seelie king your enemy?"

I chose not to mention that, thanks to our little agreement with Finvarra, we now *had* to steal the sword.

"His people allied with our enemies, marching on our people when they least expected it. They are a large part of the reason why the rebellion failed and Lucifer kept the throne."

Taraghlan would be livid when we stole the sword. But that little problem was for future Danica to deal with.

"I do not know where the sword is," the Dearg Due warned. "But I do know someone who may be able to lead you to it."

"I'll take it."

"In exchange, you will allow me to feed."

My throat closed up, my mouth went dry, and I mentally shook myself. Truthfully, I should've expected this.

Kyla let out a whine and I glanced at her. "Memories," I managed to get out. "The Dearg Due take blood and life force from men. From women, they take our memories."

Not just any memories. Memories of love. Kyla shook her head at me and I shrugged. I didn't have many choices at this point, and if I didn't figure out a way to save Samael's life, I wouldn't be making any more memories with him. The thought stabbed into my chest, arrowing down into my gut. I faced the Dearg Due.

"We have a deal."

Her eyes somehow turned even darker. "Very well."

She took another step toward me, and Kyla leaned her body against my legs, a silent support. She was also getting into position in case she needed to rip the Dearg Due's throat out. I sent her a warning look and she ignored me, her eyes on the Dearg Due as she got within touching distance.

The Dearg Due raised her hands, and I forced myself to sheath my Mark II. I definitely couldn't be trusted to have it in my hand while she rifled through my mind.

The Dearg Due seemed to be aware that I was battling for control, because she kept her movements slow as she raised her arms. She held her hands up in front of my face, a question in her eyes.

In spite of my terror, I had to acknowledge her respect. This creature who had once been a mortal woman had never once been asked for her consent. So she waited for mine.

I nodded, and she placed one hand on either side of my head, over my temples. Her hands were like ice, but they slowly warmed, and memories began flickering through my mind like pages in a book as she searched for what she was looking for.

There was Samael, standing in front of me when we first met. I was cornered, bleeding, and entirely aware that I was about to die.

"This is the male you chose?" The Dearg Due murmured in my head.

"Your opinion is noted," I snapped.

A low laugh. I grit my teeth and then she was moving on.

There was our first kiss, in the shadows of my apartment building. He'd taken me by surprise, and I'd *melted* for him. The Dearg Due obviously had access to my inner thoughts along with those memories, because she let out another creepy chuckle.

"Yes, I believe his wingspan must be enormous."

"Fuck you."

Her hands clamped tighter around my head. And there was the moment I'd decided to save him. I was sitting in my car, debating whether to let him live or die, and looking back at it now made my stomach twist.

"Interesting," she mused.

"If I wanted your commentary, I'd ask for it."

Then we were in the field. I lunged for Samael, throwing up my shield. Hoping to give him enough time to *live*. The Dearg Due snarled.

"Stupid girl."

"Would you not have done the same for the peasant boy you fell in love with?"

Silence. Then her voice turned frigid. *"Yes. And yet*

he never came for me. That should be lesson enough for you, witchling."

I flinched at the mockery in her tone as she dared to call me one of the pet names Samael had given to me. I'd heard him say that word in every tone imaginable, from disdain to disgust, desire to delight.

"I could take that from you," she said sweetly. *"But I think there is more."*

I shuddered. Dimly, I felt Kyla press against my legs, a sound like a yelp leaving her throat. It brought me back to the present, reminded me of *why* I was allowing this.

There was Samael, showing me his own memory of Lucifer slaughtering his family. It was the first time I'd gained a glimmer of understanding into why he was so overprotective, and just one of the reasons for his control-freak nature.

She moved on.

Samael and I were standing on one of the balconies outside his ballroom now. I'd just learned I wasn't unseelie.

My gut twisted in real time as I experienced the realization that I'd outlive Evie. That Samael had known what I was.

"Delicious."

The Dearg Due wanted my reactions, so I refused to give them to her.

She sighed and moved on. And then I was lying on Samael's bed. He was standing in front of me, wings spread. They snapped shut as he humored me enough to turn, glancing over his shoulder at me with a wink.

"Perhaps I can see why you would want to bone with

this demon."

I rolled my eyes. *"It's 'bone this demon.' If you're going to steal modern vocabulary from my mind, at least get it right."*

"Bone this demon. I will remember."

She watched as I slept with Samael for the first time. *"I never got to do this, you know. Never got to enjoy this experience."*

"I'm sorry that was your life."

"I have taken many other first times to make up for it. But not yours. No, I think there is something better. Something you are attempting to hide from me."

Her claws dug into my head now, drawing blood. Kyla went nuts, the sound leaving her throat almost like a roar. I managed to choke out an order for her to stand down. I wouldn't go through all of this and *not* get what I needed.

The next memory rolled through my head. And it hurt.

It was directly after I walked through that library and read the Nephilim prophecy. The moment I realized Samael knew what I was. Had known for some time.

"Now, every demon alive knows the Nephilim is alive," Samael told me.

I watched my face. I looked like he'd stabbed me in the gut. *"Tell me you didn't know who I was. Tell me you didn't know I have the power to take down your oldest enemy. The man who slaughtered your family."*

I could see Samael's expression as he gazed at me. I'd thought that expression had been blank, but I'd been so upset myself that I'd missed the devastation in his eyes.

Then I was holding Misty to his throat. The Dearg Due laughed and laughed.

"Tell me." I demanded.

He stayed silent and I choked out a dry sob.

"You knew who I was this entire time, and you let me stay ignorant. Worse, you were probably planning to use me to take down your enemies. Deny it."

The Dearg Due sighed. *"This is what men do."*

"You haven't exactly had the best experiences with men," I replied.

The Dearg Due watched the memory for a little longer. *"I believe you can keep this one,"* she purred.

I'd been holding on. Clutching desperately to the one memory I couldn't give up, but the Dearg Due had eons of experience digging out what she wanted.

She struck.

A choked sob left my throat as I watched myself in Samael's penthouse. I hadn't noticed at the time, but his expression seemed… softer. He looked almost content.

We'd just finished dinner. The remains were on the table inside, surrounded by the flowers and candles he'd arranged for me.

"I'm in love with you," I blurted out.

He hadn't believed me. I could see it in his eyes as I watched the memory in excruciating detail.

"You would play with me even now?"

I frowned at him. "I didn't expect it to happen. God knows I didn't want it to. You infuriate me, challenge me, annoy the shit out of me. You're bossy and controlling, and dealing with your ego is no fucking picnic, let me tell you."

The Dearg Due watched silently as I paced back and forth, Samael's silver gaze drinking me in like I was something he'd never thought to see. Something entirely unexpected but welcome. I knew what was coming next. I attempted to shut the memory down, but I had no hope against the Dearg Due's vicious power.

"Just a few months ago, if someone had told me I'd fall in love with you, I would've told them to get their head checked," I muttered.

"I'm not sure if that's complimentary."

I ignored that. "And now… I miss you when you're not around. I had to actively fight with myself not to come to this tower every damn day."

"Danica–"

"I want to fall asleep next to you, and fight with you, and fuck you, and complain to my friends when you're being your usual, overly possessive self. I want to be yours. But only if you're mine, too."

Strong hands gripped my shoulders, turning me, and Samael's mouth crashed down on mine. He buried his hand in my hair and the world faded away as I lost myself in the feel of him surrounding me. My demon. Mine.

"Is that a yes?" I mumbled against his mouth.

"Say it again," he ordered, and I rolled my eyes. Bossy demon.

"I love you."

I could feel tears dripping down my face as I stood in that cave. This was the moment we'd both admitted our feelings. The moment I'd stopped running.

Next to me, Kyla let out a sound like a whimper, and I attempted to close my eyes, but the Dearg Due refused to let me look away. I watched as Samael lifted me into his arms and carried me through his penthouse, laying me on his bed.

"This doesn't mean you can tell me what to do all the time," I said.

"Quiet." He nibbled on my lower lip.

"And I'm not going to give up my career for you."

He laughed. "Of course not." He pulled back long enough to strip off his clothes and my mouth went dry. I forced myself to raise my gaze to his face in an attempt to get my point across.

"I'm serious, Samael."

"I know. So many clothes in my way."

He was stripping me, but his eyes met mine as he paused. "I want you, little witch. Not a woman who will do everything I say without question. Although that might be an interesting experience for a few days."

I'd given him a dark look, and he laughed, unhooking my bra and nuzzling my breasts.

"I've had centuries of women doing as I said," he told me. "None of them could hold my attention for more than a few weeks. You? You will be mine forever. And if you didn't know I'm already yours, you haven't been paying close enough attention."

"Please," I said aloud. "Not this one."

"This is my price," the Dearg Due hissed in my mind. "It is *this* memory, and the chance to save him, or you keep your memory and lose him forever."

There was no choice at all. But I vowed that if I ever got the chance, I'd make her pay for this. How many other women had she done this to over the centuries?

"Thousands," she whispered in my mind. *"And none of them have managed to kill me yet, little witch."*

"Call me that again. I fucking dare you."

Her hands left my head, and I stared at her, my face still damp. I grasped for the memory, but there wasn't even a whisper left.

She'd taken something precious. I didn't know what it was, but I felt it like a hole in my chest.

"You will find a connection to the sword in the Middleground. Go to the Tengu," she said. "You will find what you are looking for there."

Kyla narrowed her eyes at me as we left. I swallowed around the lump in my throat.

"I had no choice."

She was silent until she'd pulled on her clothes, and we were both standing on the forest path once more.

"Are you okay?"

"No." But I would be. One day, maybe Samael would help me remember what she'd taken. Until then, at least I had a way to get him back.

CHAPTER SEVEN

Danica

By the time we left the seelie realm, it was getting dark. I didn't know if time worked the same in the Middleground, but I sent Kyla home and drove toward the blue portal I'd first traveled through so long ago.

What if I couldn't do this? What if I was merely delaying the inevitable? Was Ag right? Had I done more damage to the demons by tying myself to Samael?

It was only now, when I was alone in my car, that I could allow myself to question my decisions. That I could truly feel the terror from my choices.

It was hard to reconcile the person I'd been, just six months ago, with the person I was now.

I hadn't known what I was doing when I completed my bond with Samael. All I'd known was that I couldn't bear to live in a world without him in it. The power had poured from the deepest part of me, all of my instincts screaming that I had to do whatever it took to keep him alive.

Even knowing what I knew now, I couldn't bring myself to have any regrets. I'd bought us time. Now, I had to make the most of every minute of it.

I parked next to the portal, got out of the car, and took a deep breath.

I walked straight through the portal as if I were out for a Sunday stroll. No pain. Nothing.

The last few times I visited this realm, I was with Samael. He'd brought me here to meet his dragon, and then again to meet her daughter.

Now, instead of being flown to the cave, with Samael's arms wrapped around me, I was making my way on foot, just like I did the first time I visited, when I stole the Mistilteinn dagger from Samael's hoard.

Vas would have flown me, of course, but I needed to do this myself.

I hesitated outside the cave, taking a few deep breaths. Finally, I took a step inside, my eyes adjusting to the dim light. Something crunched, and I slowly turned my head. Scylla was currently tearing the meat from a long bone, and she chomped down on that bone as her eyes met mine.

The last time I'd visited, Nuri had been the size of a large dog. I gaped at the younger dragon as she prowled toward me. She now towered over me. Maybe I'd been an idiot to come here without Samael.

I went still as Nuri leaned down and sniffed at my hair. A picture flashed through my mind, and my heart ached at the sight of Samael's face.

"He's not here," I managed to get out. "He's in trouble."

Nuri lay down, her tail whipping back and forth across the ground as she glanced between me and her mother. Scylla dropped the bone and watched me, a clear order to speak.

So I explained what had happened. And then I explained what would need to happen if we were to save Samael's life.

My voice was shaky as I finished. "Will you help me? If I can find a way to reverse the spell, will you help me bring him back?"

Scylla took a single step closer, and I forced myself to stand my ground. Then she bowed her head, a clear answer.

"Thank you," I breathed. "I'll be back with him. As soon as I find the sword."

Danica

I knew something was wrong as soon as I got back to the tower. I double-parked outside the entrance and ran toward the lobby, my lungs tight.

Bael was waiting by the elevator.

"What happened?"

He opened his mouth. Then he shook his head and pressed the button for the elevator, gesturing for me to get in.

Samael wasn't dead. I'd *know* if he was dead.

His penthouse was packed with demons when I arrived. A few of them gave me dark looks as I stalked toward Samael's bedroom.

Ag sat next to Samael's bed with Lia curled up on

his lap. He was absently stroking her ears, his gaze on the bed.

I was dimly aware of Vas stepping closer to me, but all I could see was my demon.

His hands were gone. The hands that had held me close, carried me through the air, cupped my face as he made love to me. The hands he used to capture my chin when I was being a smartass. To brush my hair back from my face. To strip me of my clothes when he decided he needed me naked right that minute.

My knees turned to jelly, and Vas wrapped his hand around my arm, keeping me on my feet.

My lips were numb. "When?"

"A few hours ago," Ag said, his eyes on Samael. Finally, his eyes met mine, and we shared a moment of perfect understanding.

Samael was dying.

Vas pulled me toward him as the high-rise shook. The windows rattled, and the chandelier above my head swung back and forth.

I jolted. "Jesus, was that an earthquake?"

Ag turned back to Samael.

"That was the mages. They have declared war against us, in retaliation for the damage to their building."

I couldn't breathe. "Mella was the one who damaged the building."

"And you freed the selkie."

I took a moment to come to terms with that. "Will they bring the building down?"

"They're trying. Samael's wards are keeping it standing, but as he becomes weaker, so do those wards.

Never have they been able to touch the building with their power before. All the demons in our territory are attempting to bolster the wards, however most of us are also funneling our power into our bonds with Samael in an effort to keep him alive."

Albert was a dead man. I swallowed around the bitter taste in my mouth. Lilith stretched from where she was standing in front of the window, and her eyes met mine. She raised one eyebrow at me expectantly.

What would Samael do?

That was easy, he'd kick some ass.

I stalked out of the room and onto the balcony, where I closed the door behind me and pulled out my phone.

"Yes?" Nathaniel answered immediately.

"How would you like for me to owe you a huge favor?"

"I'm listening."

I outlined my plan, and he was silent for a long moment. "I would be putting all of my wolves in danger."

I sighed. "What do you want, Nathaniel?"

More silence. I ground my teeth but forced myself to stop as soon as I realized the werewolf could likely hear it.

"We require an alliance," he finally said.

"Samael's unconscious."

He chuckled. "And you're ruling the demons in his place."

"They're ruling themselves. I'm just a figurehead."

He ignored that. "It will be an alliance similar to the one Samael has with the unseelie king."

It was probably wise for me to not mention just how

shaky *that* alliance was right now.

As usual, I was out of options. "Fine. Get the paperwork drawn up. We're on our way."

I walked back into the bedroom, where Vas watched me out of dark eyes. His uncle ignored me.

"I need every demon in this apartment ready to go," I said. "We're taking him out of here."

Ag slowly got to his feet. "What exactly have you done?"

"We're going to visit our new allies."

Danica

The penthouse doors were flung open, and four demons picked up Samael's mattress, carefully keeping it steady.

I chewed on my lower lip. "What if they drop him?"

Vas nudged me with his elbow. "They're some of our best in flight. Don't second-guess yourself now."

"Okay. The mages will be watching this building," I told the demons. "I'm going to create a distraction. Don't move until you see my signal."

Asmodeus raised one eyebrow. "And what is your signal?"

"You'll know it when you see it." I stepped closer to Samael, but I was too scared to brush my lips over his. His hands were nothing but ash, which was about to get blown away in the wind. My throat burned. "If I get the counter spell, will he–"

"He'll be good as new," Vas murmured.

Neither of us pointed out the obvious—that if Samael's entire body turned to ash, there would be nothing left to restore.

"You're coming with me," I said.

Vas attempted a grin, but it was strained. "I figured."

I glanced back at the demons holding Samael's mattress. I didn't need to tell them to be careful. With a nod, I reached out for Vas, and we shot into the sky.

"Want to tell me all about your little plan?"

I shrugged. "I'm going to raise some hell and make Albert regret messing with us."

My power had been licking at my shield all day. It didn't feel anything like when I had strained to hold it at bay–when using it meant that I risked losing control. No, now I instinctively knew that I could now turn it on and off like a tap.

"They'll be waiting for us," Vas warned.

"I know. How close can you get us?"

He considered it. "Do you want to attack from the ground or the air?"

"Air makes more of a statement. Can you tell if anyone is in the building?"

He nodded. "I'll be able to see heat signatures." He gestured up at the sky, which was darkening as we spoke. "Construction will have finished for the day."

I smiled. "Good."

The facility looked like it had been hit by a bomb. That bomb went by the name of Mella. I took a moment to mourn the library. Even when I'd loathed every other inch of the Mage Council, I'd loved the library.

As soon as we were within sight of the facility, I raised my ward. It glowed around us, a purple-gold that also highlighted us like a beacon. No one would be looking at Samael's tower right now. All eyes were on us.

"Oh Albert," I sang, pushing power into my voice so it echoed over the entire neighborhood. Mages surrounded the facility, their faces tilted up as they glowered at us.

"You think you can huff and puff and blow my house down? Let's see how you like it."

"Amana!" Albert roared.

I turned my head. He was standing on a car, his face bright red. His eyes burned into mine and I gave him a finger wave.

"Don't you dare!" He actually shook his fist at me.

I laughed. "What did you think would happen, Albert? You really thought you could come for my people with no repercussions?"

He gaped at me and I laughed again, knowing it would piss him off. Because that's exactly what he'd thought. Someone had told him Samael was out of the picture, and he'd struck when we were weakest.

Now he would pay.

"Any heat signatures?" I muttered, and Vas shook his head.

"You're clear."

"Excellent."

I lifted my hand. May as well make it dramatic.

All eyes were on me as I raised my pointer finger and stabbed it toward the facility.

Power *erupted*.

I gasped as it streamed from me, bathing my every

cell with warmth. The mages attacked as one, their power smashing into my ward, but if there was one thing I was good at, it was warding.

The side of the building exploded.

I directed my power at the other side, aiming close to the ground. Mella had done so much damage that it wouldn't take long for it to–

Screams tore through the air as anyone in the vicinity of the building fled for their lives. I aimed more power at the building, and fire slammed right into the center of it.

"Danica, stop!"

Someone else was using a spell to make their own voice louder. I glanced down.

Keigan stood on the ground below me. Even from here, I could see the disappointment in his eyes.

Disappointment in me.

Behind him, the facility pancaked. Dust flew through the air, covering everything in the vicinity.

"Take us down," I told Vas.

"It's not safe."

"Just for a moment. Please."

Vas tucked his wings in, and we plummeted down. I barely refrained from screaming as he thrust his wings out at the last minute.

"You'll pay for that," I gasped.

He merely gave a low laugh, and a second later my feet were on the ground.

"Why, Danica?" Keigan asked. He was covered in dust and grime, and his eyes filled with tears as he turned toward the remains of the building.

"They came for us," I said. "They know Samael's

weakened, and they attempted to bring the tower down."

"So instead of bolstering the wards, you decided to blow up our building?"

I gaped at him. "Do you even know what happened to me in that building? Albert knew about Ben and Cara and everyone else, Keigan. I know he did. I almost died. Samael may still die."

Sadness clouded his face. "You could have come to me. We could have talked about this."

I didn't tell him I'd needed the distraction to take what was left of Samael out of the tower. I just shook my head.

"You said you were thinking about leaving the Council. Maybe it's finally time for you to choose sides."

His eyes were steady on my face. "Are we at war, Dani?"

The nickname did it, and I had to blink back tears. I pretended it was from the dust in the air.

"You and me? Never. Me and Albert? You bet your ass. He struck when I was away from the tower. While Samael lay dying in his bed. I'll never forget that, Keigan. Never."

The look in Keigan's eyes was like someone close to him had died. Behind me, Vas tensed. His arm hooked around my waist.

"We've got to go."

He launched into the sky before I could say another word.

Not that I had any idea what to say.

We were both silent as Vas flew toward Nathaniel's territory.

"You're leaking," Vas said softly.

I glanced at him. He raised one hand, wiping my tears away.

"I'm messing everything up," I muttered.

Vas shook his head. "If Samael was awake, he would've done the exact same thing. Only he would have killed every mage in the vicinity. You did them a favor."

"It doesn't feel like it."

"It's difficult. Being in two worlds."

I glanced at him. His gaze was on the forest below us.

"Does it feel difficult for you?"

The corner of his mouth lifted, but he kept his attention on Nathaniel's territory.

"I've spent time with humans, but I've never worked with them. Or for them."

I nudged him with my elbow and he laughed. "I think it's difficult for anyone. I think your sister is going to find it the most difficult of all."

My chest clenched. "I miss her."

"I know. She's safe. Our people are watching her."

"Thank you."

He grinned and nodded down at the clearing in front of us, where Nathaniel stood, his hands on his hips.

"His people are watching her too."

I frowned, but Vas was doing his drop-like-a-stone landing and the air was ripped from my lungs.

"Why do you do that?" I griped as my feet finally found the ground.

"Got to keep you awake."

I rolled my eyes and nodded at Nathaniel. He wore

faded jeans and a plaid shirt, and if you weren't able to feel his dominance from twenty feet away, you'd never know he was an Alpha.

"Thanks for this."

He smiled, and it was all wolf. "As much as I like you, Danica, allowing this many demons into my territory is not something that I've done out of the goodness of my heart."

"I know."

"Let's get the signing done, and then I'll take you to him."

Nathaniel waved his hand behind me, and I turned, finding the clearing suddenly full of both wolves and demons.

None of them looked happy.

Well, I wasn't exactly dancing for joy, so why should anyone else be having a good time?

"We've had our lawyers draw up the agreement," Nathaniel said, nodding at one of his wolves, who stepped forward and handed it to me. "However, if you would like any changes, they can be negotiated."

I read the document, my eyes so dry and tired that scanning it was almost impossible.

I forced myself to concentrate. The alliance would encompass both territories and also included a peace treaty. Both Nathaniel and Samael—or me—would be required to notify each other if one of their people committed a crime in their territory—with the punishment to be negotiated.

There was also an amendment detailing a potential trade agreement—to be negotiated and signed later. Ag appeared in front of me and I handed him the paper. "What do you think?"

He scanned it. "I want Bael to take a look."

I nodded and he stepped away. Across the clearing, I spotted Kyla, who waved at me.

I glanced at Nathaniel. "Any problems getting Samael settled?"

He gave me a sympathetic look. "No. I'm sorry for your loss, Danica."

"There's no loss. Not yet."

He merely nodded. "When will Evelyn be returning?"

"I don't know. She doesn't know what happened with Samael and I haven't told her."

"Why?"

"There's nothing she can do."

He just watched me, and I sighed. "She needs some time, and I'm going to give it to her."

I glanced around the clearing as the demons discussed the alliance. Realistically, the wolves had all the power in this little situation. We needed somewhere safe to stash Samael, and the mages knew they wouldn't get within half a mile of wolf territory without the sentries ripping them apart.

Not to mention, our little agreement included those wolves surrounding Samael—in addition to the demons who would be housed in this territory wherever necessary.

Nothing and no one would get to him.

Except time.

And I was running out of it.

CHAPTER EIGHT

Danica

I woke up early the next morning and watched Samael. I kept expecting him to open his eyes. To flash me his wicked grin and ask, in his usual imperious tone, why exactly I was lying so far away.

I'd told him all about the contract with the wolves last night, and he'd seemed pleased. But I'd constantly woken, sleeping lighter than I had in years. As a result, I'd barely gotten to spend any time with him.

Better figure this shit out, or you won't be spending time with him ever again.

Panic clawed into my gut as I carefully kept my gaze away from the empty spaces where his hands should be. Already, his wrists were crumbling the same way his fingers had a couple of days ago.

Lia purred at the end of the bed. I'd had the demons bring her when they brought Samael, just in case the mages got any bright ideas about bringing the tower down again.

Kyla would be here soon. I glanced around the bedroom of the small cabin. Sliding doors occupied one whole side of the room, allowing the demons to simply walk in and place Samael's mattress on the bed.

A second bedroom housed Ag and Vas, and Bael had slept on the sofa in the living room. I could leave knowing Samael was as safe as could be. All three of them would lay down their lives for him.

A bouncy jingle sounded from the living room. Bael had turned on the TV. I hadn't packed much when I went back to the tower last night, but I pulled on a clean pair of jeans and a long-sleeved t-shirt. Then I reached for my weapons. Lia got to her feet and nuzzled me.

"Hey cat. You hungry? The demons are going to hang out with you today."

I wandered out into the living room. The cabin was rustic, made of wooden logs, but no expense had been spared with the furnishings. This was one of the houses that the wolves who lived with Nathaniel used when they wanted privacy.

A smoke alarm blared and someone cursed. Bael nodded at me as I sat next to him on the sofa.

"Vas is cooking," he said mournfully, and I smiled.

"How *will* you guys survive without Samael's chefs?"

He grinned, but it dropped from his face as the ad ended and a newscaster appeared, a picture of Samael and Nathaniel behind his right shoulder.

"Breaking news out of Durham this morning," she announced. "The Triangle Werewolf Pack has signed an alliance with the demons. When asked for a comment, the werewolf Alpha said that the two factions share mutual interests, and he was looking forward to the alliance benefiting both the wolves and the demons."

"However, according to our sources, Samael himself hasn't been seen for weeks. The alliance was signed by Danica Amana." Footage of Samael and me played on the screen, and my heart ached so viciously, I wondered if it was bleeding. On the TV, Samael was kissing my forehead before he turned to smite the McCormick descendants.

"When asked for comment, a spokesperson for the demons said that Samael was out of town, and the alliance was handled by his mate, Ms. Amana."

I turned the TV off. "I guess the cat is out of the bag."

Bael smiled. "I leaked it."

"Why would you do that?"

"Strategy. Now that our alliance with Finvarra is on thin ice, and we're at war with the mages, we need it to be known that we're allied with the wolves."

I swallowed, my throat suddenly dry. All of this had happened to the demons since I got involved with them.

Vas stepped into the living room and handed me a cup of coffee.

"You look a little sick," he remarked.

Bael glanced at my face and shook his head. "Don't blame yourself. It was only a matter of time."

"You think Samael would have allied with the wolves?" I hadn't had a chance to ask him last night.

"If he'd needed to. He didn't need to. But *now* we need to. It was the right decision, if a little hastily executed. But the mages would have poured all of their power into our tower until it fell."

"You think they could have brought it down?"

"Our spies informed us that Albert had arranged for

three other mages at his power level to land in Durham last night. Together, they would have brought that tower down. With Samael so weakened, we wouldn't have stood a chance."

"I brought down their building instead."

Bael's grin returned. "So I heard. Wish I'd seen that."

A knock sounded at the door and Bael got to his feet, pulling it open.

"Hey guys," Kyla looked fresh as a daisy. I tried not to hold it against her. "Coffee?"

Vas stepped into the small living room and handed her a cup. "Breakfast is ready," he announced.

Kyla shot me a look as she glanced toward the kitchen and my lips twitched. If I could smell burning, she likely knew exactly just what to expect from Vas's cooking.

It was food, though. Even if the toast was a little blackened and the eggs were overcooked enough to have the texture of rubber. I covered them in salt and inhaled them.

"And where are you going today?" Bael asked as I took a final gulp of coffee, then headed into the bathroom to brush my teeth.

"The Middleground."

Shocked silence claimed the cabin. I'd expected Vas to stalk through the door, but it was Ag who appeared, his face dark.

"You think it's wise to risk your life right now?"

"I think I don't have a choice," I mumbled around my toothbrush.

"You always have a choice."

I scowled, rinsing my mouth. "Would you prefer if I sat by Samael's bed and wrung my hands? Maybe it would be more convenient for you if I fell apart and whined that there was nothing that could be done?"

Surprisingly, the corner of his mouth curled up. I almost pinched myself, but within a fraction of a moment, his expression was blank once more.

"No. Last night was the correct decision, regardless of the implications. The mages should have known not to attempt to strike at us, no matter how weak they perceived us. But if you die…"

"Who will be in charge?"

He frowned. "Me," he said, and a hint of distaste flickered in his eyes. At least I didn't need to worry about Ag stabbing me in the back in a bid for power. I grinned. Nope. The demon looked appalled by the thought of ruling.

I shrugged at him. "Samael trusts you as his second. If I don't come back, you know what to do."

Besides, we both knew it was a lot easier to judge the person making all the decisions than it was to make those decisions yourself.

He ground his teeth. In any other circumstance, I would have enjoyed his discomfort, but if we had one thing in common, it was our love for Samael.

"Don't take any stupid risks," he ordered.

I just shrugged. What Ag considered a stupid risk was probably pretty similar to what I considered the price of saving Samael's life. He heaved a sigh, turned, and stalked out of the bathroom.

"Good talk," I called after him.

It didn't take us long after that. My car was still at the tower, so we took Kyla's Nissan, driving toward the Middleground's portal.

The portal was located on the outskirts of Chapel Hill. In a strip mall. Instead of closing the mall and declaring it off-limits, the store owners close to the portal had decided it was a good way to drum up business from curious humans. There was even a gift shop selling portal-branded souvenirs at one end of the mall.

"Ooh, fudge," Kyla murmured as she caught a sign outside one of the tourist stores. "I like fudge."

I shot her a look and she grinned. "I've never been to the Middleground."

"Me neither. I don't know many people who have."

The Middleground wasn't ruled by any one ruler, but was, instead, split into different territories.

It required much less power to cross into the Middleground compared to the other realms. That made it a popular choice for refugees who were fleeing other realms, along with plenty of unsavory types who had escaped the authorities in their own realms.

It was a good thing both of us were armed to the teeth.

I was carrying my Nim Cub, my Mark II, my throwing knives, and my Colt. Misty was also tucked away out of sight—it wasn't a smart idea to flash a powerful artifact in this realm unless I had to.

I'd restocked my utility belt—the sight of it forging a vicious longing for my demon—and I'd wrapped a long, thin piece of metal around my hair band, just in case I needed a garrote.

Kyla had her own gun, several knives, and, of course, her fangs and claws.

We parked next to the gift store and ignored the curious humans who held up their phones to record us as we walked through the portal.

It spat us out in the middle of Harlen, one of the smaller territories in the Middleground. From here, we'd need to head west.

I scanned our surroundings. So far, the Middleground was a dark, dingy place, the atmosphere worsened by the sky, which was the yellow-green of an old bruise. We were standing close to the portal on the edge of the village, surrounded by wooden buildings that looked like they'd blow over with the first gust of wind. But from the decrepit look of them, they'd stood here for decades.

"Remind me where exactly we're going?" Kyla said.

"Tengu like mountainous areas. Sometimes they even live in trees."

"And what exactly are tengu?"

I took one last look at the village. There was such little movement that my neck itched. But I could feel eyes on us.

"They originated in Japan. At least, that was what we thought before the portals opened. Now we know that they may have come from the Middleground. Some people consider them demons. Others consider them gods. But they're actually unseelie. They're known for their swordsmanship, and they can also control the wind." I glanced at her. "Whatever you do, don't take anything from the forest."

She nodded and we turned toward the dirt road

leading out of the tiny village. Nothing moved.

"Creepy," she murmured.

I let my hand slide down, resting it just a few inches from my Colt. We began walking. No one stopped us.

For a city girl, I was spending far too much time wandering through various forests.

I pointed at the ominous dark line of the mountain chain to the north. "We're heading that way."

It took us close to two hours to walk through this side of the forest and into the foothills. The mountains loomed over us, and the forest seemed to grow colder as we approached, the trees growing further apart.

The forest went silent. Both of us tensed.

And then the winds started. A gentle breeze at first, but within a few moments we were being pelted by dried leaves and twigs, dirt and grass flying up toward our faces. I ground my teeth.

"We were sent by a Dearg Due," I called out, but the wind ripped the words from my mouth.

Nothing to do but wait. We bowed our heads, holding our hands up to protect our faces from the forest debris. Eventually, the wind slowed.

"Interesting welcome," Kyla murmured.

Something dropped down from a tree a few feet in front of us, hitting the ground with a thump. I had my Colt out and pointed before I realized I'd moved.

Two legs poked out of the tengu's long robes, but that was where any similarities to humans ended. He carried a large fan in one clawed hand, and his wings flapped threateningly as he blocked our way forward. His face was bright red, with a nose that must've been six inches long.

"Take us to your leader," Kyla said.

I shot her a look and she winked at me.

The tengu turned and walked deeper into the forest. We followed him. I watched my steps so I wouldn't trip over any tree roots or fallen branches. Kyla instinctively put her feet in the right places as she scrutinized the surrounding forest.

Within a few minutes, the tengu let out a low whistle. The exact same sound was replicated from deeper in the forest and he gestured for us to step forward.

In the time it took for me to blink, we were surrounded.

There must have been fifty tengu circling us. Their presence at my back set my teeth on edge.

"Half-blood," one of them said, stepping forward. "Why do you come here?"

"I'm hoping for your help," I said.

The tengu looked vaguely intrigued, his long nose wrinkling. "You wish for us to teach you magic?"

"No. We're looking for the sword that was used to kill Grendel's mother. One of the Dearg Due told us to come to you."

"And you expect that I will tell you where to find it?"

"I'm sure there's some bargain we can make."

Exhaustion suddenly washed over me like a wave. Another day, another bargain, and still, Samael faded away in his bed. Alone. For a moment, the unfairness of it all hit me like a fist to the gut.

I straightened my shoulders. The tengu was watching me out of dark eyes.

"We do not have the sword," he said.

"But you know where it is?"

"I know where it *was*. Several centuries ago."

"And what do you want for this information?"

One of the tengu approached Kyla, his eyes curious. Another followed in his footsteps and within moments, she was surrounded by tengu as they sniffed at her.

Her vicious growl ripped through the air.

The tengu backed off a few paces, but if anything, they now seemed more interested.

"My people are considering a new business venture," the leader said.

I attempted to hide my surprise. I wasn't sure what I'd been expecting him to say, but that definitely wasn't it.

"We have an opportunity to work with the seelie in your realm, selling our swords." He pulled his sword free of its sheath and paused as I admired it.

"There is a spell that we would like to use for luck in our new venture. We require the blood of a gnome who has traveled through the portals."

"Why a gnome?"

He shrugged. "You haven't heard of the luck of the gnome?"

He said 'luck of the gnome' as if it was a spell itself. I frowned. "No."

"Gnomes carry with them the luck of the gods. Particularly when it comes to commerce. Since we will be trading with your realm, the luck we create will be greater if the gnome has been in multiple realms."

"Why can't you get your hands on gnome blood yourself?"

"For the magic to work, it must be given freely."

And no gnome would hand their blood over to the tengu. Bad spells could be done with blood. I knew some people who burned their blood if they happened to bleed anywhere near witch territory.

I sighed. "And what guarantee do I have that you won't use this blood for nefarious purposes?"

"We will swear a geas."

A geas was a blood-vow. It would prevent them from using the gnome blood for anything other than the commerce spell.

I glanced around at the tengu. "All of you?"

"If necessary. This is for the good of all of us."

"I may know someone who can help. But I need proof that you can give me helpful information about the sword."

"I will tell you where it *was*. It is up to you to track it from there."

Time was slipping through my fingers like water. I wanted to shake the tengu. To roar at him. To threaten. But I knew damn well that would only lose me any cooperation I might've had.

"Fine."

We trudged out of the forest. Already, this day felt endless, and knowing that I was going to have to convince Gary to give me some of his blood was not improving my mood.

We were close to the edge of the forest when Kyla went still. It took me another moment, but I felt it too.

"They approached upwind so I couldn't scent them," Kyla whispered. "But they're close."

"What are they?"

"No idea. They smell… wrong."

Using my power here would announce who and what I was to every creature in this region of the Middleground. I didn't have time to play stupid dominance games or tussle with idiots who thought they could kill me and use my power.

Especially since I'd need to return to this area with goblin blood.

"No magic," I said beneath my breath, and Kyla nodded. The werewolf looked pleased by the thought of getting her claws dirty. The last few days had been stressful for her as well.

Giant scorpions scuttled out from between the trees, blocking us in. They shuffled through the forest on eight legs, tails held high in the air, sharply pointed and likely dripping deadly poison. They were about the size of a golden retriever, and I scanned them, counting nine of the creatures.

"Give us your weapons. And your money," one of them said, although his fangs were far too big for his words to come out clearly.

"Dude, that lisp is embarrassing."

"Now!"

Kyla threw me an amused look.

I sighed. As much as I was ready to rumble, I didn't want to waste time with this.

"Are you sure this is a good plan?" I asked them.

One of them stepped forward and attempted to poke Kyla with one of his claws.

She pulled her knife and stabbed him, so fast the

movement was a blur. Her clothes tore, and then she was a wolf.

The giant scorpions attacked en masse.

"Don't let them sting you," I called to Kyla.

I pulled my Mark II. I had no idea if the Colt would fire properly in the Middleground, and it was something I'd be checking as soon as I was done with this little party.

The closest scorpion charged, moving surprisingly fast. He swung his tail and I ducked, burying my knife in his chest. I tore my blade free as he screamed. My kick took him in the gut and sent him flying.

One down.

Kyla had killed one, too. Seven to go.

She let out a sound like a roar. It echoed through the forest, loud enough that everyone froze. I lunged forward, then rolled low, sliding down to shove my knife deep in the closest scorpion's unprotected belly. Six left.

He screamed and two scorpions leapt forward. I struggled to pull my knife free, but it was stuck.

Goddamn it.

I let the knife go, and the scorpion's front legs collapsed. I spun out with a hook kick, feeling my hamstring whine at me as I smashed the back of my heel into its face.

Fuck, that hurt.

Don't hit them in the places where they're covered in hard armor, dummy.

I pulled my Nim Cub from the sheath around my neck. The scorpion on the left charged me, tail striking faster than a rattlesnake.

I ducked, lunging to the left. My foot slid in the dirt

beneath me, but I shoved my knife in the gap between the two segments of its armor. Thick green blood poured from its throat as it fell.

Five.

The second creature was already on me. I bobbed and weaved, moving backwards across the clearing. A few feet away, Kyla had killed two more of the creatures and she sent me a lupine grin of challenge.

Three to go.

One of them backed away, darting into the forest.

Two left.

The scorpion in front of me whirled, using its tail in an attempt to sweep my feet out from under me. I vaulted over it and slashed out with my Nim Cub. He reared back.

He used its back legs to lunge forward, striking at me with his front claws. Again. Again. Again.

I ground my teeth as his claw caught my knife arm, and he let out a victorious howl.

My forearm burned. Droplets of my blood flew through the air as I ducked. If he'd cut me much higher, I would've been in trouble, but he was celebrating far too soon.

I let my arm drop, like I was losing function, and my chest heaved as if I were running out of steam. The scorpion raised his tail, telegraphing his attack to the entire realm. I stepped into him, ducked beneath his head, and thrust my knife up.

It rebounded off the thick protective armor on its chest. Missed, damn it.

Kyla trotted over to me, as if she was out for a morning stroll. She pounced, ripping into the scorpion's belly. Then she struck out with one paw and threw the creature several feet into the air.

I blew out a breath. "I had that," I said.

Her mouth fell open in a wolfish grin and I rolled my eyes at myself. "Thanks."

We surveyed the forest around us.

"We're leaving the bodies here," I announced to anyone who may be listening as I located my Mark II. "As a reminder of what happens to those who think to take from us. If you see us again, I suggest you stay the fuck out of our way."

I wiggled my blade out of the scorpion's armor and wiped it on my jeans. Then I gathered the remains of Kyla's clothes, scooping her car keys from where they'd fallen through a hole in her jeans pocket. She stayed alert, scanning the forest around us as I picked up her weapons. I attempted to wipe off some of the green blood that had splattered across my neck with the remnants of her jeans, and then we continued our trek out of the forest.

The village was just as creepily silent as we approached, and I kept one eye on our surroundings while we walked back through the portal.

Kyla raised one paw and placed it on her trunk. I unlocked her car and popped the trunk, surveying the large white containers that were neatly stacked and organized. "That's a lot of clothes."

It made sense that she'd take them with her in case she needed to shift. I hopped in the passenger seat and waited while she shifted and pulled on her clothes.

She opened her door a few minutes later, sliding into the driver's seat. "Where to now?"

"I need to go to Gary's. He's going to be more cooperative if I talk to him alone. If Gary gives us his blood, we'll head straight back to the Middleground."

"And if he doesn't?"

"I'll be calling in every favor I have left to try and get some freely given gnome blood from elsewhere. And if that doesn't work, I'm down to one option."

She glanced at me and I sighed. "Go back and start killing the tengu until they tell me what I need to know."

Kyla winced.

"Yeah." I would be moving into bad-guy territory. There was another option, of course, but I wouldn't let myself consider it. Cutting Gary out of the picture and asking his kids for their blood would only mean I wouldn't be able to meet my own eyes the next time I looked in the mirror.

I wouldn't become a monster just to save our lives. It was a slippery slope down, but it would start with betraying my friend's trust. I wouldn't let my desperation turn me into someone I couldn't recognize.

I glanced out the window and crossed my fingers that Gary would be willing to help.

CHAPTER NINE

Danica

I opened the door to Gary's store, marveling at the silence. Kyla was waiting in the car, although she'd made noises about stopping somewhere for some food. The werewolf burned through calories at an insane pace, and she got pissy when she was low on fuel.

Gary was restocking his shelves with exploding charms. The gnome had recently decided he needed to improve his branding, and all of the charms glistened in a dusky gold.

He nodded at me as I walked in. "I heard what happened to Samael."

"I guess the word has spread by now. Where are the kids?"

"At their friend's house for a playdate."

Good. Because I had a feeling Gary was going to say some incredibly bad words when he heard what I was asking for.

His gray face creased as he watched me walk toward him. "You need my help."

"Yeah. You're the only one I could think to ask." I chewed on my lower lip as he watched me expectantly. "You're not going to want to do it, but I swear on my life that I won't allow it to harm you."

He narrowed his eyes at me. "How about you swear on Samael's life, and I'll know you mean business."

I gaped at him and he shrugged. "I've seen the shit you jump into when someone you love is in danger. Samael's life is more important to you than your own."

"Fine. I swear on Samael's life that I have you covered."

The words seemed to echo in the small space and Gary nodded as if he could hear the truth in them. "What is it you need?"

This wouldn't go well. "I need some of your blood to give to a clan of tengu in the Middleground."

His mouth dropped open, revealing his pointed teeth. "Oh, is that all?"

"I know it's a lot to ask."

"I have kids, Danica. I can't risk them."

"I know. And I'd never ask you to risk them. You know that."

He watched me for a long moment. "Why do they want my blood?"

"A spell." I winced at the look on his face. "They want to start a business. Apparently gnomes are… lucky."

Gary laughed. When he realized I was serious, his laugh abruptly cut off and he shook his head.

"We're no more lucky than anyone else. Or weren't you here when my store was torn apart?"

"It doesn't matter if you're actually lucky. The tengu believe you are, and they want to trade with this realm. I'll have them swear a geas that your blood will be used in no other way. But it has to be freely given."

He stared at me for a long moment. "Why don't you explain to me what this has to do with your demon."

I took a deep breath, and it all came pouring out of me. The Spell of Three, the sword, my bargain with the seelie king, our alliance with Finvarra, and the information I needed. Gary was silent for a long moment.

"If I do this, I no longer owe you."

I gave him a dark look. "You don't owe me anything anyway. If you do this, I'll owe you."

"You know that's not how it works. I owe you a blood debt." He smiled, but there was no humor in it. "And this is the blood required."

"If you don't want to do it, I can figure something else out. It'll take me longer, but I'm not going to–"

"Hush. Swear to me that you'll protect us."

"I swear it."

"Fine."

I blinked at him and he smiled. "If you say you've got it covered, you've got it covered. If only to make sure you don't end up raising my kids if I'm killed."

My lips turned numb. I could feel the blood draining from my face as I stared at him, appalled.

"You don't mean that, right? You're fucking with me."

He bared his teeth in a feral grin. "Keep me alive, and you'll never have to find out."

I wrestled with that while he jumped off his stool and sauntered into his stockroom, obviously pleased that I was currently unable to speak.

He poked his head out of his stockroom. "Better

come in here so we don't scare off my customers."

He'd found a small glass vial and a dagger, and he handed the vial to me before cutting into the back of his arm. Gnome skin was thick, so he had to stab deep.

"That should do it," I murmured when the vial was almost full. "Thank you."

"This clears things between us."

"I told you, there was nothing to clear."

His mouth tightened and I sighed.

"Fine. The debt is clear."

"I hope you manage to wake Samael up," Gary said. "Good luck."

"Thanks."

I stepped out of the store, my hand sliding down to my Colt as someone moved in my peripheral vision. Rose narrowed her eyes at me.

"Jumpy much?"

I sighed. "You don't know the half of it."

"I guess I can't blame you, all things considered."

"What are you doing here?"

Rose sighed, turning to lean against Gary's store window. The gnome would love that. Her dark eyes were tired as she looked past me, surveying Main Street as if waiting for someone to fire on her.

"I, uh… I wanted to apologize."

Whatever I'd been expecting, it hadn't been that.

"Apologize? For what?"

She took her gaze off the street for long enough to roll her eyes at me. "For, uh, talking shit about you to everyone I came into contact with? For arresting you with Naud Chains? For–"

I held up my hand. "I get the point. Look, you probably saved my life that night at the Council."

She opened her mouth to argue and I shook my head. "If Cara had stayed alive, I wouldn't have had a chance. She was smarter than all three of those dumbasses put together, and she never would've left me alone with just Wes in that office. If not for that choice, I wouldn't have gotten to Mella, wouldn't have managed to return her pelt."

Her eyes widened. "Is that what happened?"

"You hadn't heard?"

Her mouth twisted. "The Council is keeping any information about that night very quiet. There's a ban on speaking about it at all. Not to mention, I'm not exactly working for them anymore."

"They fired you?"

She gave me a look like I was a particularly dense kind of idiot.

"There's a price on my head."

It clicked. "They know you killed Cara."

"They can't prove it, but they caught me on the cameras in the parking lot that night. They know I had something to do with it, and they've given orders to bring me in."

If they caught her, they'd torture her. Fury burned in my gut.

"How've you managed to stay off their radar so far?"

"I've been lucky. Besides, I'm not high priority right now—they're mostly trying to figure out how they can take advantage of the demons being weakened."

"I'm sorry."

She shrugged. "I wouldn't be working for them anyway. They made all these noises about how Wes, Bruce, Cara and Ben… how they were acting alone and they had no idea. But they were lying. I can tell."

"Who was lying?" My heart twisted in my chest and she shook her head.

"Not Keigan. He's walking around like a ghost. But, I'm pretty sure Albert knew. And a few of the Discipulus mages under him. It goes deeper than you think. You should be careful."

"Thanks for the warning."

She nodded and stepped past me. Then she stopped.

"I heard about your business. If you need an extra set of hands, let me know. I'm freelance now."

I grinned at that. "I will."

She nodded and began walking away.

"Wait."

Rose glanced over her shoulder, then scanned her surroundings again. Her head may think she had it under control, but her instincts weren't convinced.

"Where are you staying?"

She gave me a cool look. "Why?"

I rolled my eyes and waited her out. She scowled at me.

"In my car, okay? I can't go home because some of the bounty hunters are staking it out."

I pulled my keys out of my pocket, wiggled my car key off the keychain and threw the rest to her. She caught them automatically with a frown.

"Do you know where I live?"

She gave me a look and I grinned. "Oh, that's right,

you were hunting me for a while, right?"

She stiffened. "I apologized for that."

I shook my head. "I'm just playing with you. Look, my apartment is empty. Evie's away and I'm staying with Samael. It's warded and there's food in the freezer. You may as well stay there."

Her mouth dropped open. "Are you sure?"

If I hadn't been, the shocked gratitude in her eyes would have convinced me. "I'm sure. Get out of here before they catch up to you."

"Thank you. Seriously."

"I'll be calling you the next time I need a merc."

She grinned. "Done."

Danica

"This place creeps me out," Kyla murmured as we walked through the forest in the Middleground.

"More than the light fae forest?"

"That forest *wanted* to be creepy. This place is too quiet."

The tengu leader seemed surprised that we'd returned so quickly, his red face flushing even darker with excitement. I held the vial of blood in my hand and waggled it, keeping one hand on my Mark II.

"I need your geas," I told the leader as he approached. His eyes remained fixed on the gnome blood, alight with pure joy before he blinked and managed to snap out of it.

"Of course, of course." He turned and said something

to his people in their tongue, and they began to gather.

There were a lot more of them than I'd assumed. Probably close to a couple hundred. They jumped down from the branches of trees, and slipped through the forest soundlessly until they were all gathered in the large clearing.

Knives were handed around, and it took several minutes before all of the tengu had sliced open their arms. When everyone was bleeding, I reopened the wound in my forearm to lock the geas in place.

The tengu took a deep breath, holding his arm up in the air.

"We will never use the gnome blood brought to us by Danica Amana in any way other than for a commerce spell which will be performed on this day. If we stray from this use, any repercussions shall strike our people times three." They all intoned it, and I felt the wound in my arm flare as if in response.

I let out a long breath. It was done. The leader reached for the vial of blood, and I shook my head.

"Information first."

He gave me an unfriendly look. I merely waited him out and he sighed.

"Once, when I was a young man, I met a woman named Ilis, who claimed to have touched the golden sword. At first, I didn't take her seriously. Many had bragged about the same. However, she showed me the imprint on her palm, and I knew.

"The sword had known she wasn't fated to wield it, you see, and the hilt had heated, burning through her skin. The sword's hilt had been engraved with specific pictures and runes."

"How do you know it was definitely the right sword?"

"The rune which had left its scar on her skin is only known to a small collective of people. The tengu have been sword wielders since long before your portals opened. Our history and knowledge are vast."

"Will the sword burn my hand?" If so, I needed to make sure I was wearing gloves. My hands had to stay in good working shape to keep me alive.

"Only if you intend to wield it yourself."

"Where can I find Ilis?"

"In the unseelie realm."

I rubbed at my right temple, where a dull throb was announcing its presence. "I'm going to need better directions than that."

The tengu closest to me shuffled impatiently and the leader shot him a look. All movement ceased.

"Take the portal that opens close to the unseelie king's keep. There is a nearby town called Smolten. Once you arrive, look for a tavern called The Harpy's Hell. Ask for a bartender named Dinbel. Give him a gold coin, and he will show you the internal portal."

I held up a hand. "Hold on a second. The internal portal?"

The tengu smiled. "You didn't think the portals only functioned between realms, did you?"

I sure did.

His smile widened. "Once through the internal portal, you will find the Swamp of Ilis. Follow the path from the portal, and you will find Ilis herself."

"Okay. Thank you."

I handed over the blood and the tengu gave me a grave nod.

"I wish you as much luck as this spell will bring us."

I had a feeling we were going to need it.

We made our way back out of the forest.

"You trust them not to hurt Gary?" Kyla asked.

"I texted Gary the wording of the geas before we walked through the portal. He was happy with it. Even if they were to risk the repercussions of attempting to get around it, I don't think they would."

"Why?"

I smiled. "Because Gary has allies. I'm one of them. And even if I end up dead, I have other measures in place to protect Gary and his kids. If the tengu want to trade with our world, pissing us off is the wrong way to get started."

"You are a cunning ruler," a deep voice said.

Kyla jumped about a foot in the air, shooting me a look that told me she hadn't scented the approach. I pulled my Nim Cub as we both turned.

The man was seelie, with the refined features of the aristocracy. Weapons were strapped to his body, although he was dressed in little more than rags. His gaze scanned both of us, landing on my face.

"The creatures you killed have been targeting residents in this region for many months. I arrived last night, after a contact asked me to take care of the problem, only to find that two females had done it for me."

Kyla bared her teeth. "Is the fact that we're females relevant?"

He studied her. "I meant no offense." His gaze

switched to me. "But we are in your debt."

"There is no debt."

He waved his hand through the air at that. The dismissive action reminded me of Samael, and my breath caught in my throat.

"My name is Fotadh. I knew your parents," he said. "I have a contact who was close to your father."

"How do you know who I am?"

"I am particularly adept at memorizing magical signatures. Yours is a unique mixture of witch and demon. And I have met that demon."

I was curious, sure. But I didn't have time to waste in this realm. "My father abandoned my mother and left her alone and pregnant. I have no interest in him."

"My contact also knew of your mother."

I hesitated and Fotadh gave an elegant shrug of one shoulder. "I will be paid for the reconciliation of the problem those creatures presented to this community. My honor demands that I also pay the debt to you."

I studied him. "You're a Theon."

He gave me a courtly bow and said nothing.

The Theon were a sect of seelie who traveled the realms, removing any threats to their people. It was rumored that they were the rare third children born to seelie, and handed over to be trained in assassinations and warfare.

They had a very stringent code of honor. I trusted that Fotadh wasn't sending me into a trap, but with the clock ticking, I couldn't risk spending any more time in this realm.

But what if this contact knew something about mom

that could lead me to her killer? There were so few people who knew my mom, and if this person had known both of my parents…

"How far away does he live?"

Fotadh smiled. "Not far. I will lead you to him."

The village was beginning to come alive when we walked through it. The smell of cooking meat hung heavy on the air, and a group of goblin children played some game which involved running around the decrepit huts.

"What's going on?" Kyla asked.

"The people in this village have been too terrified to leave their homes. Every few days, those creatures would raid all of the villages in this area. There was nothing of value left, so they would steal the food. There are no warriors living nearby. Before the creatures arrived, this was a welcoming community for the poorest of paranormals."

"Why are they here?"

"Many of them were driven out during the wars centuries ago. Some of them are the descendants of those who were banished for various crimes in the fae realms, and do not have enough power to cross through the portals.

I wished I could kill the giant scorpions again. "At least one of the creatures survived."

The seelie gave me a pleased smile. "Two of them survived. I dispatched them this morning."

Excellent.

Fotadh's contact didn't live far from the village, but unlike the villagers, who had been living in poverty, his home was a large log cabin, obviously built to last.

"I'm guessing the creatures we killed didn't attempt

to steal from this guy."

The seelie nodded and it pissed me off.

"So he's been living his life, ignoring the fact that the village was being targeted every few days?"

Fotadh sighed. "Ugales is not… right any longer. After what happened to your parents, he was unable to function. Please try not to judge him by your usual standards."

I'd make my own mind up about that. From the disgusted look Kyla sent me, we were on the same page.

Fotadh knocked on the wooden door. The knock was ignored, so he continued knocking until it was finally thrown open.

I didn't know what I'd been expecting, but it wasn't a high demon.

Ugales glowered at Fotadh. Then his eyes met mine and the blood drained from his face.

"What are you thinking bringing *her* here?" he demanded. "I have no need for the bad luck that follows her family."

His wings rustled behind him, and I merely raised my eyebrow, giving him a cool look. "Is that why you've been hiding out here and leaving the villagers to be preyed upon?"

Not a hint of shame crossed his face. Instead, his expression went blank as he turned back to Fotadh. "Why did you bring her here?" he asked again.

"My honor demands it. I am hoping your honor will demand the same." Fotadh gave the demon a meaningful look that made him glance away.

"Fine."

Fotadh turned to us. "I leave you both here," he announced. "Are you able to make your way back to the portal?"

We nodded and he gave Ugales a final warning look before giving us a courtly bow. "It was a pleasure to make your acquaintance."

He walked away, the sword on his hip glinting in the sunlight.

Ugales let out a low growl but opened his door further.

"Come in then."

The cabin was larger than it looked from outside, but it was sparsely decorated with little more than a wooden sofa—complete with ancient-looking cushions and a small table. There was a bed in one corner of the room and a tiny kitchen.

"Ask your questions."

This guy was pissing me off. "Why are you here?"

"That's my business."

"How did you know my parents?"

A hint of sorrow flickered in his eyes. "Agates and I… we were… not quite friends, because friendship was never encouraged amongst Lucifer's court. But we never actively plotted against each other."

My father's name was Agates. I filed that away to think about later, but I wasn't here to learn about the man who'd gotten my mother pregnant and abandoned her.

"What about my mother?"

He clamped his mouth shut and I let out a low growl. Next to me, Kyla was so still she could have been made of stone. I recognized that expression on her face. It was her "this guy deserves my teeth in his throat" look.

"Your mother should have known better than to get involved with a demon."

"There, we can agree. But she got involved with him anyway. Tell me what you know."

His wings spread wide. "Don't think to order me, halfbreed."

This was a waste of time. I turned to go, and he let out a low growl. "You may be of Lucifer's line, but you won't prevent me from fulfilling my debt to that fae bastard."

Ah. Someone owed Fotadh a favor. There was a fair amount of that going around.

"Then cooperate with me," I said. "Tell me why you're here and not in the underworld—or even in my world."

He let out a bitter laugh. "Those loyal to your father were purged. I was nearly caught, and only escaped because Lucifer had more important traitors in his sights. Should I have crawled at Samael's feet?"

"I've never known Samael to expect his people to crawl for him."

The look he sent me was coolly amused. "And you believe your demon would have gladly welcomed one of Lucifer's most powerful advisors to his ranks?"

I shrugged. "So instead you fled to this realm?"

His expression darkened at the word *fled*. Yup, I'd already figured out how to get under his skin.

"I waited to see if Samael would retake his throne. He was no match for Lucifer, once the new underking bargained with the underworld to keep him from using his power. Then the portals opened, and it was *Samael* and his people who fled."

He was trying to get under *my* skin now. I gave him a slow smile.

"And my mother? What do you know of her?"

His mouth twisted. "I know she should have known better–"

I leapt at him.

I'd used this move before on Samael, and the memory of it attempted to steal my concentration. The demon hadn't been expecting me to move, and I hooked my leg behind his, unbalancing him.

He landed flat on his back with a thump, and I smiled at him from where I'd positioned myself over his torso, Misty at his throat.

"Wow," Kyla remarked. "I didn't see that coming." She walked around us and placed her boot lightly on the demon's forehead.

Even with Kyla's strength, we were really only able to keep Ugales flat on his back thanks to the element of surprise. Werewolves were strong, but demons were usually stronger.

Unfortunately, Ugales had been hiding away in his cabin for far too many years.

He glowered up at me, and I could feel him gathering power.

I let a hint of my own power out to play. He was a high demon, but he wasn't anywhere near as powerful as the demons I hung out with on a daily basis. And as he'd been so quick to remind me, I was of Lucifer's line.

"Tell me what you know about my mom, and who killed her. And keep in mind," I let my gaze drop down to

Misty, "I'll know if you lie."

A dull flush worked its way up his cheeks. It looked like Ugales and I wouldn't be exchanging Christmas cards this year.

"Ask your questions," he spat.

"You may have opted out of politics, but I've got a feeling you've been keeping up with everything that's happening in both realms. So why don't you tell me what you know about my mom's death."

He didn't bother denying the fact that he'd been gathering information. Instead, he gave me a nasty smile.

"You believe Lucifer only just learned you were alive? He had his suspicions all along. Because one of your father's friends betrayed him and told him all about your mother."

The edges of my vision turned red. "Lucifer killed my mother?"

"Of course not." He snorted, turning his attention to Kyla. "Get your foot off my head."

I nodded at her and she stepped back, but not until she'd given the demon a low growl of warning. Misty hadn't glowed. So far, Ugales was telling the truth.

"Why didn't Lucifer have my mom killed?"

He gave me a look that said he wasn't impressed with my level of intelligence. I refrained from digging Misty into his skin.

"Lucifer learned of her when she returned to Durham. Which was perhaps the stupidest move she could have made." I didn't have it in me to snap at him. He was right.

"So then what?"

"So his men were planning to snatch her."

"Which men? The demons who crossed into our world were loyal to Samael."

He smiled. "All of them? Really? Your naivety would be cute if it wasn't so embarrassing."

I gritted my teeth and ignored that. "So someone else killed her before Lucifer could take her?"

"That's right. Removing Lucifer's ability to torture her and discover if the rumors were true, and if your father really sired a half-breed bastard with her."

"Vercan was one of those demons, wasn't he?" He'd been seen near my mom's body soon after she'd died, and he was the demon I'd been looking forward to questioning before someone killed him in Samael's club.

Ugales shrugged. "Probably. All I know is that Lucifer raged through the underworld when he learned someone had killed your mother before he could take her. I heard it was the biggest cull of his men since he learned Agates had visited your realm."

I winced at the thought. Ugales lifted his hips, and I was suddenly straddling him. He gave me a sour look.

"That's all I know, half-blood. Now leave."

Kyla held out her hand and helped me climb off the demon, and I slid Misty back into its sheath. At least now I knew for sure that Lucifer hadn't killed my mom. Because Ugales was right about one thing—he would have killed her in the underworld, after torturing her until she begged for death.

The thought made bile climb up my throat.

"Are you okay?" Kyla asked as we left the hut.

"I don't have time to not be okay," I said. She pinched me and I sighed. "Not really. The letter Evie left for me...

She said she knew, down to her bones, that she was the reason Mom was dead. I don't think she's to blame in any way, but I think she's right about some of it—whoever had our mom in that lab likely killed her."

Kyla opened her mouth, but a deep voice cut in from behind us.

"You never asked about your father."

I kept walking. "He's irrelevant."

"He's alive."

My mind turned blank and I froze. "I don't care."

"You don't wish to know where he is?"

If he was alive and he'd never come to help my mother, never shown up to meet me…

"No."

The demon let out a bitter laugh. "Looks like you're more like your grandfather than you know, halfbreed."

I whirled, but he'd already slammed his door closed.

I gave myself one moment to process that information, and then I pushed it out of my mind.

We walked toward the portal silently, and my chest ached like someone had taken hold of my heart and twisted. It wasn't the first time I'd actively longed for Samael, but it was the worst. All I wanted was to talk to him, to hear his voice. Our dreams weren't enough. I *needed* him.

Just a few months ago, I would've been shocked at that thought. I hadn't needed anyone. Hadn't wanted to.

I stroked the gold mark on my hand and poured the love I felt for Samael down our bond.

I pictured him, there in the cabin, deep in wolf territory. I didn't let my fear enter the equation, just sent him all of the feelings I hadn't wanted to admit to until it was almost too late.

We should've had more time. If I hadn't been so stubborn, so damned determined to listen to my mom this *one* time... so sure that the demon would never be able to wrestle back his most overprotective instincts...

And now he may never truly hold me again.

Tears filled my eyes. Kyla kept silent, her gaze on the forest around us, giving me a moment to collect myself as I *reached* for my demon.

For the first time, I could see every inch of the bond—a shimmering gold. And at the end of the bond, I could *feel* Samael in a way I hadn't before.

"I miss you," I told him.

"I miss you too, little witch."

I tripped over my feet, falling to my knees. Next to me, Kyla gaped at me. I held up my hand, and she went silent.

"You can hear me?"

His voice was very faint, but it dripped with the smug amusement that was so... Samael.

"I can. I didn't dare to hope that our bond would be strong enough for you to speak to me in this place without the benefit of our dreams. But you strengthen it with your will."

"Does it weaken you?"

"Our bond strengthens me, witchling."

"You know what I mean. Does speaking to me like this weaken you?"

"Slightly. Not enough that I would give up the chance to hear your voice."

A tear dripped down my cheek. *"I miss you so goddamn much. I can barely function."*

"I can sense you in another realm, little witch. I have a feeling you're doing much more than barely functioning."

I let out a choked laugh. *"I just talked to someone who knew my parents. He said my father is alive."*

"And you believe him?"

"I used Misty."

A long silence. *"My spies have not informed me of this. If he's alive, he must have fled to a pocket realm, or else he was smuggled somewhere he could fly under the radar."* I could practically hear Samael's frown. *"Where exactly is my body right now, witchling?"*

"Uhh, I'm walking through a portal. Gotta go. Talk later!" I sent him an image of me blowing him a kiss and got a chuckle in response. He didn't protest, though. I had a feeling speaking to me this way wore him out more than he wanted to admit.

"I was talking to Samael," I told Kyla. She raised one eyebrow.

"That's freaky. Werewolves can communicate in a similar way with their mates but never between realms."

"When Samael was hit by that spell, I completed my end of the bond. I had no idea what I was doing, but now I can see him in my dreams."

She stared at me. "I guess you've been wishing you could spend more time asleep."

"You've got that right."

"Where to now?"

I sighed. Truthfully, I was worn out. And I'd bet

Kyla was too. "It's getting late. We should get some sleep before we head to the swamp."

Of course, there was always the chance that we'd arrive in the unseelie realm in the middle of the night. Time didn't exactly work the same in all of the realms. But we'd cross that bridge if we came to it.

Besides, I had a niggling feeling that whatever I was about to face in that swamp would require me to be at my best. And I was learning to listen to my instincts.

CHAPTER TEN

Samael

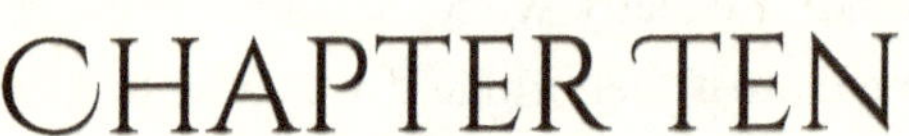

I pulled Danica into my arms as soon as she appeared, rolling her beneath me. "I thought you'd never fall asleep."

She sighed. "Turns out, the anticipation of needing to fall asleep isn't conducive to actually falling asleep."

I smiled at that. But the smile quickly fell from my face. She frowned up at me.

"What is it?"

We needed to have a difficult conversation. The kind of conversation that my little witch was not going to be pleased by. Her frown deepened, and I forced myself to broach the subject.

"We need to discuss what will happen if it becomes too late for the counter spell."

She stiffened. "You mean if I fail. That's loser talk, Samael."

"I would be remiss if I didn't ensure you were prepared for all possibilities."

She shook her head, and I tightened my hold on her. "This is important."

She sighed. "Fine. What do I need to know?"

"If we run out of time, and you are still alive…" she flinched at the thought, but I pinched her pert nose lightly. I would do whatever I could to ensure that I didn't take her with me. If there was one thing I knew, down in my gut, it was that Danica wasn't fated to die this way.

"Ag will help you," I murmured. Danica's chin stuck out stubbornly, but she was listening. I had a feeling it was just an effort to humor me, but if the worst came to pass, one day, she would remember this conversation.

"Lucifer will come for you. It's why he had the black witch perform the Spell of Three in the first place. He has obviously been kept informed of my tendency to act first and think later when it comes to you."

Her lower lip trembled, and I nuzzled her tiny ear. "I wouldn't have it any other way," I assured her.

Danica scowled up at me. But I could see the retribution burning in her gaze. She hadn't allowed herself to think about what would happen if she were left alive. But I knew my little witch, and she would burn with vengeance.

"Tell me everything I need to know about Lucifer," she ordered.

I smiled. "We won't have time for me to tell you *everything*, but that's what Ag is for. He will be your closest advisor, and he, too, will be chasing revenge." I could only hope that he would respect my wishes and keep Danica safe while he found that revenge. I pushed that thought away and focused on my little witch.

"I have seven of the nine Black Books. Lucifer made a mistake when he banished Cyprianus from the underworld. Cyprianus was furious enough that he left a small piece of a spell in each of the grimoires. When pieced together, the spell will weaken Lucifer's connection to the underworld, making it possible to kill him."

Danica took a deep breath, then slowly let it out, her expression deep in thought. "Do you know where the other two grimoires are?"

"I know where one of them is. Before you went missing, I sent Belphegor to Peru, where a tribe of humans was rumored to have last seen the eighth book."

"I wondered why I hadn't seen Bel around," Danica murmured. "Okay, and the ninth book?"

I growled. "It escapes me still."

Danica shot me a teasing grin. "Something's not conforming to your expectations? Must be difficult."

I tucked a lock of her hair behind one ear. "I'm becoming used to such things," I said meaningfully.

She laughed. "I'm assuming you guys have notes and theories on the location of the ninth book."

"Yes. Ag has access to everything."

"Okay," she blew out a breath. "So if you cark it, and I'm left hanging around, grief-stricken and gunning for revenge, my best bet is to get my hands on the nine Black Books."

Her tone was light, but I caught the flicker of terror in her eyes. "Correct."

"What else do I need to know?"

"Lucifer's main assassin is called Daimonion."

She nodded. "He killed Vas's parents."

"Yes. He's extremely dangerous. Lucifer keeps him close, as he has enough supporters of his own to make him a threat. However, he remains the assassin with the highest kill rate."

Some of this information, Ag could tell her, and yet I felt the need to pass the torch, to do everything I personally could to prepare her for the fight of her life.

And the thought of not being there for that fight, of leaving her vulnerable…

It tore into me.

Some of what I was feeling must have made it onto my face, or down the bond, because Danica's expression softened.

"It's okay," she whispered. "Tell me what you need me to know."

Danica

I found Agaliarept as soon as I woke up the next morning. He was meeting with several of the other demons, most of whom nodded at me when I arrived.

I nodded back, then shifted my attention to Ag. "Can I talk to you?"

Within a few minutes, we were in Samael's room—the quietest room in the cabin.

"The eighth black book," I got straight to business. "Has Bel managed to find it yet?"

Surprise flickered in Ag's eyes, and he glanced at Samael. "He's been telling you of his plans."

I nodded and his expression tightened with a hint of grief. But he pushed it away quickly, his expression turning inscrutable once more. "Bel is still in Peru. The tribe is remote, hidden deep in the Amazon. While he has been searching for weeks, the rainforest canopy is exceptionally thick."

"Okay. Please keep me updated."

He nodded, but it was noncommittal. I watched him.

"You don't think I'll be able to help. Why?"

"Because I know the truth," Ag said. "In all likelihood, Samael is going to die. I don't say this because I'm looking forward to it. Samael has been an excellent ruler and he would bring peace to the underworld."

I studied Ag's face. He spoke so clinically, and yet I knew better. From everything I'd seen so far, he considered Samael to be almost like a son—just like Vas.

He turned his head to look at me. The gold flecks in his eyes looked brighter today. Judging by the dark circles beneath them, he hadn't slept properly in weeks. Demons didn't need as much sleep as humans, but I had no doubt he could use eight straight.

"You won't care about any of this if Samael is dead," he said tiredly. "You won't care about facing the Underking, about the fate of our people. You won't have it in you to give a shit when Lucifer finds a way to leave the underworld. And by the time your grief has cleared enough for you to care, this realm will be lost."

I swallowed. He was right.

If Samael wasn't here, I wouldn't care about Lucifer, about the underworld, about the crown. I wouldn't care about any of it.

He nodded again at whatever he saw on my face, returning his attention to Samael, and I left him to his grief.

I had enough grief of my own this morning.

Kyla was meeting me here at seven. I glanced at my phone. I still had twenty minutes. The demons guarding the cabin stopped talking as I stepped outside, but I couldn't find it in me to care.

I walked past them and into the forest. I could sense eyes on me, but I ignored them as I chose a path and walked.

A human woman strolled toward me, giving me a nod. One of the werewolves' mates. Most of the wolves had been keeping the humans far from our demons—our alliance too new for them to trust us completely.

I nodded back and kept walking, attempting to process my conversation with Samael.

He'd been working toward his revenge for centuries. He'd been so close to striking out at Lucifer, to taking his throne back, to saving his people.

And then he met me.

Lucifer had known exactly where to strike. I was the chink in Samael's armor. His blind spot. The weakness Lucifer had been searching for.

It was worse, knowing that I'd been the method used to take him out. That our love—so new and fresh—was twisted and wielded against us.

I'd been attempting to ignore the very real chance that Samael could die. That I'd done nothing but prolong his life by a few days, maybe a week at most.

Here, where no one was watching, I let the tears roll down my cheeks, let my shoulders shake, and replayed Ag's words.

He thought I'd just give up if Samael died. To be

honest, *I* didn't know how the hell I'd be able to keep it together.

But the demons deserved someone who would fight for them.

I wiped the tears off my cheeks and squared my shoulders. I'd never imagined that I'd stand for the demons, but they deserved to be able to live in their homeland. And Lucifer deserved to die for what he'd done to us.

My grandfather could never understand just what it was to love someone so much that you'd do anything for them. And ultimately, that would be his downfall. Because if Samael died, and I stayed alive, I would pick myself up off the floor, and I would make Lucifer regret the day he ever learned I existed.

I stalked back toward the cabin and made my way back into Samael's room. Ag was now standing by the window, his expression shadowed as he stared outside.

"I won't give up," I told him. "If... if he dies, I'll do everything I can for your people."

"Your people," he told me, his gaze still on the forest outside. But his shoulders relaxed enough that I knew he understood.

"My people," I said. And something shifted inside me. A weight found its way to my shoulders, but it was a good weight, a comforting weight.

I turned and strapped on the last of my weapons. It was time to get back to work.

Kyla met me by her car. "Well, you look like shit."

I shrugged. Then I slid into the passenger seat and relayed my conversation with Samael.

"So much intrigue," she murmured. "Does he know anything about the ninth black book?"

"Not so far, and he's been searching for centuries."

"These old paranormal guys are just set in their ways," Kyla said. "They need a fresh, young, optimistic perspective."

I couldn't help but grin. "Damn right."

The portal crossing was uneventful, and within half an hour, we were standing in the unseelie realm. I shivered, glad I'd worn my leather jacket. "Okay, we need to find Smolten."

Kyla nodded, her gaze fixed on a group of goblins. They walked next to a cart full of vegetables, the driver spurring on a horse that looked so old it could drop dead at any moment.

"Oi, you," she called.

The closest goblin turned, baring its teeth at us. "Fuck off."

"Cute. Where's Smolten?"

He'd obviously spent time in our realm, because he flipped up his middle finger. Kyla just stared at him, her eyes turning lighter as she channeled her wolf.

He swallowed and lifted one shaky finger, pointing left. "That way."

I examined him. Then I pulled my Mark II and a cloth, slowly cleaning the blade. "If you're lying, we'll come back for you."

He paled. His friends had already left without him, unconcerned. "Fine. It's that way," he snapped, pointing in the opposite direction. "Two miles. You can't miss it."

"Gee, thanks," Kyla said sweetly. He flipped us off

again and hurried to catch up with his friends.

Without a word, we both kicked our pace up to a jog. By the time the town came into view, I'd stripped off my jacket and my muscles were feeling limber. Next to me, Kyla wasn't even sweating. I shot her a dark look and she chuckled.

"Don't hate me 'cause you ain't me."

I rolled my eyes.

Smolten was close enough to Finvarra's keep that it was obviously a center for trade. We joined the line at the entrance to the town. Fae guards were positioned on either side of the entrance, and I lifted my gaze.

There. The wall was dotted with more guards, likely wielding crossbows.

The line moved quickly, and other than one bored scan of our faces, the guard we passed didn't pay us much attention. I rolled my shoulders and examined the town.

"We're looking for The Harpy's Hell," I reminded Kyla.

"Catchy name. I vote we go that way," she nodded to her right. I shrugged and turned, heading in the direction she'd specified.

"Why?"

She tapped her nose. "Because I just got a whiff of beer and unwashed creatures."

Perfect.

The Harpy's Hell was a small, plain building with gray walls and a dark, wooden rooftop—like all of the buildings on this avenue. We stepped around a drunk gnome, currently losing his stomach three feet from the door.

The tavern was packed. I had no idea what time it was here, but the sun was still high in the sky. I felt eyes on me as I slipped the gold coin from my utility belt.

Kyla's expression was relaxed, but the way she stood–feet planted and slowly running her gaze around the patrons in the tavern–made it clear that she wasn't prey. I stepped up to the bar and nodded at the lesser fae currently polishing a glass with a filthy rag.

"Dinbel?"

One sharp nod.

"I need access to the internal portal."

"You got coin?"

I held up the gold coin and he scowled. "The price has increased. You ever heard of inflation?"

I gave him a steady stare and his scowl deepened, but he plucked the coin out of my hand with a bad-tempered sneer.

"Let's go."

He stepped around the bar and jerked his head toward a door leading to what I assumed was a back room.

There was nothing here. I tensed, ready to reach for my blade, but he threw the closet door open, revealing the glimmer of a portal.

"Didn't see that coming," Kyla remarked.

Neither had I.

Dinbel pushed a collection of brooms and mops aside and gestured for us to walk into the portal. "Go on then, ain't got all day."

The portal was multi-colored, reflecting rainbows which danced through the room like it was a crystal. I really, really hoped the Tengu knew what he was talking about and we weren't going to end up in the wrong place.

"Alrighty then," Kyla said. She gave me a 'what are you gonna do look' and strolled into the rainbows. I sighed and stepped through after her.

"You're welcome," Dinbel snapped as I strode into the closet.

The first thing I noticed was the humidity. The portal had spat us out in a region so unlike the one we had just left that my mind struggled to process it. If anyone had attacked, we would've been sitting ducks as we both blinked dazedly and gaped at our surroundings.

Sure, the tengu had said we'd be going to a swamp. But whatever I'd pictured, it hadn't been this.

The path was bordered by trees on either side. The trees themselves were blue-green, with dark, inky black leaves. Vines climbed up the trees, a greenish yellow that reminded me of poisonous snakes.

The path cut through the wetlands. If we were to step off the dry ground, our boots would be swallowed by a thick, dark mud.

"You take me to the creepiest places," Kyla muttered.

I sighed. "Let's get this over with."

Kyla hummed the Yellow Brick Road song while we walked along the path. Within a few minutes, the path had widened, finally giving way to a springy ground that was damp but stable enough to walk on.

To our left, giant grasses gave way to the same blue-green trees, clumped together in a dark forest. To our right, it was all sandy swamp, the water dark and murky. I had no doubt that various creatures lay in wait beneath that water.

An unseelie woman was digging at the edge of the swamp. I had no idea what she was looking for, but she lifted her head as we approached.

"Ah," she said. "You've come."

Either she had a glimpse of the sight, she had access to a seer, or she wanted me to wonder. I just shrugged.

"My name is Danica," I said. "I was sent by–"

"I know who you were sent by. You're looking for the golden sword."

"Yes. Can I see your palm, please?"

She smiled at me and held up her hand. The scar was deep, as if she'd been branded with the strange runes. I peered at it. I'd never seen those runes before.

"Are you ready to do whatever it takes to get that sword?"

"Yes."

She gave us both a faint smile. She was beautiful, as all of the fae were, but there was something more… human about her than I usually saw with the fae.

"You may learn to regret that answer," she said wryly. She got to her feet and walked toward me, the bottom half of her long dress soaked in water and covered in dirt. She didn't seem to notice.

"I was present when the sword was given to its last owners several years ago. I can tell you who they are. If they have passed it on, it will be up to them if they tell you the details or refuse to divulge that information."

"We can make them tell us," Misty sounded amused, if that was possible for the enchanted dagger. *"They can't refuse me."*

"Slow your roll," I advised it. *"We don't even know*

*if they'll talk to us yet. We need to get their details from
Ilis first."*

Ilis tilted her head. "Come and eat with me. The
sword isn't going anywhere. At least for now."

I opened my mouth to protest, but Ilis was already
turning away.

Kyla glanced around at the swamp. "Where exactly
are you thinking of eating?"

Ilis grinned over her shoulder at us and waved her
hand. I jolted as the mists parted, revealing a huge house
on stilts.

From the way Kyla stiffened, I was guessing even
her natural wolfy power hadn't allowed her to see through
that glamor. Her eyes lightened in annoyance, but we
followed Ilis up the wooden stairs.

Ilis opened the door, revealing a cozy kitchen.
Semi-sheer kitchen curtains framed the closest window,
the warm breeze making the butterflies printed on them
appear like they were taking flight. The counters were
mint green, standing out against the black and white
checkered floor.

Ilis gestured to the bright red table in the center of
the room and strode toward her gray fridge. We sat down
as a small white cat strode into the room, hissing at Kyla.

Lia loved everyone as long as they fed and pet
her. I'd forgotten most animals weren't exactly fans of
werewolves.

Watching that cat wind around Ilis's legs made
me long for a peaceful morning, making breakfast with
Samael, Lia silently ordering us to add to her already
emptied food bowl. We hadn't had enough normalcy, my

demon and I.

Ilis pulled out a large container, poured something into a pot, and set it on the stove, stirring occasionally. Within minutes, a rich, spicy scent filled the room and my stomach rumbled.

We sat and ate bowls of a thick stew which seemed similar to gumbo. Ilis handed us both a piece of fresh, buttered bread, and for a few minutes, there was no sound as we all ate.

"Now," Ilis said finally as she sat back in her chair, pushing her bowl away from her. "We will talk about the necessary steps for the information you need."

I nodded. Ilis may have fed us, but it didn't mean she wasn't going to make us jump through the necessary hoops for whatever knowledge she had. Thankfully, the brief respite—and the food—had given me a little of my energy back.

"What do you know of the sword?"

I took a deep breath. "When Hrunting failed Beowulf, he found another sword in Grendel's mother's lair. He used it to slay her, and her blood melted the sword until only the hilt was left."

She nodded. "Some speak of the radiant light which filled the cave once the monster was dead. However, most believe the light came first, allowing Beowulf to see the sword hanging on the wall of the cave."

I chewed on that. "So the sword wanted to be used?"

A tiny smile hovered around her mouth. "What else do you know about the golden sword?"

I shrugged. "I know the seelie king wants it, because of a prophecy which says he could use it to kill the unseelie king."

"And why do you believe this prophecy exists?"

I felt like I was a pupil who was missing the point of a lesson. I frowned. "Because fate is a fickle bitch?"

Ilis laughed. "My king is Taraghlan's most loathed enemy."

Ahh. "So the sword appeared for Beowulf because in that moment, Grendel was his greatest enemy?"

She beamed at me, and it was as if the kitchen lit up with her pride. "That's right."

"If this prophecy says the sword will be used to kill your king, why would you help me?"

She raised one eyebrow. "The prophecy says it *could* be used to kill my king. I happen to believe that it won't be."

"Why?"

She gave me a sly look and glanced at Kyla. "That is a theory for another day. There are many myths surrounding this sword, but one of them is of great importance when it comes to your search for it."

"What is it?"

"The sword may only be located by those with a warrior's heart."

Well, shit. I was many things, but I wouldn't say I was a warrior.

"How do you know if someone has a warrior's heart?" Kyla asked.

"I will give you a task. Completing it will tell me everything I need to know."

Alrighty then.

Kyla and I got to our feet. Ilis shook her head. "This

task is for Danica to do alone. Eat some more, wolf. I can practically feel your hunger."

Kyla glanced at me. I nodded, and she narrowed her eyes warningly at Ilis. Finally, she shrugged and turned to the pot on the stove, refilling her bowl.

If I didn't come back, Kyla would kill whoever she had to. And I knew she'd take up the hunt for the sword.

Ilis led me back out the door and down the stairs. Sweat instantly beaded on my forehead as my feet hit the spongy ground.

"I had to take an internal portal to get here," I said. "Is there another portal that will take me back to Durham?"

Ilis frowned. "No. But… it is possible for me to stack two portals for a short amount of time, allowing you use a kind of shortcut–bypassing the internal portal. I'll work the spell while you're completing your task and you can take the same portal you came through."

That would save us some time. "Thank you. And what is my task exactly?

Ilis turned toward the water. Her gaze sharpened, her fae senses likely seeing something I couldn't. I narrowed my own eyes. This place creeped me out.

"There are creatures of myth here," Ilis said. "Creatures which fled the more populated areas of this realm. One such creature has made its way into your human mythology."

Well that was as clear as the mud beneath my feet. Amusement flickered through Ilis's eyes at whatever she saw on my face.

"In order to prove yourself as a warrior fated to claim the sword—even for a short period of time—you must slay one of these creatures. Bring me its head, and I will tell you who I once saw with the sword.”

My mouth dropped open. Well, that took a dark turn. I glanced around at the wetlands. “Any hints about where I can find this creature?”

She shook her head. “You must use your own inner compass.”

Awesome.

CHAPTER ELEVEN

Danica

I surveyed my surroundings. Edward–the guy my mom had somehow convinced to train me from the time I was a teenager–had ensured I trained under various conditions, but it had been a long time since I was in a swamp.

Next to me, Ilis waved her hand and a canteen appeared. "Water," she said, handing it over, and I clipped it onto my utility belt.

"Thanks."

Obviously, she wasn't expecting this to be a quick little trip.

"You may not use your power for this task," Ilis said.

I gaped at her. "Why?"

"True warriors use their skills and their cunning to complete tasks such as this."

I gave her my best "are you kidding?" look. "True warriors use whatever advantages they have available to them."

"These are my terms."

Her terms sucked. I clenched my teeth so hard my jaw ached. "Fine."

"One more thing." She smiled at me. "I need your dagger."

I didn't bother offering her my Nim Cub or my Mark II. I merely narrowed my eyes at her and clamped my hand over Misty's hilt. "Why?"

"You may not have help for this task," she said, her gaze steady on my face. "I will keep it safe for you."

She gave me a moment to silently debate the wisdom of handing over a fae artifact I knew damn well they'd kill to get their hands on.

Kyla would likely know Ilis had Misty when she returned. Unless Ilis stashed it somewhere. The werewolf would be keeping a close eye on her. And it wasn't as if the dagger was likely to be helpful, unless I needed someone to cheer me on and encourage me to use it for the gruesome parts.

My mind flashed to Samael, slowly crumbling away. It wasn't like I had a choice at this point. I slid Misty from its sheath and handed it over. Ilis's eyes widened as she clasped the hilt.

"I will return it to you once you have completed your task," she said. "This I swear." She gave me a nod. "I wish you luck."

And then I was alone.

Unless I wanted to go for a swim, there was really only one path to take. I turned right and headed into the dense foliage of the island.

As usual in the fae realms, I could feel eyes on me. I pulled my Mark II and scanned my surroundings. Nothing jumped out at me, so I kept walking.

This place was hellish. Why Ilis would choose to

live here was beyond me. Insects buzzed around my head, biting at me whenever I was too slow to slap them away. Within a few minutes, sweat was dripping into my eyes and I rubbed the sting of it away.

"Miserable place," I decided. With no idea where I was going, I took a long look behind me, memorizing the way back to Ilis's, and took a right, through a small gap in the trees.

"Jesus fucking Christ!"

I jumped backward, my shoe landing in a puddle of thick mud. The snake was larger than anything I'd ever seen on earth—even in a book or movie. Its body was as wide as the tree trunk it was wrapped around, and the length of it went on and on, disappearing into the foliage to my left.

"Who entersssss my territory?"

And it talked too. I was Alice, and I'd fallen down the wrong damn rabbit hole.

"I have been given a task to complete," I replied, and the snake watched me out of slitted yellow eyes.

"I know your tasssssssk. You want to passssss?"

"That's right."

"When you return, bring me blood from the creature you will sssssssslay."

"Why?"

"Blood of thissssssss power will nurture my young."

Nurturing its young definitely didn't seem like the smart play. The snake coiled back. In the blink of an eye, its tongue had darted out to taste my cheek. I slashed with my Mark II, and it swiped through empty air.

Its point had been made. I was fast. But compared to

the snake, I'd moved with the speed of a glacier.

Time was ticking. If I refused, I'd be brawling with this creature, since I'd agreed not to use my power. Not only was it entirely too big, but it had zero business being as fast as it was.

"Fine," I agreed.

"Make your vow," it told me, swaying slightly in place.

"I'll bring you back the blood," I agreed.

The snake slowly moved away, allowing me to pass. I really, really didn't want it at my back. I gave it a warning look, tightened my grip on my knife, and scampered past it.

It didn't wrap itself around me and crush me before swallowing me whole, so I counted that as a win.

A small trail opened up. Realistically, it couldn't be considered a path, but Ilis likely used it when she was navigating this area.

I focused on putting one foot in front of the other, counting my footsteps. I refused to think about all the things outside my control right now.

Eventually, the tree line opened up, and my foot sank into the water. I pulled it free, but there was nowhere else to go.

In front of me, another small island waited. I turned and scanned the direction I'd come from, but it was becoming increasingly obvious that I was being led toward the creature I was supposed to kill.

I could swim, but it wasn't my best thing. Fighting in water didn't appeal in the slightest, and I took a moment to imagine all of the terrifying creatures hidden beneath the water, waiting for a stupid ex-bounty hunter to wade into their territory.

They didn't even need to be fae creatures. A crocodile from my world could hide underwater for hours before it struck.

I allowed myself a few moments to imagine all the things that could kill me, and all the long, painful ways I could die. Then I forced myself to put it away.

"You are frightened, little witch." Samael's voice was a soothing presence in my head.

"You should be resting."

"Your fear called to me." I could suddenly feel his presence, closer than I ever had. He let out a low growl.

"You are in the unseelie swamplands. Why are you there?"

"I had to see a woman about a sword."

"You will not enter that water. It's too dangerous."

"I love you, but you don't get a say in this."

"I always get a say." His haughty tone made me do something I hadn't thought I could do in my current predicament.

It made me laugh.

"My weakness amuses you?"

I sighed. *"Of course not. It's just... you're half-dead and you're still attempting to handle circumstances outside of your control. I'd probably be doing the same thing. I don't know what that means for the long-term success of our relationship."* I kept my tone light, teasing, and Samael echoed my sigh.

"It means we are alike in many ways. Luckily, we have enough differences that our lives will never be

boring."

I liked that he was talking about the future. About us having our lives together. It meant he trusted me to get the job done and return to him. Even if he didn't like that, he couldn't help me.

"You're too distracting," I told him. *"Go back to sleep."*

I could practically feel him scowl at that, but he knew I was right. A moment of inattention here could mean I accidentally used my power, making my agreement with Ilis null and void. Or it could mean I was too slow when a creature from the swamp decided to attack. I forced myself to push that thought away.

"Be safe," he told me. *"I love you."*

His presence faded away, and I scanned the brackish water in front of me. Our little conversation had helped me push most of the remaining terror away. Even if I didn't have to wade through the water to find the creature I was hunting, Samael's decree that I wouldn't enter the water pretty much guaranteed that I would.

A girl had to keep her independence in any relationship.

And I was procrastinating.

I stepped into the water before I could talk myself out of it. The mud sucked at my boot, and I shifted for balance as I took the next step. This wasn't so bad.

The next step took me chest-deep and I cursed up a storm.

My utility belt was waterproof, and hopefully the canteen Ilis had given me was as well. But I was off balance and quite literally out of my depth. I needed to get out of this water *now.*

The mud was so thick that it would have been faster for me to doggy-paddle through the water. But my boots were far too heavy, and the thought of taking them off…

Nope, nope, nope.

I kept my Mark II clutched in my fist, so I wasn't exactly moving quickly. Water splashed into my mouth and I spat it out with a grimace.

My next step took me underwater. I had no idea how deep it was, but I panicked, swallowing my next mouthful of the filthy water.

I flipped onto my back and gasped for air, kicking out with my feet and using my hands to propel me backward.

Just a few feet to go.

There was no gentle incline up to this island. I leaned both hands on the damp grass and *pushed.* The mud sucked at my boots and I wiggled them free, straining to escape the water.

The ground felt better than I could have imagined. I flipped onto my back and caught my breath, staring up at the sky.

I had to keep going.

I took stock of my weapons—all of them miraculously still in place. I didn't bother checking the inside of the utility belt. Samael had given it to me, so it would hold up, and opening it would mean dripping water inside.

I waved away the insects that were attempting to feast on my bare skin and got to my feet. Something shrieked nearby—a bird, probably—and I jolted.

I was ridiculously jumpy for someone who was armed to the teeth. But I'd have felt a lot more secure if I was allowed to access my power.

You went most of your life with no power to speak of. Don't start relying on it now.

My salty inner voice had a point.

I was standing on the bank of the island, although there wasn't much bank to speak of. I could reach out and touch the nearest tree.

The water may have washed away some of the sweat gathering on my skin, but I was already replacing it. I'd been trying to conserve the water Ilis had given me, since I didn't know how long this little task would take, but I couldn't risk getting dehydrated. I uncapped the flask and took a small sip. The water tasted clean, with a hint of underlying sweetness.

Another shriek. This time, I didn't jump, but I did twist the cap back on the flask and replace it with my Nim Cub. Time to get moving.

The trees were sparser here, the ground damp enough that took an extra jolt of energy to lift my feet.

The next shriek tore through the air. Closer this time, but further to the left. Either one of the creatures was approaching, or there was more than one, and they were surrounding me.

Goody.

Hopefully, they were the creatures Ilis wanted me to kill, and I could get the hell out of here.

The edges of my vision turned blurry and I rubbed at my eyes. It was so goddamned hot and humid in this place, it was as if I was inhaling warm water.

If I saw Finvarra again, I'd be sure to let him know exactly what I thought of this part of his realm.

The forest went quiet in the way that told me the creatures in it were attempting not to draw the attention of the larger predator in their midst. I kept my steps quiet, but I wasn't made for creeping through the forest. *I was the one being hunted.*

And it knew I was here.

CHAPTER TWELVE

Danica

I planted my right foot behind my left, turning my body sideways to present a smaller target. My power licked at me, pure temptation.

Nope. I wasn't going through all of this crap just to fail based on a technicality.

I pushed my power back and waited. I probably had seven to eight feet of clearing around me, and it was unlikely that I'd find a better spot if I needed to fight. If something was hunting me, I wasn't going to walk straight into its trap. I'd force it to attack here, where I had more room to move.

"I know you're there," I said softly. "Let's go."

A bush in front of me rustled, and I forced my knees to bend slightly, loosening up. The edges of my vision turned blurry again. I was probably getting dehydrated already.

Something stepped into the patch of sunlight, snuffling at the ground.

My shoulders slumped. A six-legged animal.

It looked like some kind of wild pig, only with more legs and an extra set of eyes on either side of its head. It paid me no attention, simply sniffed around and moved on.

I let out a deep breath and turned away from the small clearing.

Something slammed into me.

I flew several feet, my trajectory only stopped by the tree I hit before I crumpled to the ground. I'd miraculously managed to keep my dagger clutched in my hand, and since I hadn't accidentally stabbed myself with it, I got to my knees and stared.

I'd seen pictures of this thing in a book somewhere. Likely when Edward was teaching me about various mythological creatures. Unfortunately, he hadn't told me how to kill it.

Chupacabras had been reported in our realm since before the portals opened. But the pictures I'd seen had put them about the size of a kangaroo.

Those pictures were wrong. It was at least three times that size, and I had a feeling it would prefer my blood to the livestock it was reputed to attack.

I made it to my feet, and a groan left my throat as I took stock of my body. My back ached from its rendezvous with the tree behind me, but I didn't think I had any permanent damage.

The chupacabra hopped forward, likely planning to give me some more of that damage.

I had to hope my knives would pierce its green-gray scales. But first, I needed to see how fast it was.

I slipped one of my throwing knives free of its sheath on my utility belt and threw.

The chupacabra dodged to the right and let out a shriek of rage. Red eyes glowed with fury as it bared a mouthful of sharp teeth.

Fast. That was my answer. It was fucking fast.

I was pressed up against the tree still, and I needed room to move.

I threw another knife, resisting the urge to slam my hands over my ears as it shrieked again. This time, I came closer to hitting it, and the chupacabra crouched, muscles trembling as it prepared to lunge.

I had to time this perfectly.

The chupacabra launched itself at me, its powerful back legs propelling it through the air. I ducked and rolled beneath it, pushing myself back to my feet. I was in the middle of the clearing now. It would have to do.

It didn't waste any time. The creature jumped toward me again, this time staying low. It had learned its lesson.

Time slowed to a crawl. I dropped, my back flat against the ground. My legs came up, and I slashed at its vulnerable underbelly.

I could suddenly feel Samael, but he was silent, obviously unwilling to distract me. His presence helped though, and I drove my Nim Cub further up into its gut as its thick, black blood poured onto my stomach.

The chupacabra's breath was hot on my face as it leaned over me. It stunk of rotting meat as it shrieked, now attempting to escape my blade. It reared back, then struck, its teeth aiming for my face. I lifted my left hand as I almost lost my grip on the Nim Cub with my right. The chupacabra's blood was making the hilt slippery.

Its teeth clamped onto my left arm, and this time, I

was the one to scream. Samael's fury engulfed me, cutting through the pain.

The chupacabra was bleeding out. I just had to hold on. I twisted the knife, and it shrieked again, almost blowing out my ears. It was trying to escape now. Its hind legs scrabbled at the dirt, kicking into my legs. I gritted my teeth and hung on.

It slumped against me, weakened by blood loss. I heaved, but the angle was wrong, and it was heavy.

Not to mention, my left arm was almost useless. I needed to wrap it up. Hopefully, it didn't need stitches.

Great. I was trapped beneath its body. Awesome.

"Need some help, my love?"

"Don't even think about it, Samael."

The last thing I wanted was for him to give me any of his energy.

The chupacabra gasped out its last breath, and I gagged as the scent of rot washed over me.

I wasn't allowed to use my power in my task, but surely I could use it for this?

I blew out a breath. I couldn't risk it. I managed to wiggle my right leg higher up and pushed against the chupacabra, using it as leverage as I wiggled out.

Thick, black blood warred with the mud and dirt covering my clothes.

The world swam around me as I sat in the clearing. I needed to get moving. All the blood was likely drawing more predators.

I reached for the flask and gulped more water, sighing as it alleviated the dryness in my mouth. Then I pulled my t-shirt off. I was wearing a sports bra, and it would have to do.

Enough procrastinating. I took a deep breath and looked at my arm.

Shit.

It felt like the chupacabra still had its teeth in my arm and was gnawing away at it. The wound bled steadily, and I rummaged in my utility belt for some clean bandages. I slapped them on, wrapped my arm in my t-shirt, and after a moment of indecision, I reached for the last low-level pain charm Samael had slipped into my utility belt when he'd replaced it.

It didn't remove the pain, but it softened the edges enough that I could function.

"Are you okay?" Samael's voice was a low caress, but I could feel his frustration at not being able to click his fingers and summon a healer.

"I'm fine. Thanks for the pain charms, by the way."

My vision was still blurry, and I took a few more sips of water. Then I turned and trudged past the chupacabra's body, in the direction I'd been heading.

I kept my steps as light as possible. Ilis had said I'd know the creature I was supposed to kill when I found it, and now I could *feel* that I was heading in the right direction.

Dizziness swept over me and I stumbled, leaning against the closest tree. I hadn't lost enough blood for this level of mental fog. And I hadn't sweat enough for dehydration to cause it either. What the hell was going on?

"Drugged," Samael's voice dripped with cold fury. *"You've been drugged."*

"That's impossible," I said aloud. Then I froze. I pulled the canteen free and opened it, pouring some of the water into my hand.

I sniffed. No scent. No weird taste. I mean, sure, it was a little sweeter than normal water, but I'd figured it was just because it was from the unseelie realm.

And I'd also figured Ilis could be trusted. She'd had no reason to kill me.

I dropped to my knees as the realization swept through me. Kyla was alone with her. And she'd been eating her food, too. Was my friend already dead?

Bile flooded my mouth, and I leaned over, heaving.

I had to get back. I would kill Ilis for this.

The pulling in my chest increased. I ignored it. If Ilis wanted me to go that way, it was likely she had something nasty planned while I was weak and disorientated.

My instincts roared at me, the invisible leash incessant. I could feel the creature, close enough that I should at least check it out.

I deliberated. Samael's presence was gone, and I had a feeling I knew why. He'd be collecting his strength so he could pour it into me and help me return to Kyla. I needed to prevent that from happening.

I wouldn't make it back like this. The forest was swimming around me, and strange colors were beginning to fill my vision. There was no way I'd be able to swim back through the swamp to Ilis's island.

Kyla was a wolf. She would've scented poison in her food. I had to trust that she could look after herself. And I had to find somewhere safe to rest—maybe up a tree or something.

I took a hesitant step forward. When the ground didn't hit me in the face, I took another.

The strange forest was coming to an end. I could see more sun between the trees, and it seemed to glow like a beacon, dragging me forward.

I pushed through the gap and froze.

Creatures filled the huge clearing. Creatures of myth.

They curled up together in groups, some of them wandering the space as they nuzzled at each other. There must have been twenty or thirty of them. I didn't know what to call them. A herd? A pack? A… pride.

All of them were a stark white, only the word didn't even come close to describing the pure beauty of their fur, or the gleaming sheen of their feathers. All of them had the body of a lion, with the magnificent wings of an eagle.

Yet some of their heads were eagle, and some of them were lion. As if there was a genetic component, or as if these were two prides formed into one.

Griffins. They were griffins.

And I was supposed to kill one of them.

I tensed at the thought, and a branch broke beneath my foot. As one, the griffins looked at me, then turned their attention away, ignoring me.

All except one. He lay on the other side of the clearing, his head on his paws. His eyes were a dull gold, and they were stuck to my face. There was a… kindness in those eyes. He looked at me almost fondly.

The other griffins had paired up, and I didn't know if it was the drug in my bloodstream or my own instincts, but I knew they were mates. All except this one.

He shifted as if to get more comfortable, and I saw it.

One of his wings was damaged. Twisted in a way that made it lie awkwardly against his body. I doubted he could fly. Our eyes met once more, and his golden orbs held sorrow and acceptance. He would never take to the skies like the rest of his brothers and sisters. He was forced to run after them, trailing them by scent and often only arriving when they were readying to leave once more.

I blinked. How did I know that? Was he showing me his reality in my mind?

The other griffins began to spread their wings. One by one, they took to the skies, leaving the last griffin alone. He looked unperturbed, now well-used to loneliness.

My heart ached.

The world twisted once more, and I tightened my hand around the hilt of my Mark II.

Two different futures unraveled in front of my eyes. Whatever Ilis had drugged me with, it showed me the repercussions of my actions.

As if I didn't already know.

In the first choice, I shoved my blade into the Griffin's throat. It roared, pain and betrayal stark in its kind golden eyes. In this vision, I ignored it and continued slicing. Eventually, its head hit the ground, separated from its body. I watched as I leaned over and threw up next to it. Then I made my way back to Ilis. Ilis beamed at her when she arrived, holding out her arms.

I scowled. The bitch drugged me. We certainly wouldn't be hugging it out when I arrived.

Ilis leaned forward, whispering the secret I needed in my ear. Then Kyla was there, and we made our way through the portal. The vision skipped ahead, and my eyes filled at the sight of Samael, love and gratitude in his eyes as he opened them for the first time since the Spell of Three took hold.

And then the second choice played out in front of me. I turned and walked away from the Griffin. Ilis shook her head in disappointment as I arrived, all of this time wasted, and for nothing.

Ilis whirled and strode toward her house, and a few days later, I watched as Samael turned to ash in front of my eyes.

Fuck. That.

I ground my teeth until pain shot through my jaw. Ilis wouldn't give me what I needed unless I killed this magnificent creature? Fine. I'd figure it out without her. Between us, Kyla and I would tear these realms apart until we found the location of the sword. It would cost us time, but it wouldn't cost a piece of my soul.

At this stage of my life, I had very few lines I wouldn't cross. But this was one of them. I wouldn't kill an innocent, defenseless being just because it would make my life easier.

"Fuck you, Ilis."

In front of me, the griffin slowly stood. Was it limping slightly? It stopped a few feet from me, as if waiting for me to make up my mind.

It confused me. The griffin may not be able to fly, but even if I attempted to kill it, it could more than put up a good fight. It was much, much larger than the chupacabra, and in my current condition, it would likely take me down.

It stepped forward again, and I gaped as it bowed its

head. It was offering me its throat.

Ilis could have sent me to this place to kill one of the many creatures who preyed on others. I could've killed an entire pack of chupacabras. But instead, she'd decided to toy with me, to send me to kill this magnificent beast, who was simply unlucky enough to be unable to fly away.

No fucking way.

"I'm not killing you," I told it wearily, and the griffin lifted its head. Could it understand me?

It slowly moved even closer, keeping its posture unthreatening, although even now, it could have opened its mouth and swallowed my head whole.

Exhaustion swept over me, and my whole body went weak. I gave myself the pleasure of imagining slipping a blade between Ilis's ribs.

I slumped to my knees, cursing the unseelie's name. Warm fur brushed my skin, and the griffin curled its body around me as I passed out.

CHAPTER THIRTEEN

Danica

I don't know how long I slept for, but the sun had lost much of its heat as I blinked open my eyes. The griffin was still curled protectively around me, and contentment gleamed within its eyes as I glanced at it.

My mouth was so dry, I'd give almost anything for a sip of water. But my head was mostly clear, although a headache had burrowed behind my right eye and stayed there.

I had to get moving.

And even the thought made me want to curl up and close my eyes again.

"I appreciate you being my snuggle buddy," I told the griffin, "but I've got places to go, houses to burn down."

Ilis had told me not to use my power for her little task, but she'd said nothing about using it when I arrived back, hungover and exhausted from being magically roofied.

Oh yes, she would pay.

The griffin chuffed as I got to my feet. Then it leaned down and nuzzled my hair.

"Yeah," I told him. "You too. Uh, good luck with everything."

I pivoted and strode out of the clearing, back the way I'd come. Thanks to the time I'd lost, I now needed to move my ass.

My chest was heavy. Samael would have killed that griffin for me. He would've burned this realm down if I was the one dying and he had to come up with a plan to save me.

"Your heart is soft beneath the barbed wire you wrapped it in to keep yourself safe," Samael purred. *"Your compassion and mercy are two of the things that drew my attention before I came close to admitting what I felt for you."*

I tensed. *"Are you reading my mind?"*

"No. But I can feel your guilt."

"You would have done it for me."

He was silent. *"And you would have been disappointed in your male when you had learned what I had done."*

"That disappointment wouldn't have stopped you."

"No." Amused tenderness radiated from his end of the bond. *"But I have been alive for much longer, have been forced to do things that would make you turn away from me if you were to learn of them."*

"I wouldn't turn away from you. I told you. I'm all in."

"Then you will understand that I could never turn from you for the kindness that comes naturally."

I didn't feel particularly kind. I resented the hell out of the griffin, and I'd been planning on stabbing Ilis ever since I realized she'd drugged me.

"Even if that kindness means you die?"

Just the thought made me itch to turn in place, stalk back to the griffin and slay it.

"You will come up with another way. And if you don't, I will be waiting for you when it's your time."

The thought of being forced to go on for centuries without him… loneliness almost swallowed me whole.

Something rustled behind me, and I whirled, crouching into a low fighting stance.

The griffin eyed me.

I eyed it back.

"What are you doing?" I asked it.

Of course it didn't answer, merely waited, as if expecting me to move.

"You shouldn't follow me. There are bad things in this place. Things that would probably love to eat nosy griffins."

The griffin ignored that. Samael gave a low laugh and faded from my consciousness.

I sighed and turned back toward Ilis's. The griffin would get tired of following me, eventually.

I made it back to the edge of the island without any further surprises. My arm throbbed with every beat of my heart and I hoped it wasn't infected. I glanced over my shoulder at the griffin as he watched me prepare to enter the water.

The look in his eyes said I was crazy for leaving the safety of firm ground.

He wasn't wrong.

"You should follow your friends before you lose their scent," I told him. He ignored that, his gaze dropping to the water. His lips pulled back from his teeth.

"Yeah, I'm not exactly stoked about it either."

I sat and dangled my legs into the water, took a deep breath, and slid down. The griffin paced back and forth on dry land, clearly unhappy with my decisions.

He wasn't the only one.

The water was still murky, and various bugs took the opportunity to dive bomb my face and neck as I focused all my attention on making it to the other island.

I was halfway across when the griffin roared. He gave me enough warning that I took a deep breath as the creature struck.

Half of the breath shot from my lungs as the water closed over my head and I was dragged down, down, down.

I slashed out with my Mark II, but I was uncoordinated in the water. Whatever had attacked me currently had its teeth clamped around my ankle. I folded in half and stabbed with my knife, this time making contact. Blood filled the murky water, and I saw a flash of furious orange eyes as I swam like hell toward the surface.

I should have taken my fucking boots off. That decision had sure come back to bite me in the ass.

The surface was within a few inches now. I reached for it, desperately kicking, using my free hand to push myself through the water.

My fingertips broke the water.

And I was pulled down again.

My lungs screamed for air, my body already weakened from my injuries and the drug Ilis had slipped me. I kicked out, thrashing in the creature's grip, and it ignored me. I caught a flash of scales in my peripheral vision. I stabbed once more, making contact, but my blade slid off thick scales.

All it needed to do was wait me out. I didn't have much longer in me.

White filled my vision. The shock of it made me lose more of the precious breath in my lungs. The griffin didn't stand a chance in the water with his wings and heavy bulk.

The creature released me, turning to new prey, and the griffin somehow rolled beneath my body.

He shot up, lifting me out of the water. I inhaled, gasping precious oxygen as I flew through the air. He'd angled me toward Ilis's island, and I landed in the mud, still chest-deep in the water, but out of immediate danger.

The griffin, on the other hand…

The water was murky with blood. He'd jumped in to save me.

I couldn't let him die.

I took a few deep breaths, hyperventilating in an effort to store more oxygen. Then I dove.

I cut through the water, driven by pure panic. The thought of the kindness in the gentle griffin's eyes, replaced by a vision of that kindness being snuffed out…

The murky water gave way to white fur. The griffin filled my vision as he swam toward me. And I understood, without knowing why, that he wasn't pleased that I'd gotten back *in* the water.

He shoved his head into my chest, propelling me

back in the direction I'd come. Where was the creature who'd dragged me down?

I struggled in an attempt to peer around the griffin to the scaled creature, but the longer I took to get out of the water, the longer the griffin was prey for the creature lying in wait.

I gasped for air as my head popped above the water, lunging out of the way so the griffin could make it onto the shore. Once there, I rolled onto my back, dragging precious cool air into my lungs.

The griffin collapsed beside me. I rolled onto my stomach and eyed him.

"What, exactly, were you thinking?" I snapped.

He gave me a look full of gentle reproach and I made it up onto my knees, looking him over.

"Are you even going to be able to find your friends now? What do I call them—your herd? Your pack? Your gang?"

One of his back legs was dripping blood in a steady stream. Shit. I unzipped the main compartment on my utility belt, no longer worried about contaminating it with dirty swamp water. I'd replace what I needed to when I was back in my realm.

The griffin showed me his teeth as I approached him with the bandages and I paused. Now was probably a good time to remember that his head was all lion, and that lion could chomp me into tiny pieces if I pissed him off.

"Are we going to have a problem here?"

I leaned forward and his teeth gleamed at me, his eyes making it clear that he wasn't happy. I scowled at him.

"Your blood is going to be drawing predators for miles. If we don't stop the bleeding, we'll be stopped by hungry creatures who want to snack on a griffin. And I'm not exactly at my best right now."

That was putting it lightly. My arm was killing me after spending so much time flailing in the water. My ankle ached, although those cuts were relatively shallow, and I was bone tired in a way that warned me I needed to sleep soon.

The griffin huffed out a sigh and lowered his head on his paws, closing his eyes. I took that as a sign that he would allow me to bandage him up.

"It's tricky with all this fur," I told him. "And I'm not a vet."

He opened one eye and stared at me. I couldn't help my grin. He not only understood me, but he knew what a vet was, and he was offended.

"Just kidding. I'm just going to wrap this around you for now. When it's no longer bleeding, you can chew the bandage off or remove it with your claws. Deal?"

He didn't give any indication that he'd heard that, and I shrugged, slowly climbing from my knees to my feet. The world turned fuzzy at the edges. I was likely still fighting off the remnants of whatever Ilis drugged me with.

Oh, she would pay.

"Right. This is where I leave you. Thanks for, you know… covering my ass in that water. Although I didn't kill you and I should've, so I guess we're even." I reached out and petted his soaked fur and then turned in the direction of Ilis's house—at least I was pretty sure that was the right direction. I slid my Nim Cub out of my sheath. I was really, really hoping I wouldn't need to use it.

I squeezed through a gap in the brush, the mud sucking at my boots.

"Not long now," I muttered. I was very carefully not thinking about Kyla, left alone with the traitorous unseelie, and I was most definitely not thinking about all the time I'd wasted here, while the sands in Samael's hourglass trickled down.

My body ached for water. I *was* dehydrated by now, but I hadn't seen a freshwater source since I arrived in this humid cesspit.

Something moved behind me and I spun, Nim Cub ready. The griffin stared at me. I glowered at it.

"You gave me a heart attack. What are you doing? You're going to lose track of your friends." The thought of the griffin wandering alone made my chest clench. "Although, to be honest, they seem like complete jerks for not waiting for you."

He ignored all that, waiting patiently, and it clicked.

"You can't come with me."

Nothing. I sighed.

"Seriously. You can't get anywhere near Ilis. She sent me to kill you. Do you understand what that means?"

His gaze moved past me, as if he was impatient. Was I assuming he could understand me when he couldn't? No, I was sure he had some level of understanding. I narrowed my eyes at him.

"Lookit, you're on team Danica now, which frankly surprises the hell out of me. But if she tries to hurt you,

I'm going to have to kill her, and then I'll be in even deeper shit with Finvarra."

He stayed where he was, and I threw my hands in the air. "Fine."

I blew out a breath and turned back toward Ilis's house. The sun was getting low in the sky now, and if I ran out of light in this place, I would be in big trouble.

It must've been around half an hour before I recognized some of the landmarks around me. The griffin stepped silently behind me, looking for all the world like he was out for a stroll. I glanced over my shoulder at him, and he snarled.

I jumped, but he was looking behind me.

That couldn't be good.

"Where issssss my blood?"

Oh fuck. It wasn't that I'd forgotten about the snake, it was just that… okay, fine. I'd forgotten about the snake.

"Change of plans," I told it, gripping my Nim Cub a hair tighter and arming my other hand with a throwing knife.

"You broke your vow," it hissed furiously.

"Extenuating circumstances."

Behind me, the griffin trembled, and I risked a quick glance. He wasn't trembling in fear. He was crouched, muscles vibrating in a way that told me he was readying himself to launch at the snake.

That would get ugly. We were both wounded, and the snake was mammoth in size and much faster than it should've been.

"I'll give you blood," I said tiredly. The snake's tongue darted out as it tasted the air.

"The creature behind you. That wasssss the deal."

"New deal. My blood, or we'll all rumble. You may kill us, but I swear, I'll do enough damage that you'll regret it."

The snake stared at me silently.

"Fine."

I didn't want to unwind the t-shirt from my arm, so I sliced a shallow cut further down. The griffin let out a low growl.

"I hear you."

"Don't you dare," a low, furious voice snapped.

Samael had mentally reached for me again, just in time to weigh in on my decision. Awesome.

"I don't have much choice, and before you say anything, the griffin is hands-off."

My demon was a silent, enraged presence as I took a step forward. To be fair, he had a point. This was the height of stupidity. If the snake wrapped itself around me, the griffin may attack, but I'd still be dinner.

I'd done a lot of difficult things recently, but taking my next step was one of the hardest. The griffin stepped forward, ready to shove me aside, and I bared my own teeth at him.

"Don't even think about it."

He roared.

I almost dropped my knives with the urge to clamp my hands over my ears. The sound rumbled through my body, quiet at first, the threat raising the hair on the back of my neck. Then it grew impossibly loud, until it sounded like a 747 taking off. When he was done, the marsh was eerily silent.

No birds chirping. No insects buzzing. Nothing.

Despite the situation, I was impressed. "A little dramatic," I told him. "But I think you got your point across."

The snake didn't exactly show any fear, but then, he was a snake. He drew back slightly though, waiting us out.

"I don't like this," Samael's voice was hard.

"I mean, death by giant snake isn't exactly my preferred method of carking it either."

"That is not amusing."

"Come on, it kinda is. Don't worry. I've got this."

I wasn't entirely sure I did have this, and from Samael's snort, he could feel my uncertainty.

I smiled at the snake. "Let me tell you how this will go. You try anything, other than tasting my blood, and my blades will sink into you. Then the griffin will tear you apart."

"I undersssssstand."

"Fine."

I shot the griffin a warning look. His eyes were on the snake, but he didn't seem like he was about to attack, so I took one more step forward.

Then I held out my arm.

I kept my throwing knife in that hand, my Nim Cub poised in my other hand. The snake slowly lowered toward me, taking its sweet time.

I couldn't blame it. We were all on edge.

The snake's tongue darted out, tasing my blood, and I shuddered. It took every ounce of my willpower to keep my arm raised, and to not bury my knife in its scales.

"Half-blood," it said, tasting once more. The feel of its tongue brushing against my skin made bile crawl up my throat.

"The things I do for you," I teased Samael.

"Still not amused."

So much for breaking the tension with humor. I slowly pulled my arm away, and the snake pulled back, as if to strike.

"You got what you wanted," I ground out. "Now let us pass."

"Your blood tassssstessss like sssssuffering."

"Cool story. We're leaving now."

I slowly backed away, waiting for the snake to climb further up its tree. I wanted to walk past it about as much as I wanted to jump back in the water with the creature who'd wanted me for a snack.

Knowing the griffin was guarding my back helped. Although I worried about him walking back this way alone.

My body was so tense my muscles ached as I forced myself to stride past the snake. I didn't let out the breath I was holding until I could see Ilis's house between the gaps in the brush.

I glanced at the griffin. "Do me a favor and at least stay out of sight while I talk to Ilis. Then I can have Kyla take a look at your wound. She'll have more experience with four-legged first-aid."

We'd figure out how to get him back to his friends later.

I squinted through the trees as a figure walked down the stairs. Ilis. She'd known I was almost here.

I left the griffin crouching behind a tree and stepped out of the brush.

Danica

Ilis's smile was wide and gentle and oh-so welcoming. The audacity.

I didn't slam my fist into her face, but it was close.

"You made it," she said.

"Yeah, no fucking thanks to you."

A hint of regret crossed her face. "I apologize for the effect of the drug. I was… unaware of human biology. The drug should have done nothing more than open you to your basest self."

"I don't want to hear it. Where's Kyla?"

The door to Ilis's kitchen opened and Kyla stepped out. My shoulders slumped.

Ilis was examining my face.

"You believed I would harm the wolf."

"You drugged me and left me vulnerable in your hellish swamp. Why wouldn't I believe that?"

I looked past her, waiting impatiently for Kyla to make her way down the stairs. All I wanted to do was get the hell out of here.

"Don't you wish to learn about the sword?" Ilis asked.

She was taunting me now? I glowered at her. "I failed your little task."

She smiled. "A true warrior is merciful. They are

compassionate. They do not slay innocents for their own benefit."

A muscle next to my eye twitched. Twice.

I slapped my palm over it and moved my hand away from the hilt of my Mark II before I was tempted to do something I'd regret.

"Let me get this straight. You sent me into a swamp, instructed me to kill a mythical creature, drugged me, and now you're telling me it was all some kind of *morality* test?"

Ilis nodded. "Compassion is one of the most ignored, yet most important, traits. If you were the kind of person who would slay the griffin for your own gain, I would not want the sword to fall into your hands. You would save your demon, and then one day, the power you gained would corrupt your soul."

"You drugged me. I almost died."

"The drug was only supposed to allow you to make the decision of your heart."

I shook my head at that. I didn't want to hear her excuses.

"Fine. Where can I find the people I'm looking for?"

Her gaze moved over my shoulder and surprise darted across her face. "The griffin has followed you."

I ground my teeth. Of course he wouldn't stay put, because that would be too easy. Although, since Ilis had told me I *wasn't* supposed to kill him, at least I knew he wasn't in any danger around here.

Kyla stepped gingerly across the spongy ground and stared at the griffin. "What, exactly, is that?"

"Your replacement. I didn't know if you'd still be

alive when I got back."

She narrowed her eyes at me. "Hilarious."

Kyla didn't look any worse for wear, and I decided not to mention the drug in front of her while we were still here. You're welcome, Ilis.

"Where's Misty?"

Ilis handed the dagger to me and some of the tension drained from me as I slipped it back in its sheath.

"Who has the sword?"

"The queen of the merfolk."

"I thought they were a myth."

She merely glanced pointedly behind me at the griffin. I followed her gaze. The mythical being was lying in the sun, his eyes heavy-lidded as he watched us.

"Okay. How sure are you that she has the sword?"

"I gave it to her. She will have kept it safe all these years."

"Fine." I was too pissed about the magical roofie to say anything else.

I turned without another word, and Kyla fell into step as we walked back toward the portal. Ilis better have kept her word and stacked them for me.

The griffin watched us out of huge, adoring eyes as we approached. Despite myself, I slowly held out one hand, stroking his ears. Now that I wasn't in danger, I could appreciate just how rare this experience was. I'd hung out with an honest-to-God griffin.

Vas would lose his mind when I told him.

"Thank you for your help," I said. "You need to go now."

The griffin lay down, as immovable as a mountain.

If he wanted to stay here, who was I to argue? Maybe Ilis would find it in her heart to help him get back to the rest of the griffins.

We turned to walk away, and Kyla let out a choked laugh. The griffin was following us. I whirled around and he lay back down.

"Your life is a circus," Kyla said.

I shook my head and stalked away. If he wanted to escort us to the portal, that was his business.

"I'm looking forward to getting out of this place," Kyla muttered as we approached the swirling colors.

I gave her a sour look. Her clothes were still pristine, and she looked fresh enough that she might've taken a nap.

"Difficult day eating Ilis out of house and home?"

She merely grinned at me. "Jealousy is the ugliest emotion."

"Blah blah."

"Real mature."

"My maturity disappeared when I was wandering drugged through the forest."

Kyla went still. Her head angled, eyes narrowed in a way that told me she was on the hunt.

"Excuse me?"

Whoops. "Hey look," I started, pointing toward the griffin.

She turned her head, and I shoved her through the portal. I gave the griffin one last pat and then stepped through myself.

Kyla gave me a dark look from where she was sitting on the ground. "Unnecessary."

"We don't have time for you to rip Ilis's throat out, and Finvarra already hates you."

"Not as much as I hate him," she muttered darkly. Then her mouth dropped open.

Soft fur brushed my hand, and I slammed my eyes shut.

"You've got to be kidding me."

The griffin had followed us home like a stray dog.

Kyla laughed. We both turned to examine the griffin who gave us a "what are you waiting for?" look.

"From the state of his wings, I'm guessing he can't fly," Kyla said.

"Nope. And," I said meaningfully, "if he doesn't march himself back through that portal, all of his friends and family are going to have moved on without him."

The griffin didn't look concerned. He just lay down once more.

I pinched the bridge of my nose as Kyla marveled at the size of him.

"How the hell are we going to fit him into my car?"

CHAPTER FOURTEEN

Danica

We ended up lowering the back seats in Kyla's Nissan. Both of us pushed our own seats forward as far as we could, but even then, to say it was a tight fit was the understatement of the century. White fur spilled from the back windows, which were far too small for the griffin's huge head to fit through, although he seemed to be enjoying the fresh air, anyway.

Who wouldn't, after spending an extended amount of time in that marsh?

The werewolf sentries knew Kyla's car, and we drove slowly through their territory, parking outside of Nathaniel's ranch-style home.

I shut the passenger door as Kyla opened the trunk for the griffin.

Vas dropped down from the sky, likely on sentry duty for the demons. No one would be taking any chances with Samael out of commission. His mouth dropped open at the sight of me, before curling up in a shit-eating grin.

"Wow, what the hell happened to you?"

I snarled at him. "I don't want to talk about it."

All I wanted was a shower and to curl up next to my demon. Vas must've seen the longing on my face, because he opened his arms, offering a hug.

I took it.

"If I haven't told you, I'm proud of you," he squeezed me tight, his voice gruff.

A fraction of the tension in my neck disappeared. Somewhere along the way, Vas had become the brother I'd never had.

"Thanks," I said, my throat tight. "How is he?"

"The same. If he lives through this, it'll be because of you. My uncle knows it too."

I sighed at the thought of Ag. "Is he there?"

Vas's body shook, and I realized he was laughing. "Go shower. You stink."

I pushed away from him. He glanced down at his body, and I winced. I'd transferred a healthy amount of wet mud onto his own clothes, which were now filthy.

He looked so put out, I couldn't help but laugh. Kyla ambled up to us and grinned at him.

Vas went still as he spotted the griffin. "What the hell?"

Kyla opened her mouth, but a deep voice carried over the chatter of the birds around us.

"Kyla."

We both turned at Nathaniel's voice. There was something in it… some hint of warning that made me edgy.

A man stood next to him. I didn't need to ask who he was—he was like a male reflection of Kyla, with the same creamy brown skin and bright blue eyes.

I smiled at him in greeting, but my smile fell as I took in his expression. His nose was wrinkled, eyes narrowed, and his mouth a thin line. Disgust practically radiated from him, and if I could sense it, it was likely stabbing into Kyla's heightened senses.

I was covered in mud, water, and blood, and I stank of the swamp. Vas likely wasn't much better. But it wasn't us he was looking at—other than the quick glance of contempt as he took us in. No, that disgust was all for his sister.

Kyla flinched.

I gaped at her. I was so used to her tough exterior, I'd forgotten she had a vulnerable side. I'd only seen it a few times, and one of them was when she'd told me about how she'd been psychologically tortured, and then turned against her will by her ex. But her voice had broken when she'd talked about how disappointed her brother would be at how she was turned.

This wasn't disappointment, though. This was pure fury.

"Ian–" Kyla attempted a smile and took a step toward him. He just shook his head.

"Not only are you a werewolf, but you're colluding with filthy demons?"

Ouch.

Kyla narrowed her eyes at him, but her voice was shaky. "These are my friends, Ian. This is Danica and this is–"

"I don't care."

She flinched, and Nathaniel took a single step closer.

"Watch how you speak to her," he warned. Dominance lay heavy in his voice, and Ian tensed.

"Kyla is my sister."

"And she's *my* wolf."

Ian swallowed at that, his gaze returning to his sister. "So that's how it works? You've completely turned your back on us?"

Now Kyla growled. It was low, deadly, and her brother turned white. She stalked several feet closer.

"You accuse me of turning *my* back on you? Where were you when Joel was preventing me from seeing my friends? When he declared we were moving two hours from my office and I had to quit my job? When I didn't get to say goodbye to granddad before he died? Where the fuck were you then? Oh, I know. You were best buddies with Joel's friends, and you didn't want to piss any of them off."

Vas stiffened, but it was Nathaniel's snarl that made the hair on the back of my neck stand up. Obviously, he hadn't known that little tidbit from Kyla's life.

Ian slowly turned, finding Nathaniel practically breathing down his neck. The Alpha's eyes had turned that eerie pale blue, so light it appeared almost white, and his canines had lengthened.

Nathaniel had perfect control most of the time, so if he was allowing a hint of his shift, it was because he'd decided to scare the crap out of the asshole next to him.

Fuck it.

I called my power to me, darkening the air around us. Next to me, Vas let his wings appear, spreading them wide. The griffin, obviously feeling left out, decided that was the perfect moment to let loose one of his ear-splitting roars.

Nathaniel gave me a look that said we would definitely be talking about the creature I'd brought into his territory.

Ian's gaze darted between all of us. To his credit, he didn't piss his pants, but his hands trembled as he took a step back.

Nathaniel had allowed him to visit, obviously unaware that he was a judgmental fuck. I had a sneaky suspicion that Ian wouldn't be invited back.

"Why did you come here?" Kyla snapped.

"To find you. I've searched for you since you went missing."

"Why? To see if you could tolerate being around a werewolf?"

He stayed silent and she laughed. "These are my friends. That's the future Underqueen who you just insulted. She's guarded my back for the past several weeks. Oh, and she gave me a job."

"Kyla–"

"Leave, Ian. There's nothing for you here."

Ian gave us a sweeping glance. A muscle jumped in his cheek. He gave Kyla a sharp nod, and then he whirled, stalking back toward his car.

Kyla moved past me.

"Hey–" I started, and she shook her head.

"I don't want to talk about it. I'll see you later."

Fair enough. I'd had my share of sibling drama over the years. No one could fuck you up like family.

Nathaniel stared at the griffin as Kyla walked away. The griffin bent his front legs, lowering his head in a regal bow. It wasn't a submissive move. It was the acknowledgement of one dangerous creature to another.

Nathaniel studied him for a long moment. Finally, he lowered his head in a shallow nod. The griffin rose and wandered after Kyla.

Nathaniel raised one eyebrow at me.

"I need to clean up, then I'll fill you in."

He merely nodded. I wasn't fooled by his patient demeanor. It was unlikely the Alpha was used to waiting for anything.

Lilith was sitting in the living room when I arrived back in the cabin. Her mouth dropped open at the state of me, and I pre-emptively flipped her off. Surprise flashed through me at her amused grin.

A low curse sounded, and I turned toward the kitchen. Ag was standing in the doorway, expression displeased.

What else was new?

"What have you done?" he snapped.

I was so tired I could barely get the words out. "I danced to an unseelie tune and now I know where to get the sword."

"To your arm," he clarified, stepping forward.

Oh, that.

I'd avoided looking at it. Since I'd wrapped my shirt around it, it had settled down to a dull throb, but I sure wasn't looking forward to peeling my sad excuse for first-aid off of it.

Ag was instantly next to me, and I jolted back, but he'd already caught hold of my arm and was untying my t-shirt.

"I didn't realize you had mother hen tendencies," I murmured as Ag unwrapped the bandage.

"Quiet."

I rolled my eyes. Behind Ag, Vas stepped into the room and grinned at me.

"It looks worse than it is."

"And how would you know that?" Ag raised his voice. "This needs the healer."

"No it doesn't," I started, and he merely ignored me.

"Go bathe. You're of no help to Samael if you die from a nasty infection before he can wake."

My mouth dropped open as Ag got to his feet and stalked out the door, likely to contact Eldan himself.

"I would've thought he'd be happy for me to get a nasty infection," I said sullenly.

Vas shook his head at me. "He may not like your choices, but he doesn't want you dead."

"He hates me."

"He thinks you're a loose cannon."

"I'm independent and proactive."

"Uh-huh."

He gave me a look, and I scowled. "I'm going for a long, hot shower. You'll have to arrange to shower elsewhere if you're hoping for hot water today."

"Brat."

I stepped into the room I'd claimed as my own, my gaze going straight to Samael.

No change.

I let out a shaky breath, stepping closer to the bed.

Lia hissed at me as I approached. I paused, narrowing my eyes at her. "You live with demons and cuddle up to werewolves, but it's the griffin's scent that's the problem?"

She ignored me, lifting her leg to wash.

"That's just peachy."

I rummaged in my suitcase for clothes and carefully removed my weapons so they could be cleaned. My jeans, sports bra, and underwear would go straight into the trash.

I allowed my mind to take a few precious moments to go blank as the hot water pounded down on me.

When I was done, I dried my hair with my good arm and wrapped myself in Samael's towel. Less than two weeks ago, he watched me shower, his eyes hot and feral with desire, until he was interrupted by business.

I should have told Azazyel to fuck off and jumped Samael. Should have spent the day in bed talking and laughing with him while I had the chance.

I glanced at Lia, who showed no further interest in approaching me, even though I was now griffin-scent free.

"You can be a real dick, you know that?"

A low laugh sounded behind me, and I glanced over my shoulder at Bael.

The demon grinned at me, slipped his hand into his pocket, and pulled out one of Lia's fish-shaped treats. I gaped at him.

"You're bribing my cat now?"

He shrugged. "She was best friends with Vas, and I couldn't let him win her affections without demonstrating who had the superior ear-scratch."

I pondered that, and he handed me the treat. I scowled at Lia, who'd opened one eye.

"This is the one and only time I'll bribe you," I told her.

Her other eye opened. We both knew I was full of shit.

I offered the treat, and she slowly got to her feet, stretched, and sauntered across the bed toward me.

The treat disappeared from my palm, and I stroked her silky head. She purred and nuzzled me.

"Friends again, huh?"

"Ag wants to see you," Bael said.

"My arm is fine."

"Don't make me come in there," Ag's deep voice said from the living room. I sent a filthy look in his direction, and Bael laughed.

"Better get it over with."

I cinched Samael's robe tighter around my waist and stepped out of the bedroom.

Ag sat on the sofa and gestured for me to sit next to him. The other demons made themselves scarce, and I scowled at Vas's back as he disappeared. Traitor.

Ag seemed content to let the silence stretch, and I shifted on the sofa.

"I hope you cleaned that," he said.

I scowled. "Why do you even care?"

He attempted to keep his blank face on, but I caught the surprise in his eyes. "I'm unsure what you mean."

"Clearly, you don't believe I can save Samael, so why do you care if my arm gets infected and I end up losing it?"

He sighed. "I believe you will do everything you can to save him, and if I haven't told you, I admire your stubborn commitment to saving his life."

Lucifer must be livid right now, since the underworld had clearly frozen over. "Uh, thanks."

Ag gave me a faint smile and got to his feet at a knock on the door, opening it for Eldan.

The light fae healer nodded at him, but his gaze shot straight to me, sweeping over my body clinically, as if he could sense my injuries from several feet away.

"Danica," he murmured as he stepped inside. "I heard you were in the unseelie swamplands."

"Yeah."

"I need to see any open wounds you have so I can check for infection. Lots of nasties in that neck of the woods."

"You have no idea."

Now that the coast was clear of any potential talk of feelings, Vas stepped back into the room. I shot him a filthy look, and he grinned back at me, unrepentant. Eldan examined my arm. "Does that hurt?"

His hands were cool and efficient. I shook my head.

The door opened. Belphegor stood there, hands on his hips, expression pissy.

"Does someone want to tell me why, exactly, everyone is out here in wolf territory and not in our tower?"

My mouth twitched. Eldan did something that made pain shoot through my arm, and I winced as Vas filled Bel in.

Bel grinned at me, a dimple appearing in his cheek. "You blew up the Mage Council?"

"They started it," I shrugged.

"I like your style." The grin fell and he swallowed, his expression turning grave. "I want to see him."

Ag jerked his head toward the bedroom and Bel followed him in to see Samael.

Eldan released my arm. "Since you don't want to sleep yet, I used a light touch. You'll still be in pain. When you're ready to get some proper rest, let me know and I will complete the healing."

I raised my arm. It ached, a steady throb, but it was nowhere near as bad as it had been, and the wounds were closed, scabs already formed.

"This is great. Thank you."

At Eldan's insistence, I showed him the teeth marks in the skin at my ankle. He winced. "Do I want to know?"

I shivered at the memory of the attack. It was scarier not knowing exactly what that creature had looked like.

"Nope."

Bel returned. His eyes held the same sadness everyone's held when they saw Samael so close to death. But he reached into his canvas bag and pulled out a book, holding it out to me.

"Is that what I think it is?"

He nodded. "The eighth Black Book," he said tiredly. "And let me tell you, getting my hands on it wasn't exactly a walk through the park."

I'd tucked my hands against my chest, but I forced myself to reach out and take the book. The magic resonating from it was both dark and familiar, but the book itself was faded black leather with absolutely nothing remarkable about it.

Vas wandered out and winced at the book. "Smells worse than a black witch."

"I'm assuming the other grimoires are still in Samael's safe?" I asked him.

He nodded. "Best place for them. The mages aren't going to attempt to take the tower down again anytime soon. Not only are we not there, but apparently the fae are *pissed.*"

I smiled. Many of the buildings around Samael's tower were owned by both the seelie and unseelie. If the tower came down, so would those buildings, not to mention the economic disruption in the city.

I held out the book. "Can we put this one in the safe too?"

Ag leaned around Vas and took it from my hands. "No. After Gloria borrowed one of the black books without Samael's permission, he ordered her to return it and changed the code on the safe. He didn't have a chance to give me the code before…"

I swallowed around the lump in my throat. "Okay. For now, can you keep it safe?"

"Yes."

My phone vibrated, and I pulled it from the pocket of Samael's robe. I hadn't expected it to still be working after the adventure I'd had today.

Come see me, child. There are things you need to know.

Hannah. I sighed. I'd be an idiot not to go. She'd given me hints of my future before, even going as far as to insist I wear the bone bracelet around my wrist. If there was a chance she could help, I'd take it.

Vas leaned over my shoulder, his body tensing. He loathed black witches. Something told me he'd had a bad experience with one in the past. It wasn't like Vas to despise someone for no reason.

"You're not going alone," he declared.

I gave him a look that said he'd better rewind. He ignored me. "The last time you were lured somewhere by someone you trusted, you were almost sent straight to Lucifer. If Gloria taught us one thing, it's that no one can be trusted."

I sighed, but he had a point. "I'll text Kyla. She might be done for the day though."

"If she can't make it, I'll come." I raised my eyebrow. Vas really was worried. He pulled out his own phone, likely to text Kyla, and I turned my attention back to Eldan.

"Have someone call me when you're ready to have your healing completed," he said.

"Thank you."

He gave me his most reassuring smile and opened the door.

Kyla stood there, her hair damp and in fresh clothes.

"That was fast," I said.

She shrugged. "Let's go."

I glanced at Vas. He gestured that he'd stay put.

"Good luck," he mouthed.

I nodded. If Kyla wanted to ignore the whole nasty encounter with her brother in favor of burying her head in work, I could support that. I'd been known to do the same thing myself more than once.

The griffin insisted on coming. I didn't have it in me to argue. We piled into Kyla's car, keeping the windows rolled open to give the griffin a fraction more space.

"Anything I need to know about this witch?" Kyla asked.

"She feeds on negative emotions."

Kyla's expression turned sour. "In that case, she's about to attend an all-you-can-eat buffet."

I opened my mouth, and she glanced at me before

turning her attention back to the road. "I still don't want to talk about it."

"Fair enough."

Kyla raised her hand as we rounded a bend on our way out of wolf territory, and an answering howl sounded from a hidden sentry.

"All I'm saying is he has some fucking nerve showing up here," Kyla said.

I turned in my seat. Apparently, we were talking about it.

"And then to say I turned my back on *him*?"

I'd never heard Kyla sound so hurt. I opened my mouth, but she continued talking. "The worst part is, we used to be so close. He practically raised me after our parents died. He worked as a mechanic, and I'd watch him work while I did my homework. I met Joel when I was still a teenager. He worked with Ian, and they became best friends. Then, I guess, me and Joel hit it off."

I winced. "How old were you?"

She shot me an amused look. "Seventeen. He didn't touch me until I was nineteen—much to my dismay. I followed him around like a shadow. Eventually, we started dating. Within a few months, we'd moved in together. Ian loved it at first. He got to hang out with one of his best friends whenever he saw me."

"I'm guessing that didn't last."

"No. We had a good life, you know. A life I loved. I was social, I had hobbies and a large group of friends. Both of us had separate lives, but we still spent more than enough time together. Then Joel started drinking more. He… changed. Well, either that or I missed the warning signs.

"I was young, and I was lonely. Looking back now, I can see how sick our relationship was. When someone loves you, they don't try to alienate you from your friends and family. They don't make you financially dependent on them."

"I'm sorry."

She attempted a smile. "I was planning to leave him, you know. That weekend he went on his hunting trip. I think he must've had an inkling, because he told me if he returned and I wasn't there, he'd tell Ian I'd cheated on him."

My hands fisted. "What a piece of shit."

"Yeah. I didn't care what my brother thought by then. I'd been secretly working under the table—odd jobs—and I'd saved enough for a flight out of there. My flight was delayed, and I was at the airport when I got a call from one of Joel's friends' moms, asking if I'd heard anything. When I realized he was missing, I was relieved. I loved him, but I was relieved."

"We're not meant to live in fight-or-flight mode," I told her. "You can love someone and still know that they're bad for you."

She nodded. "Yeah, I know that now. I missed my flight and went back to the house. I didn't leave, because by that stage, his friends had been found dead. I mourned for him, and I started to plan my next move. If I'd just left on that flight… if I'd never gone back to the house…" Her voice trailed off and she swallowed a few times, as if she was having trouble getting the words out. "And then Joel showed up, and he'd been turned." She glanced at me.

"You know the rest. I attempted to pretend I didn't know he had turned. He played along for a while, and then he turned me. And I killed him."

"And then you met Nathaniel, and he ordered you to move to Durham."

It must've been tough. Especially being surrounded by a pack of dominant males. Although, from what I could see, Kyla more than held her own.

We'd made it to Trinity Park and Kyla glanced at me. "Which way?"

I directed her to Hannah's. By the time we parked, Kyla's face was blank. "I'll be okay," she said at whatever she saw on my face. "It's just… he was my only family. It's going to take me a while to accept that he wants nothing to do with me."

"You have a family, Kyla–" I started.

My door opened, and Kyla snarled.

"Calm down, wolf." Hannah narrowed her eyes at me. "Why are you wasting time out here? Didn't I tell you I had information for you?"

I sighed and got out of the car. The griffin waited patiently, his gaze on Hannah. By the time he was out of the car, huge and majestic on the sidewalk, Hannah's mouth had dropped open.

She gazed at the teeth, the wings, the patient, amused eyes.

"That can't be what I think it is."

I smiled, pleased to shock the witch. The griffin nudged my hand with his and I stroked him on his soft head.

"You can't take a griffin as a pet, halfling."

I frowned at her. "He's not a pet. He's my friend."

The griffin let out a sound like a purr and Kyla gave me a look that said she remembered exactly how pleased I'd been when the griffin followed us through the portal.

Hannah threw up her hands as if she was tired of my shit, and turned to stalk down the path and into her house. We caught up to her within a couple of steps.

Kyla glanced around, wide-eyed, as she took in Hannah's crowded home. The griffin somehow managed to delicately pick his way between the antique furniture. The witch had added to her collection since I'd been here last, all of it smelling of the oil she'd recently used to polish it. We followed her through the dining room and into the living room, where she gestured for us to sit on the sofa.

Her eyes rolled back in her head and she was silent for a long moment. Then she blinked. "You," she said, pointing to Kyla. "You will lose everything one day."

Kyla scowled at her. "You sure you're not looking at my past?"

Hannah gave her a slow smile. "No. When you are ready, you will come here and allow me to feed on your misery, and I will give you the advice you will need. Eventually, if you're not an idiot, you may find happiness in the place you least expected it."

Kyla's scowl deepened. "I don't need your advice."

Hannah opened her mouth, likely to scold her, but I shot her a look. The wolf had been through one hell of a day, and the interaction with her brother had been the cherry on her shit sundae.

Hannah merely shook her head, the hint of a smile dancing around her mouth. "He won't even see you coming," she murmured. "Oh, how I hope I live to see you turn his world upside down."

Kyla bared her teeth, and I winced. If it were up to her, Hannah wouldn't live to see her next sunrise. I cleared my throat.

"It's been a long day. What is it that you wanted to tell me, Hannah?"

She sat back in her chair, and her eyes went cloudy as she gazed at me.

"I had a vision. You will attempt to visit the merfolk."

"Yes. Can you tell me anything that will help?"

"The dagger on your hip will be useful. You will be tempted to leave it behind. A little saltwater will do it no harm, and you will need it for what you face in the dark depths."

I shuddered at the thought of those dark depths. But if Misty could help me stay alive, I'd take it. The griffin nudged my hand, a silent show of support.

Hannah smiled, inhaling my fear.

I ignored her. "I need you to look for someone for me. I'll pay you."

"You wish to know where Samael's black witch is."

I nodded. "Is she alive?"

"Yes. In order to find her location, I will need to search the veils."

She shuffled away, returning a moment later with several crimson candles. Kyla stiffened a second before Hannah lit them with a wave of her hand, and I nodded at her. Yup, that was blood she scented.

Hannah murmured an incantation and closed her eyes, beginning to slowly rock.

From the look on Kyla's face, she'd be comparing notes with Vas when she got back to her territory.

"The witch is beyond you, child. At least for now."

"She's in the underworld?"

Hannah nodded, her rocking picking up speed. "You may take some comfort in knowing she got far more than she bargained for out of her alliance with Lucifer. He is… displeased."

Good. I hoped she was suffering. "What else can you see?"

"Lucifer waits for you. You must keep close all you hold dear when you meet him."

"I'm not planning to meet him."

Hannah laughed. "Fate cares nothing for your plans, child. You may think that harnessing your power will save you, but you will quickly learn otherwise."

"Then what will save me?"

"The things that you keep hidden from all."

I groaned. "Like what?"

Hannah quit rocking and opened her eyes. "I can't tell you. I can only see so far, and you've exhausted me."

She gave me a look as if I'd personally tired her out, and I got to my feet.

Time to figure out how to get to the merfolk. Because I'd had so much luck with water so far.

CHAPTER FIFTEEN

Danica

I rolled over, frustration coursing through my veins. I couldn't feel Samael's presence. If I wanted to talk to him, I needed to fall asleep. But I was overtired, exhausted deep in my bones, and yet too stressed to be able to relax.

I switched on the lamp next to the bed and reached for a pair of jeans. Five minutes later, I strode past Vas, who was snoring softly from where he'd fallen asleep on the sofa.

I opened the door and gaped. On the porch, Kyla was curled up in wolf form, snuggled against the griffin. She looked almost petite next to the huge half-lion, half-eagle creature. Their fur was almost the same shade of white.

She opened her eyes. I closed my mouth.

"I can't sleep. I'm going to Mere's," I told her. "Can I take your car?"

She nodded and closed her eyes again.

I ducked out of sight as a demon flew overhead. Sitri.

The drive seemed shorter than it was, the roads empty, the solitude welcoming. The suburban houses I drove past were dark, blinds pulled, doors locked as families slept. For a moment, I longed to be tucked up in one of those beds, with a normal life, with no prophecy attached to me.

What would that be like? To grow up in this world and go to an ordinary job, day after day? I couldn't even imagine it.

Light spilled from Meredith's like a beacon, the sound of laughter and conversation reaching my ears as I parked Kyla's car. For a moment, I thought loneliness would eat me alive. I kept expecting to see Evie around every corner, her delicate brow creased in thought as she helped me plan my next move.

A cool breeze blew my hair back as I locked the car and walked toward the bar's entrance. A group of goblins were gathered outside, shooting the shit. They focused intently on me as I approached.

"She just blew up the Mage Council," one of them stage whispered, swaying unsteadily on his feet. "I heard Albert put a price on her head."

"That skinny runt? We could take her," his friend puffed up his chest, and I slowly turned my head.

The goblins went silent, and I opened the door, keeping my gaze on them. One by one, they looked away, and I stepped inside the bar.

Meredith's was slowly clearing out, even the regulars heading home at this time of the early morning. I slid onto my usual stool, and Mere worked her way down the bar until she was standing in front of me.

"You saved my bacon, by the way," I told her as she

poured me a drink.

"Hmm?"

"You and Riona. Driving to the Mage Council, calling Samael, and following the car."

I had vague memories of seeing her ashen face, not long after Samael had been struck by the spell. I'd screamed until my throat was raw, and one of the demons had knocked me out. I'd woken up after surgery.

"I'm just sorry it happened," Mere murmured. "It's difficult to wrap my head around Lucifer turning so many of the mages."

"Cara was the one who hurt the most," I admitted. "Out of all of them, she was the only one I considered a friend."

Mere leaned on the bar. "You've had a rough few months."

I choked out a laugh and raised my drink. "Tell me about it."

"Can I help in any way?"

"Actually… if Evie isn't back in time for me to complete the counter spell, I'll need another witch. Apparently, the spell requires a representative from each faction. Something tells me Gemma and the others won't jump at the opportunity to save Samael's life."

"Of course," Mere said. "Just tell me where and when."

She stepped away to serve a group of seelie women, and I brooded into my drink. When I finally raised my head to gesture for a refill, Mere had her gaze fixed behind me.

Vas had arrived.

The bar went quiet, and I knew what they saw. A large, pissed-off demon stalking toward the bar.

A gnome slid off the stool next to me and made himself scarce. Vas took the seat and gave me a steady look. "Leaving alone isn't smart. The Underking will do anything he can to take us down."

My throat was so tight I could barely get my words out. "Lucifer has already mortally wounded us. Now he's just waiting for us to bleed out."

"Hey," Mere said. "That's loser talk."

I choked out a laugh. It hurt my throat. I caught the look Vas sent her, his eyes full of gratitude. They both glanced away.

"We know what you're dealing with, you know," Vas said. "Me, Bael, Lilith, and everyone else. Even Ag. If the others can't look at you, it's because they're ashamed."

I squinted at him. "Ashamed of what?"

Mere slid me another drink. "Ashamed of giving up on him."

I stared at her, and she rolled her eyes. "I run the only bar for paranormals. I hear things. And everyone knows most of the demons went straight into mourning while you were figuring out what needed to be done."

"I'm making it up as I go along. It might not work."

Vas nudged me. "And if it doesn't, we'll all know that you did literally everything possible."

"I probably won't be around to deal with the repercussions," I said. I only wished that I'd had more time to spend with Evie.

Vas stiffened and I glanced at him. Something flickered in his eyes, and I went still.

"What?"

"Nothing."

Mere shook her head at him, and I narrowed my eyes at her. "Do you know?"

"Nope. But I can guess." She sighed. "I'd bet the demons have some kind of plan to make sure you make it even if Samael dies." She raised her eyebrow at Vas, who stole my vodka soda and took a hefty slug.

"You may as well spill it," I told him.

"Samael managed to reach out to my uncle. If it looks like he's getting too close to dying and taking you with him… Ag is supposed to find a way to break the bond."

"There is no way to break the bond."

Vas shook his head. "Not usually. But while your bond with Samael is in place, it's fragile, held together by sheer will. Samael thinks it can be broken, and he has no intention of taking you with him if he dies."

Samael had kept that quiet. Oh, he'd talked about how he'd wait for me, but he hadn't mentioned he'd actively reached out to Ag.

I couldn't blame him. I would have done the same thing.

"Thanks for the pep talk, you guys."

I got to my feet. I needed to talk to Samael, and I'd drug myself to sleep if I had to.

Vas slid off his stool and looked at Meredith. "I need to talk to you."

Mere drew back, and I eyed her. She moved faster than I'd expected, in a way that told me she had some level of combat training. She sent me a pleading look, and I lifted my phone.

"Sorry, I've got to take this."

"No one's calling you at 3am, Danica!" Mere's voice carried over the bar as I scampered toward the door.

Would you look at that? I suddenly wasn't feeling as depressed as I had been when I walked in here.

I leaned against the brick wall and waited for Vas. I'd expected him to be in one of his dark moods, as he usually was whenever the subject of the sloe-eyed witch came up, but this time he looked more than a little satisfied.

"What happened?"

He held out his arms, and I was too curious to whine when he carried me like a child. One of the demons could grab Kyla's car in the morning.

Vas's expression was thoughtful as he shot into the sky.

"I told her how it's gonna be."

I blinked at that. Meredith had managed to keep the peace in that bar for years, through sheer willpower and stubbornness. She had a steel core.

"Ah, you did, did you? And how is it going to be?"

He smiled, his gaze on the stars.

"I'm not standing for her avoiding me anymore."

I winced. "And Mere took that well, did she?"

He rubbed his jaw. "She punched me."

I gaped at him, and he smiled. "She's got a mean right hook. And I never saw it coming."

"That's all you have to say?"

"It's the first time she's voluntarily touched me." His smile widened. "I'm wearing her down."

"There are so many things wrong with that, I don't know where to begin."

He ignored me, his dreamy gaze shifting to the forest below us.

Not my business. I had more than enough of my own problems. And if I was secretly looking forward to the fireworks…

Well, who could blame me?

His gaze sharpened as something crossed his mind. But he kept his gaze on the forest.

"If you ever go up against Lucifer…"

A shiver swept through my body, my mouth went dry. As Vas shifted into the wind, I let him think it was the cool air that made my shoulders hunch.

"Yeah?"

"Leave the assassin for me."

"Vas–"

"He killed my parents, Danica. He left me lying in their blood. I owe him."

Something wrenched in my chest at the desolation in his voice. Vas never talked about his family, about what it had been like to grow up here, knowing his parents were killed before Ag managed to get him out of the underworld.

I took a deep breath. "If I ever go up against Lucifer, the chances of me living through it are minimal."

He shook his head, and his eyes finally met mine.

"Swear it."

"I swear."

Danica

To say that Samael wasn't pleased when I finally fell asleep was an understatement.

"You're growing weaker," Samael said. "I can see it, even here."

"I'm just tired, that's all."

"If you get too tired to function–"

"I don't want to talk about this."

He showed me his teeth. "We will talk about this."

"I'm doing everything I fucking can."

I'd been looking forward to falling asleep, wanted nothing more than for Samael to wrap his arms around me, to reassure me that it was going to be okay.

Instead, he was looking at me like I was a limb he was considering cutting off.

"You *promised*," he snarled.

I reached up and cupped his cheek. His eyes slid closed before opening to slits.

I couldn't help but smile. Both of us were so goddamned stubborn. "I know you've been putting plans in place to break the bond. I know you talked to Ag."

He stiffened. "You won't convince me otherwise," he warned.

Warmth unfurled in my chest. Even now, while he was literally falling to pieces, his only thought was of protecting me. What had I done to deserve this man? And why hadn't I recognized who he'd be to me sooner?

"I don't need to convince you of anything," I told him. "Yes, I'm tired, but that's because I've had so many adventures over the past few days."

"Don't lie to me."

I sighed. I'd felt it, of course, the decreased stamina, the bone-deep exhaustion. But I could still function. Could still save his life.

"I need you to trust me."

He snorted, although his eyes softened minutely. "You can't be trusted not to put your life on the line when it comes to those you love. It's up to me to protect you from yourself."

I eyed him. "That's not the right approach to take if you want to get laid."

He smiled, but there was no humor in his eyes. "Come here."

He led me to his bed. Of course, it wasn't really his bed, but it was exactly where I wanted to be. I'd thought we'd be stripping each other out of our clothes by now, but Samael merely lay down next to me and pulled me into his arms, stroking my hair.

My eyelids grew heavy. He moved his other hand to the back of my neck, where I stored so much tension. Skilled fingers massaged away the knots until I almost purred. I inhaled his scent and listened to the beat of his heart.

"Love you," I mumbled.

He brushed his lips over mine. "I will love you until death and beyond, little witch."

CHAPTER SIXTEEN

Danica

Kyla and I left early again the next morning. My eyelids were heavy, but if I had any chance of making the next part of my plan work, I needed to talk to Mariam.

Thankfully, she was in her office downtown, so we didn't need to drive to Hope Valley. I parked on the street and considered my approach as we walked toward the fae representative's building and took the elevator up to her floor.

I'd already played my hand with her, and I didn't have any other favors to hand over. But negotiation was overrated.

More of Samael's body had crumbled away when I woke up this morning. Mariam would help me, or she would regret it.

Kyla gave a low whistle as we stepped inside, her gaze tracking from the white silk wallpaper, accented in gold, to the thick creamy carpet beneath our feet.

"Is she expecting you?" Mariam's receptionist,

Adelina, asked as we approached the long marble counter that served as her desk. Her disturbingly long eyelashes fluttered. Next to me, Kyla went still, her gaze fixated on them as if she'd quite like to trap them beneath her paws.

"She's not expecting us," I said. "But it's important."

Adelina sighed, well used to dealing with me.

"Her current meeting ends in ten minutes. Take a seat and I'll see if she can fit you in."

There were no pixies here this morning, which made the office seem more formal. We sat in the padded white armchairs and waited quietly. I attempted to tear my mind free of the need to fixate on Samael.

Ten minutes later, a light fae guy stepped out of Mariam's office, nodded at us, and walked out. Mariam appeared, her expression resigned as she gestured for us to follow her into her office.

"I don't have long," she began.

"We won't take up much of your time. I need to know where to find the selkies."

It wasn't often that I managed to surprise the seelie woman in front of me, but that question managed to do it. She frowned at me.

"I'm not sure why—"

"It's personal. One of them was my friend."

She nodded. "Mella. Yes, it was unfortunate what happened to her, and her case is currently in litigation with the Mage Council."

I tensed. Next to me, Kyla let out a disbelieving growl. "Want to run that past us again?"

Mariam slid her a cool look. "The selkie was being punished according to the Mage Council, and yet she did unspeakable amounts of damage to their library, practically obliterating it." She glanced at me. "Obviously, that is now a moot point, since you brought the entire building down. Either way, Albert demands punishment."

I went very still. Next to me, Kyla was barely breathing. Mariam threw up a ward, her eyes wide as she stared at us.

"Have you ever worn Naud chains, Mariam?" I asked softly.

She swallowed. "No."

"I have. I wore them for several hours that night. And it was one of the worst experiences of my life. Not only did I not have access to my powers, but they drained me of energy. I could feel them, slowly eating away at my body's will to live."

I had to take a deep breath, forcing my mind away from where it wanted to linger. "Your people allowed the Mage Council to abuse Mella for over thirty years," I said softly. "She was locked up, away from her people, without her skin, and viciously targeted by every bully in that facility."

"The political situation with the Mage Council–"

I held up my hand. Mariam's face drained of color at whatever she saw in my eyes. "I'm low on time, so let me be clear. If the seelie don't protect Mella, if you hand her back over to the Mage Council, my people will step in."

Mariam's lips were bloodless as she stared at me. "I'm not sure I know what you mean."

I smiled. "Yes, you do."

Silence. But I was happy to spell it out for her. "I'm the current ruler of the demons in this territory. If Samael dies, I will remain in charge." It was unlikely that she knew my life was tied to Samael's. The demons were keeping that very quiet. "Mella owes me a blood debt from that night."

She opened her mouth and I held up a hand. "Consider how you'll choose to act in this case. Because if Mella is harmed or killed before she repays her debt, I *will* consider it an act of war. Think very carefully about whether your political dealings with the Mage Council are worth the repercussions from every demon in our territory."

Mariam was silent for a long moment. Next to me, Kyla watched her intently, her claws extended.

"I will think on what you have said," Mariam said finally.

"Good. Now where can I find Mella?"

Mariam frowned and I shook my head at her. "You don't want to prevent me from calling in my debts," I purred.

She narrowed her eyes at me and finally pulled a notepad and pen toward her, scribbling something on a piece of paper, which she ripped off and handed to me. Then she opened a drawer and handed me a small cloth bag. "You'll need these as well. One would wonder why you would be pursuing such a debt while Samael barely clings to life."

I shrugged and took the bag. "One may wonder whatever one likes."

We stalked out of her office. Next to me, Kyla's shoulders shook as we passed the receptionist, who gaped as Mariam slammed her office door shut.

"That was incredible," Kyla said as we stepped

outside. "I kind of want to applaud."

"I guess hanging around all these arrogant paranormal rulers is rubbing off on me."

She waited until we got back into my car before she asked. "Does Mella really owe you a debt?"

"Yeah." I started the car and pulled out. "I got her pelt to her that night. That's why she was able to break the Naud chains. The girl had thirty years of power stored, and she *exploded*. I thought I was going to die. I was lying there, wondering how the hell I would relocate my knee when she strolled over and told me her people owed me a debt."

I shivered at the memory of Mella's teeth, and the shredded meat of Bruce's heart that had been stuck between them.

"Why didn't she help you get out of there?"

"Her mind had… cracked," I said. "I guess she'd been trapped in her human form for too long, and by the time she got her powers back, she was… different. There was nothing remotely similar to the Mella I knew."

"You think she went crazy?"

I shrugged. "Either way, her people owe me." I glanced down at the piece of paper in my hand. "I never would've thought I'd take her up on the debt, but now I need to collect."

"Where are we going?"

I sighed. "The Outer Banks. We're going to the Outer Banks."

Danica

We went back to the cabin to make sure we had everything we needed. The griffin wasn't pleased that we were both leaving. He'd growled and attempted to climb into Kyla's car. He'd also ignored Nathaniel's Alpha stare until, finally, I explained that I needed him to help guard Samael.

He'd glanced toward the cabin where my demon lay and heaved a sigh. But he stayed.

Vas nodded at me as we climbed back into the car. Between the demons and the wolves guarding Samael with their lives, nothing would get to him.

I glanced at Kyla. We'd decided to take turns driving, and she was currently relaxed in the passenger's seat, her brow furrowed in thought.

"If anything happens to me, I need you to convince the demons to protect Mella from the mages."

She slowly turned her head. "And just how do you suppose I'll do that?"

"Let them know all about my conversation with Mariam, making sure to mention how it would be a sign of weakness if demons fail to do exactly what I said."

She smiled at that. "Done."

According to the information Mariam had given us, we had the best chance of finding Mella if we headed to Cape Hatteras. I guess it was a good thing Mariam had been keeping track of Mella, even if it was because she'd planned to hand her over to the mages for punishment.

It was a four-and-a-half-hour drive to Cape Hatteras. By the time we'd ruined Mariam's day, and then stopped by the cabin, it was already 10am.

I could feel time ticking away as we drove. I'd considered asking the demons to fly us, but it would likely take the same amount of time. At least if we were driving, we weren't hurtling through the air.

"It's going to be okay." Kyla had returned her attention to the window, and I let out a breath, rolled my shoulders, and attempted to unclench my hands from where I was white-knuckling the steering wheel.

"It's difficult not to second guess my every decision when everything is riding on those decisions."

"You can only do what you can do. Mella will help you if she can."

"I hope so."

Thankfully, Kyla had an iron bladder, so we only stopped once. By the time we were driving through the Outer Banks, I was crossing both my fingers and toes that Mella would be there.

We made it to the cape and parked, walking across the parking lot and onto the beach. To the right, a herd of wild horses were frolicking, and Kyla tensed in a way that told me she'd like to put the fear of God into them.

"What is it with you and horses?"

She opened her mouth and I shook my head. "Never mind." I pulled one of the small white stones out of the drawstring bag. "Can you hold this?"

She held out her hand, and I used a throwing knife to slice open my forearm. This arm was turning into a mess of silver scars, but I shrugged that thought off, wincing as I allowed a few drops of blood to drip onto the stone and then took it back from her.

Then I pictured Mella's face in my head and threw the stone into the air.

It exploded like a firework, greens and blues shooting across the cloudless sky. The horses took off, and I stared at the beach and waited.

Nothing.

I took a deep breath and grabbed another stone.

Still nothing.

We had one left.

"Come on Mella. Do me a solid here."

I threw the final stone into the air, watching as the sparks drifted across the sky, raining down into the ocean. Then I sat on the sand and stared blankly at the water.

We waited for half an hour. My eyes burned, and Kyla glanced at me, opened her mouth, and then snapped it closed.

Another half hour passed.

I'd failed.

I buried my head in my knees. I couldn't bring myself to get up and leave. I ran through every scenario in my brain, attempting to figure out how to get to the merfolk without Mella's help, but I was coming up empty.

"We'll figure something out," Kyla reached out and gave my hand a squeeze. "This isn't the end, Danica. I swear, we'll—holy shit."

I lifted my head and gaped. Seals were beaching themselves, moving toward me. The lead seal seemed to waver, and then I was staring at what had to be the leader of this group of selkies.

She was beautiful. I'd only seen the nightmare that was Mella as she burned down her prison, but this selkie had long, pale blue hair, and eyes the color of topaz.

"You have called to us, Danica Amana, and we have come. My name is Acacia. It appears we owe you a debt for saving our sister."

A tiny spark of hope burned in my chest. "May I ask you a question before I call in that debt?"

She inclined her head regally. "You may."

"Are the legends true about your pelts—may someone who can't breathe beneath the water use it to temporarily grant them this power?"

The selkie stared at me silently for a long moment. "Yes," she said finally. "This is true."

"I would like to know if this would be an acceptable use of my blood debt."

"You wish to borrow one of our pelts?"

"Yes."

Curiosity lit her eyes at that. "I will need to speak to my queen. This has never been asked before. To allow a human that level of trust…"

"I promise I'll return it."

The selkie laughed. "Mortals have promised the same since the dawn of time."

Fair enough.

"I'll do it," a voice said. We all turned. Mella leaned against a rock, her gaze on my face. I smiled at her.

"You look better than the last time I saw you."

Sharp teeth gleamed as she grinned back at me. "It would be impossible to look any worse."

"Albert is still alive."

The grin fell from her face. "I know. But he won't be forever. The word is spreading amongst our people, along with others who owe us favors. That bastard goes near any shoreline in the country, and he's dead." Curiosity shone in her eyes. "Why do you need a pelt?"

I glanced around, checking there was no one listening. Kyla nodded at me. She wasn't picking up any new scents.

"What I tell you needs to stay between us," I said, and both selkies nodded.

Once I'd filled them in, they glanced at each other. "This will be highly dangerous."

"Yeah. Story of my life. But will it work?"

"Yes," the selkie said. "But your blood debt only extends so far. You may borrow one pelt only."

Kyla looked displeased, but I nodded. We'd expected that.

"And," the selkie said, "if you don't return to us with the pelt, there will be no realm you can flee to where you can escape us."

"I'd expect nothing less. When will you know if your queen approves?"

She tapped her head, indicating that she could speak to her queen psychically. "Momentarily. She is considering your request now."

A group of humans were gathered in the parking lot, staring at the two naked selkies, surrounded by their family in seal form. They gaped, and one of them lifted his phone, obviously recording this little interaction.

Mella glanced at him, and the phone disappeared from his hand. His curses carried across the beach, but the entire group turned and made tracks.

"Our queen says we may help you," she announced,

and my hands shook as relief swept through me. Mella smiled at me.

"I'm glad my debt will be used for something so important."

"If I wasn't desperate, I wouldn't have called in the debt," I told her. "I don't truly believe you owe me anything."

"Then she would have been shamed to not help the one who set her free," the selkie leader said. "You have kept her from having to bear that shame."

"Okay. How does this work?"

Mella smiled. "Well, since I'll be stuck in human form, I'll hang out with your wolf."

Kyla grinned at her. "I'm Kyla. I've heard a lot about you."

"Mella. And I'm sure you have." She shot me a rueful grin and I laughed, feeling lighter than I had since I left Durham.

We checked into the closest hotel. Kyla and Mella ordered room service, with the wolf ordering enough that the kitchen must have assumed we had a football team up here. She hadn't had a chance to grab breakfast that morning.

Mella, now bundled in the hotel's robe, reclined on the bed and flicked on the TV, laughing at my expression.

"I didn't get to do this kind of thing either when I was chained up in that library. I'll be fine, Danica."

Kyla sent me a look. "I don't like you going alone."

"I'm not exactly thrilled about it, but it has to happen."

"They could kill you before you get near their

kingdom."

Mella shook her head. "The merfolk aren't exactly used to humans finding a way to take the trip down to them. Their kingdom is magically protected from ships, submarines and the like, and a scuba diver wouldn't be able to get deep enough.

"But I can?"

She nodded. "My pelt will protect you. Whatever you do, don't remove it."

I had a vision of myself drowning, hundreds of feet below the surface, the pelt floating away, just out of reach.

I took a deep breath and slowly let it out. Then I did it again.

"Not a fan of the water?" Mella asked.

"I can swim, but it's not exactly something I did a lot of, growing up."

"I wish I could go with you. But even if one of my friends followed you, they would be turned away as soon as they got near the merfolk's territory."

"I understand. I'll be fine." I focused on the steps I'd need to take, since thinking about being beneath the surface of the ocean wasn't exactly helpful. "How will I know which way to go?"

"My pelt will guide you. All you'll have to do is relax."

CHAPTER SEVENTEEN

Danica

I'd never been scuba diving. I'd never even been snorkeling, and my lack of experience in the water was biting me in the ass right now. My teeth chattered—from the fear more than the cold—and Kyla shot me a sympathetic look.

"You've got this," she said. "I wish I could come too, but you heard what Mella said. All you have to do is trust the pelt to guide you. The hard part will be convincing their sentries to let you talk to the queen."

I scowled at her. "Thanks for that." But her crappy pep talk had at least helped me focus on what I'd say to the merfolk to convince them to allow me entry.

"If I don't come back…"

"Try to save Samael, kill Lucifer, find Evie, yadda yadda."

I grinned. I'd asked Mella if I'd need flippers and a wetsuit, but she'd merely smiled and told me her pelt would help propel me through the water, and it would also keep me warmer than a wetsuit.

May as well get this over with. The pelt was soft and silky, almost like being covered with a warm liquid as I wrapped it around my shoulders. I chewed on my lip as I realized I was going to have to hold it in place with both hands, making it difficult to defend myself. But I couldn't risk it falling off my shoulders.

"Here," Kyla held out her hand. She'd taken the claw-shaped clip out of her hair and when I stared at it, she took both ends of the pelt from where I'd wrapped it over my shoulders and around my neck. A simple twist and she'd tied them in two, fastening it with the claw clip. I'd still need to hold it in place with one hand, but I could keep my Nim Cub in the other hand.

That reminded me.

I took the pelt off, removed the lanyard holding the jeweled knife sheath Samael had given me, and then lifted the string wrapped around the rowan arrow over my head.

It was invisible to demons, and since the suppression spell had finally crumpled from my power, I could no longer see it at all. I held it out to Kyla.

"Can you see this?"

"Of course."

"Keep it safe."

I plopped it in her hand, feeling suddenly naked without the rowan arrow and my lanyard. But there was a pretty good chance all the salt water would damage them.

I slipped the pelt back on, finally ready. No more time to waste.

With a final nod at Kyla, I turned and padded across the sand until the waves tickled my feet. I'd swapped my jeans for black leggings, tucking my t-shirt in so it wouldn't float up and distract me.

I glanced over my shoulder. Kyla waved at me. By now, I was chest deep. I was going to have to get this over with.

I took a deep breath and dunked my head.

No dummy, you don't need to hold your breath.

I lifted my head once more and gasped for air. Shivers wracked my body. It wasn't particularly cold, with the pelt wrapped around my shoulders and neck. No, this was terror.

I lowered my face into the water.

Take one breath. Just one breath.

I lifted my face out of the water again, inhaling sweet, sweet oxygen.

I couldn't convince my body that it could breathe beneath the water. My every atom was telling me that I was an idiot and if I attempted such a stupid thing, I would drown.

My eyes burned. After all of the steps I'd taken to get here, I'd never imagined it would be my fear that would be the biggest issue.

I swam out a little more, until only my tiptoes were touching the ground. The water came up to my chin now.

Samael's face flashed in front of my eyes. The feel of his arms around me. The smell of his cedar and citrus scent. The ash surrounding his body as he slowly crumpled into nothing.

Fuck this.

I lowered my head into the water. Before I could talk myself out of it, I took a deep breath.

Logically, I'd known it would work. But even though air flowed into my lungs, I still gasped and raised my head above the water.

No time for that. Now that I knew I wouldn't drown, I dove deep, making myself inhale. The pelt seemed to hum, and I could feel which way it wanted me to go.

I let it take me, forcing myself to take deep even breaths, instead of the shallow pants my adrenaline-flooded body wanted to take.

I'd wondered if I would need weights to help me swim down into the depths of the ocean, but the pelt seemed to take care of that, almost propelling me through the water.

Below me, a city of coral unraveled, and I floated within a few feet of the bright colors. A fish darted out, striped in orange and black, and I backpedaled, my movements ungainly in the water. The lionfish ignored me, and I was enveloped in a school of tiny silver fish as they swam past, going about their business.

I suddenly understood why people did this. It was an almost meditative experience, and I'd forgotten to focus on my breath as I stared, entranced, as a lobster scuttled out from where it had been hiding beneath the coral.

I couldn't wait to tell Samael about this.

The thought was enough to get me moving again.

The pelt was a presence in my mind, urging me deeper. I ignored the little I knew about how deep the human body could go and how long it could stay underwater, forcing myself to trust the selkies.

It was darker now. I didn't know how deep I was, but I craned my head, spotting the glimmer of light on the surface of the water far above me. My hand tightened around the pelt. If something happened now, I'd never make it to the surface before running out of air.

Focus.

Steel wrapped around my foot. I kicked out automatically, flipping onto my back and swinging my Nim Cub. My attacker simply bared his straight white teeth in a nasty smile. I'd found a merman. He watched me some more. Then he reached for my pelt.

I lashed out with my blade. He jerked his hand back and surveyed me. But he didn't attempt to take the pelt from me again.

His hand was still around my ankle, and he turned. With a flick of his tail, he was dragging me through the water. All I could do was hold on to the pelt and grind my teeth as he hauled me behind him.

I studied the merman as he swam. His back was all hard muscle, wide shoulders, beefy arms. And that tail, which powered us through the water, gave me no opportunity to strike out.

I had a feeling he was enjoying pulling me behind him like a ragdoll. He was swimming fast enough that the pelt streamed behind me like a cape, my hold on it the only thing keeping it from coming loose. I had no doubt that if it did, the merman wouldn't stop to prevent me from drowning.

If I could remove his hand from around my ankle, I could bury my Nim Cub in his side. I had a kidney shot in this position, but all I could do was hold on to the pelt and wait for him to stop moving.

I was so intent on studying him for weaknesses that

I almost missed it.

A figure appeared in my peripheral vision, and I swiped out at him, but it wasn't me he was after.

He slammed into the merman, who was forced to release my ankle. I kicked out, driving myself backwards in an effort to give the fighting mermen some room.

Strong arms clamped around me, keeping me in place. I slammed my head back and the arms loosened slightly, but whoever had grabbed me managed to hold on. My knife hand was trapped down by my side, but at least I'd retained hold on the pelt.

For now, whoever had grabbed me was merely keeping me in place. The merman who'd been dragging me through the water was now surrounded by more of his kind, all of them wearing identical, pissed-off expressions.

They were having some kind of argument. Not only were their mouths moving in an unfamiliar pattern, which told me they weren't speaking English, but I couldn't hear anything they were saying.

The merman who'd taken me glanced my way and then back to the others, throwing up his hands and saying something that didn't exactly appear to be complimentary. I gaped as a merman with long red hair hauled back and smashed his fist into the first merman's face.

I knew a broken nose when I saw it, and it appeared the merfolk bled blue. Interesting.

The other merman turned their backs on him as he cupped his nose, and, finally, he got the hint and swam away.

All attention was now on me.

The arms holding me let go, and I attempted to swim

free, but he'd only released me in order to grab the pelt.

I shook my head, silently begging the mermen in front of me, but they merely folded their arms and watched clinically as I fought to hold on to the only thing keeping me from drowning.

Cold sons of bitches. My arm was finally free, so I lashed out. From the way the hands stopped yanking on the pelt, I'd made contact, but it wasn't enough.

I had enough time to take one deep breath as the pelt was ripped from my shoulders, and then I was swimming desperately for the surface as the merfolk watched.

My lungs burned. There was no fucking way I was getting all the way up to the surface.

I was dead.

Samael

Panic woke me.

I'd gone from being unable to sleep here, to spending most of my time resting in an effort to conserve my strength.

I reached along the bond as sheer, unadulterated terror swept through me. There was no logic to temper it.

The fear gave way to grief. And I knew what that meant.

No. No. No.

She wasn't dying. Danica couldn't die. I wouldn't accept it.

She didn't get to die attempting to save my life.

My lungs burned and realization punched into me. Suffocating. Or drowning. A bad way to go.

"I'm here, little witch."

She was unconsciously reaching for me, so it was a simple matter to solidify the connection.

"I'm sorry, Samael. I tried."

I ignored that. *"You will live."*

I could feel her light, dimming faster than I could have imagined. This was my fault. If she had never met me, Danica would still be hunting her mother's killer. Would still be a bounty hunter working for the Mage Council. Wouldn't be dying, far enough from where my useless crumbling body lay that I could barely feel her.

I poured my energy into her. If I could even give her a few more moments of life, I would do it.

She reached for me down the bond. All I could do was give her as much comfort as I could.

"Fight for me, Danica. I love you."

She couldn't even respond. I'd burrowed deep enough into our bond to sense her brain begin to die, starved of oxygen. Lights flashed in front of my eyes, followed by a strange feeling of peace. Danica's body attempting to soften the blow of death.

The roar that broke from me was so loud it seemed to shake the strange between-world I was trapped in.

I refused to accept this. Refused to so much as entertain it. I closed my eyes and poured every ounce of my will and strength down the bond.

CHAPTER EIGHTEEN

Danica

It was so quiet. Quiet and still in a way that should have been peaceful.

There had been so little peace in my life up to this point that I didn't trust it for a second.

I was in a garden. But there were no sounds of birds chirping, no buzzing of insects, no scent.

So I was in a fake garden. I scowled, surveying the lush greenery, the bright flowers. A fountain bubbled noiselessly behind me, and I narrowed my eyes, turning as a path opened up before me.

Where was I? How had I ended up here? Something stronger than grief, more poignant than regret, swept through me. It was the feeling that I'd forgotten something, something I never should have forgotten. Something crucial.

With nothing else to do, I walked along the path. My hand tightened around my knife, and water dripped from my clothes. I touched my t-shirt and then licked my finger. Saltwater.

There wasn't room for fear here. A strange

sort of calm enveloped me, but I trusted it about as much as a stranger in a dark alley, so I pushed it away.

And there was my mother.

The air disappeared from my lungs in a whoosh. For a split second, I could feel intense pressure on my chest, and then it was gone.

"Mom?"

She turned, and my heart broke a little. Memories began to trickle back, slowly at first, and then faster, until it hit me.

She was dead.

Mom smiled at me, and my eyes burned, my vision turning blurry as she stepped toward me. I'd forgotten how beautiful she was. Here, the dark circles that had been constantly beneath her eyes were gone. The frown lines that had etched their way into her forehead had disappeared. Every sign of the difficult life she'd lived, of the stress she'd dealt with every day... none of it remained.

"My darling."

I choked out a sob, and then I was running, throwing myself into her arms.

"I missed you. I missed you so much."

"I know. I can feel it, every time you think of me." She pulled back slightly. "I'm so proud of you."

My shoulders hunched. "Are you sure?"

She gave me a look and a laugh bubbled out of me.

Her lip trembled slightly. "I love you, Danica. But you have to go back."

I frowned. "What do you mean?"

Her hands tightened around my upper arms, her eyes

intent. "It's not your time."

The memories had paused while I talked to her, and now they punched into me, one after the other.

"He's waiting for you," Mom whispered. "He loves you so very much."

"He's a demon."

She grinned at me, and I frowned. "You told me to stay away from the demons."

"One benefit of crossing over is the ability to see the bigger picture. You had to meet him, and you must stay alive for what comes next. This isn't your time."

I was being torn in two. Samael waited, and if I died, he died too. But seeing my mom, being wrapped in her arms…

"I'll always be here," she told me firmly.

"I can't do this," I said. "I'm not strong enough."

She shook her head. "You're stronger than you could ever imagine. Tell Evie I love her."

"Wait. Who murdered you?"

She shook her head. "You know I can't tell you that." The smile left her face, and her chin jutted out in an expression so much like Evie's that my heart howled. "You'll find what you need in the attic."

I frowned. "The coven burned down. There's no attic left."

Mom opened her mouth. A hint of frustration flickered in her eyes. Then she reached out and punched me in the chest.

I gaped at her, and she did it again. "Goodbye, Danica."

"Wait. Mom."

"I love you." She punched me again.

I jolted back, attempting to get out of her range.

"Ow, what the fuck."

An amused laugh. "I believe she is alive," a male voice said.

I opened my eyes. Everything hurt. Mom was gone. And I was lying flat on my back, staring up at a merman. A merman who'd calmly watched as I drowned.

It all came flooding back. I hauled back and swung at him. He jerked his head to the side and my fist merely grazed his cheek. I was as weak as a kitten.

My chest felt like Scylla had been sitting on it.

I could feel Samael, closer than I'd felt him in days. As if he was staring out of my eyes. And yet he didn't speak. I had a sinking feeling that he'd poured his energy into me, and now he *couldn't* speak.

"You better not have done something that stupid," I thought at him.

The silence was deafening. Anxiety took up a steady residence in my gut.

"Sit her up," an amused feminine voice said, and someone stepped up behind me, pushing me until I was staring at the most beautiful woman I'd ever seen.

Long, lavender hair curled wildly around her face and over one shoulder, reaching down to her waist. Her eyes were almost the same color, glowing like amethyst stones in the sun. Her skin was the gold of sunrise, and she wore a long, gauzy gown, decorated in seashells.

She sat on a throne made of coral. She wore no crown. She didn't need one.

Her lush lips curved at my silence. "Greetings,

Underqueen."

"I'm not the Underqueen," I said automatically. She merely leaned back on her throne and regarded me out of shrewd eyes.

I scrutinized my surroundings. I sat a few feet from the throne. I could feel more of the queen's people at my back. I turned my head, memorizing their faces. They'd allowed me to keep my weapons, and I was back on solid ground. Sure, I was heavily outnumbered, but things were looking up.

The queen was silent, giving me a moment to come to terms with my new situation. I scanned the room, my gaze lingering on the walls despite myself. They were tiled from floor to ceiling, in various shades of glimmering blue and green. They'd been designed to look like fish scales, each bordered by gold.

We were in some kind of palace.

But how was I breathing? And why did the merman who'd watched me drown suddenly have two legs? And where the fuck was the pelt?

"My apologies for the way you were brought to me," the queen of the merfolk broke the silence. "Those who caused you such pain will be punished."

I raised one eyebrow. "I died, didn't I?"

"You stopped breathing. Your heart temporarily ceased beating."

I gave the queen a look, informing her that yes, I considered that to be dying.

Her mouth curved. "But we brought you back."

"I was told I wouldn't come to harm if I visited this place."

Not strictly true, but I watched her reaction. Her jaw tightened just a touch as she glanced behind me. "Yes, well, one of my guards was bringing you to me when some of the others believed you were a threat."

"Uh-huh. Where's my pelt?"

She gave me a level stare. "We both know that is not *your* pelt."

"I have permission to borrow it."

"Which selkie would allow such a thing?"

"A selkie who owed me a favor." I was tired of sitting on the floor while the mermen surrounded me, and I slowly stood up. My body ached. Dying sure took a lot out of a girl.

I took a deep breath and explained my bargain with Mella and why I was here. Snorts sounded behind me. "You believe we will give you the golden sword?" one of the mermen almost choked on the words. I ignored him.

The queen held up one hand and everyone went silent. Cool trick. If I tried it on the demons, they'd probably crack their ribs laughing at me.

"You were prophesied to come to me, Underqueen."

I didn't bother correcting her. If she chose to believe I was the Underqueen, who was I to argue? I'd probably have a better chance at bargaining with her as Danica, Queen of the Underworld, than I would as Danica, ex bounty-hunter and cat owner.

"Oh yeah? And what did that prophecy have to say?"

I *loathed* prophecies. All they'd ever done was complicate my life.

The queen tilted her head. "It says you will bring me the Mistilteinn Dagger."

I froze, my hand automatically slid protectively over Misty. Behind me, the mermen went on high alert. The queen's gaze landed over my shoulder, and she made a gesture that made the merman protest in low voices.

She ignored it all and made the same gesture again. All of the mermen filed out of the room.

"Why do you need the Dagger of Truth?"

She sighed. "I have ruled the merfolk for nine hundred years," she said. "Before me, my mother ruled. And her mother before her."

A maternal line of succession. I was here for it. Fuck the patriarchy and all that. But from the grief-stricken look on her face, things weren't exactly hunky dory right now.

"What's the problem?"

"I have three advisors who have been part of my family since I was a small child. They advised my mother, and when she died, they continued to advise me. However, over the past few decades, it has become clear that one of them is betraying me."

I'd never get used to the way paranormals spoke about decades and centuries, the way I'd refer to weeks and months. "And you think the Dagger of Truth will help you find out who the traitor is? Have you considered torture, 'cause Samael usually finds that works for him."

A hint of amusement flickered through her eyes.

"Torture would break one of our greatest laws."

I refrained from rolling my eyes. These people had watched me die, but apparently torture was a hard no.

"So, what, you want to borrow Misty?"

"Misty?"

I felt my cheeks heat. "I gave it a nickname."

She shook her head. "The Mistilteinn Dagger can't be borrowed." Her gaze studied my face. "Tell me, what exactly do you know about the dagger you stole from Samael's hoard?"

It weirded me out that these people knew so much about my life, and, until recently, I hadn't even known they'd existed.

"Um, I know it glows when you're questioning someone and that someone decides to tell a lie." I refused to tell her all of the other things Misty had done. Like, say, replicating a look-away spell that time I'd been stuck in Samael's bedroom.

"That is a good idea," Misty said in my head.

"I thought you were asleep."

If the dagger could radiate disdain, that's exactly what it did. *"Each time I spoke, your eye would twitch and you would consider locking me in a safe. I preferred to watch and listen."*

The Dagger of Truth had been spying on me for close to a year. Awesome.

The queen shook her head at me. "The dagger chooses its owners. If it decides you are worthy, it will work for you for as long as you hold it. If, however, the dagger does not choose you, it will allow you to use it three times before it becomes magically null."

Whoa. "Magically null?"

She nodded. "Until it finds its way to its next owner. The dagger is driven by fate."

I scowled. That was my least favorite f-word.

"And how do you feel about this?" I asked Misty.

I could practically feel the dagger shrug. *"You are the one who will lose the ability to question those you wish to question. I will find my way back to your family. But you may wish to ask the cunning queen exactly what would happen if you were to give me to her."*

"If the dagger chose me, and I hand it over, what does that mean?"

The surprise that danced across her face made it evident that I'd asked the right question. Her gaze dropped to my hip and turned thoughtful.

"Once the dagger has chosen someone, it will work for them for as long as they hold it. The moment they give it up, freely and without reservation, it will never serve them again."

Dread settled into my stomach and stayed there.

"Ahhh," Misty said. *"Now you are understanding."*

If I gave the dagger up, I would lose the one edge I'd had when it came to finding my mother's killer. Grief welled up, choking me. I'd never expected to see her again, and I would gladly take another temporary death just to have a few more moments with her. Talking to her had reopened a wound that had almost healed.

Misty would never work for me again.

The queen's expression turned somber as she watched the realization hit me. "I have the sword you seek. I will trade you for the ability to discover which of my most trusted advisors has been betraying me. I've learned enough about you, Danica Amana, to know that you have no choice."

She was right. Hand over Misty and Samael lived. There was no choice at all. I took a deep, shuddering breath. I had to trust that Evie knew what she was doing. She'd begged me to let her take over the reins and hunt our mother's killer.

"I want the pelt back. And I want your word that your people will let me leave *and* reach the place I entered the ocean."

She nodded. "Done." She looked past me to someone she'd obviously trusted enough to remain in the room. I'd been standing here this whole time and hadn't realized we weren't alone. Great.

The others filed back in. The queen's gaze held death as it darted between three of the mermen. One of them was not going to have a good day, and I hoped it was the one who'd watched me drown. A small part of me wished I could stay and watch the fallout. I could get behind some drama that wasn't my own for once.

"Bring me the golden sword," she said. Gasps sounded. She simply waited and didn't expand on her order. I could respect that.

The sword appeared and she took it, gesturing me forward.

"My pelt," I said, and a merman appeared. His swollen nose looked familiar. He was the one who'd held me around the ankle. The one who'd been bringing me to the queen. "You should have someone set that," I told him, and he shot me a filthy look. He pushed the pelt into my hands and I wrapped it around my shoulders. Kyla's hairclip was long gone.

I stepped toward the throne. The queen stood, striding down the steps toward me. She held out the golden sword and I glanced down at it. The engravings on the hilt matched everything I'd been told about it so far.

I took a deep breath. *"Goodbye,"* I told Misty. *"Thank you for your help."*

"I will see you again, although you will not be able to hear me. Your family's journey to the truth is not over."

I frowned, but the queen was already reaching for it, her gaze sharp. My hand clamped around the hilt of the golden sword just as she took Misty, and our eyes met.

Hannah's words ran through my mind. "A little saltwater will do it no harm, and you will need it for what you face in the dark depths." I'd thought she meant I would need to use it, not hand it over to someone else.

Damned if it didn't feel like fate had brought me to this moment. A faint smile hovered around the queen's mouth, and then the deal was done.

Well, half of it anyway. I still had to trust them to allow me to get home.

"I will lead you to the barrier," she told me. From the shock on her guard's faces, they weren't expecting such a thing, but the Merqueen ignored them, and they fell into step behind us as we walked toward the two doors.

They opened, and we were suddenly in a long hall. I stepped up to the closest window and gaped at the city spread out in front of me.

Even with everything that had happened since I first met Samael, all the places I'd seen, the creatures I'd met—and killed—I could still feel awe.

It rose up in my chest as I blinked a few times. The queen gave me a moment, and I got the feeling she was proud of her kingdom.

She should be.

The palace stood at the end of a broad avenue, which unraveled down a hill. Side streets ran from the avenue, and merfolk strolled across what should have been the ocean floor, all of them on two legs.

And there were plants. And trees. And flowers. They looked nothing like any greenery I'd ever seen before, but they swayed in what felt like a cool breeze as it rustled my hair.

"I don't understand. Did I go through a portal while I was swimming and not notice it?"

"We have always been here, below the sea. Too deep for humans to reach, and then, when their technology could find us, the inherent magic of our people kept our city hidden. Although, the barrier has not always been in place."

"But… how could you exist when the portals hadn't opened… when magic hadn't reached this world yet?"

The queen smiled. "Magic was always here, for those who knew how to find it."

She turned, and we continued on down the hall, her guards still in step behind us. Another set of doors was opened, and my breath caught in my throat as I took my first steps outside.

High above us, a huge, incandescent dome spanned the entire city. It glowed softly, reflecting all of the colors of the rainbow and lighting the kingdom with jewel tones.

"This is why I can breathe down here, even without the pelt."

"Yes."

"But I don't understand. You guys don't need to breathe underwater."

A hint of sorrow crossed her face. "You have a tale in your world, about a merwoman who left the ocean to walk on two legs."

It took me a moment, but I nodded. "Yeah. The Little Mermaid."

Her lips quirked at that, but her eyes remained serious. "While most of the story is incorrect, there are, as usual, some details that retain the truth. However, that is not where the story began." She sighed. "My great, great grandmother was born on land. She was a poor fisherman's daughter, destined for a life of poverty if not for the striking nature of her face. Her father decided to sell her."

I winced. "I'm guessing she didn't want to be sold."

"No. But that was expected. One day, she ran to the edge of the sea, crying out to her gods to save her from such a fate. Her gods didn't answer. But my great, great grandfather did. To hear him tell the story, it took him merely a single glance for him to fall deeply in love.

"However, she considered him a demon and attempted to flee, slipping on some rocks. She fell and hit her head, and it seemed as if she had escaped her fate after all."

"But your great-great-grandfather had no intention of allowing that."

"No," she smiled. "He dragged her as far beneath the sea as he dared, using his power to breathe for her as he engaged one of our healers. When she was able to open her eyes, she kissed him in thanks."

Big mistake.

The queen nodded at my expression. "Yes, with that,

she sealed her new fate. The king decided he would have her, but he needed time to adjust his home so she could live. Prior to this, our people lived in the depths of the ocean, spending little time on land and in our two-legged forms. But the king went to the fae. He bargained with both the seelie and unseelie, and both agreed to give him what he needed. Our dome was created on the next full moon, and the night before she was to be married, the king traveled to her village and stole her away. When she awoke, she was below."

Claustrophobia rose up, sharp and violent. The kingdom was beautiful, but the idea of being stuck down here, of never feeling the sun on my face again... I shuddered, and the queen gave me a regal nod.

"Yes, the new Merqueen felt the same way. She was grateful to her mate for ensuring she wouldn't be sold, but she ached for her world. The king refused to take her back, believing it was best for her to accept her new life."

I scowled. "He sounds like a real dick."

Her laugh rang out. "Any love she may have had for him died. And she mourned, longing for the world above. Mating with the king had given her his lifespan, but she faded away within a couple of decades. Many say she died of a broken heart."

"But the dome remained."

She smiled. "While it was unpopular at first, my people had become used to it by then, and it was seen as a sign of their king's great love for his queen. They decided they enjoyed living two lives."

I frowned at that, and she gestured for me to follow her once more. We walked behind the palace, where the side of the dome met the ocean floor. The queen nodded at one of her guards, and he strode forward, walking *through* the dome. As he did, his legs disappeared, replaced by his long, glimmering tail.

They all waited, and I jolted as realization swept through me. *I* had to walk through that dome, only I wouldn't grow a tail or the ability to breathe normally without the pelt.

My breath came in sharp pants, and I attempted to pull myself together.

How could I trust that the merfolk wouldn't take the pelt away once more, strip me of the sword, and leave my corpse to float amongst the coral?

I was showing far too much fear in front of these creatures, but I couldn't help it. Shudders wracked my body and the queen sent me a sympathetic look. "You have my word," she said quietly. "None will touch you."

I bit my tongue before I was tempted to remind her that her guards had already watched me drown once, and she had a traitor as an advisor. She studied my face and gestured to one of the guards.

"My cousin," she murmured. "The person I trust the most. He will escort you to the surface." She glanced down, untucking a large shell from her dress. "May I?"

I nodded, and she gathered the ends of the pelt in front of me, using the shell to hold it in place. There was some kind of magic in play here, but if it helped me keep the pelt around my shoulders, I'd take it.

"Thank you."

The Merqueen's cousin gave me a reassuring nod. "I will protect you," he declared. With that, he strode through the dome, waiting for me on the other side.

The golden sword wouldn't fit in Misty's sheath, so I wrapped my hand tightly around the hilt and took a deep breath.

Then I forced myself to step through the dome.

CHAPTER NINETEEN

Danica

The swim back to the surface was uneventful, apart from the fact that I was breathing underwater and shaking with barely suppressed fear. The queen's cousin stayed within a few feet of me, his gaze continually sweeping our surroundings.

As soon as we were around twenty feet from the surface, he caught my arm. He gestured that he was returning and gave me a grave farewell nod.

I nodded back and turned, kicking out. The pelt propelled me for the most part, but now that I was so close to being on dry land, desperation drove me forward.

My head broke the surface and I sucked in air. Precious, cool, fresh air.

"Never again," I said aloud as I paddled toward the beach where Kyla was pacing back and forth. "Not in a million years."

Kyla had her hands planted on her hips as I hauled my water-logged self through the waves.

"You look like you went through something dark."

"You have no idea. I got this though."

I held up the sword and she whooped. "Nice."

I splashed through the knee-high waves and finally made it onto the beach. "If I never go near water again, I'll be perfectly content."

"Tell me everything."

I filled her in as we made our way to her car. I'd packed a change of clothes, and after a quick glance around the parking lot, I stripped off, so damn thankful to be clean and dry that I could've danced.

Kyla gaped when I got to the part where the merfolk watched me drown. "Are you serious?"

"Serious as a heart attack. Literally." Now that I was away from the water, I could almost look back and laugh. Almost. Kyla shook her head at me, handing me my lanyard, Nim Cub, and my rowan arrow. I instantly felt more secure as I slipped them around my neck.

"Let's get that pelt back to Mella."

The selkie was bingeing daytime TV when we arrived. I'd lost all sense of time and glanced at the alarm clock next to the bed. 1pm. I'd lost an entire night and the next morning. Time obviously moved differently in the underwater kingdom. I glanced at Kyla.

"Tell me you didn't wait on that beach the whole time."

She shrugged. Now that I was looking at her, I noticed the dark circles beneath her eyes. "I'm driving the whole way back," I said. She shrugged again. She must be exhausted if she wasn't arguing.

I handed the pelt to Mella. The tension visibly

drained from her body as she stroked it.

"Thank you for this," I said. "I know it can't have been easy."

"I would've done it without the favor." She smiled at me.

I grinned back. "Now you tell me."

Her expression turned somber. "Seriously Danica. I know you were probably just being nice, but some days, knowing that you would be kind—that you'd stick up to Bruce for me… it was all that got me through the day."

"No one should be tormented that way, should be made to feel like they're unworthy. I'm sorry I didn't do more."

"You did more than enough."

"I'm glad you killed Bruce."

"Same." She smiled, and it was wicked.

"We need to get moving."

Mella nodded. "Don't be a stranger. Oh, there's a portal to the seelie realm near here if it's easier."

"I have a stop to make first." Now that I had the sword, I was practically vibrating with the need to give it to the seelie king and swap it for the counter spell. Samael's silence was freaking me out.

But there was something I had to do first. Kyla frowned at me and I shrugged. Mella handed me a few more of the white stones Mariam had given me. "If you need anything… or just want to hang out…"

"Sounds great. I'll take you up on that."

Kyla snoozed on the way back to Durham. I barely managed to keep my eyes open myself, finally opening the window so the cool air could help me stay awake.

By the time we pulled up outside Selina's house, Kyla was opening her eyes.

"Why are we here?"

I blew out a breath and climbed out of the car. "Because your bargain with Finvarra wouldn't have happened if you weren't helping me. So we're going to talk to Selina. If anyone can give us some information to help, it's her."

"We don't have time."

"I'm making time."

I had to believe that there would be life after this. That we'd all survive. And if we survived, there were consequences for the decisions I'd made over the past few days. I refused to let Kyla deal with those consequences alone.

We got out of the car. Selina's house was painted in soothing colors—the dusky light blue welcoming and peaceful. Maybe it was something to do with Selina's wards, but simply being here made me take a long, deep breath and let it out.

Selina opened the front door. I was betting she'd expected us. Today, she wore apricot-colored pants with a wide leg, a cozy white cardigan, and a wide smile.

"I hope you're hungry," she said. "I made lunch."

Kyla grinned at her. "I'm always hungry."

Selina led us through to the kitchen, and I inhaled the rich, savory scents.

"Sit, sit. What would you like to drink?"

She gestured to her kitchen table, which she'd already set with three place settings. Kyla raised one eyebrow.

"You knew we were coming."

"I had an inkling."

Selina filled our plates with spaghetti Bolognese, then cut into what smelled like freshly-baked bread.

"This is incredible," Kyla said.

She beamed. "Well, thank you. I enjoy hosting, and it's nice to have friends visit." Her face sobered as she sat, and we all dug in. "I heard what happened to Samael. I'm sorry, Danica. Let me know if I can help in any way."

"Well, there is one thing now that you mention it." She laughed at my wry tone, and then her mouth dropped open as I pulled out the sword from the duffel at my feet.

It wasn't often that I saw Selina as anything other than perfectly composed. I grinned at her.

Her eyes grew even wider. "That's the golden sword."

"It sure is."

We ate while I told her everything that had happened since the Spell of Three took effect—Kyla jumping in to provide commentary when necessary.

"A griffin?" Selina asked.

"Yep," Kyla took a bite. "Huge. He's a sweetheart."

"I'd love to meet him." Excitement flickered in Selina's eyes. The griffin had another fan.

By the time we were finished getting her caught up, she was piling more food into Kyla's bowl with a wink.

"So, you made a deal with Finvarra," she mused.

"Yes. But there's something else. Ilis said she doesn't believe the sword will be used to kill her king. She said there are other myths surrounding it."

Selina raised her eyebrow. Then she rubbed her hands together. "Gimme."

I handed it over. She stiffened, and Kyla paused with

her fork halfway to her mouth, staring at the witch.

"The sword may be used to kill the unseelie king," Selina whispered. "But if wielded by the seelie king's hand, he will die too."

"Sounds like a two-for-one deal to me," Kyla mused.

I nodded. "If they want to destroy each other—and themselves in the process—who are we to get in the way of that?"

"Shame about that pesky bargain," she scowled.

I sighed. "Yep."

Selina's hands were still clamped around the hilt of the sword, and she ignored us, watching whatever it was she saw.

"The sword is a lynchpin in the future. Of such vital importance that those who have their fates tied to it are considered marked."

For the first time, a hint of nervousness flickered across Kyla's face, but was quickly gone, replaced by sheer arrogance.

"Marked as a badass, amirite?"

Selina's lips curved as she slowly opened her eyes and placed the sword on the table.

"Your fate is tied to the sword, but it is not the *same* as the sword. Do you have—ah. May I look with your bracelet?"

Kyla's eyebrows shot up, and she covered her bracelet with her hand. It was plain, beaded, and now that I thought about it, I'd never seen her not wear it. Even after shifting to wolf form and back.

She slipped it off and handed it over, expression somber. Selina took it from her, and we both watched as she entered her trance.

"You will trust someone who will betray their word," Selina told Kyla. "But you will find allies in the places you would least expect. You must return the sword to its rightful owner."

I frowned. "Finvarra isn't its rightful owner."

Selina was still talking. "The bargain has been struck, but you must return the sword to its true sheath, or the realms will burn."

Well, that took a nasty turn.

"You will have a choice to make," she continued. "Choose wrongly, and you will be chained to a throne. Choose correctly, and you will sit on one."

Kyla swallowed. "How do I know what to choose and when?"

Selina smiled. "You must remember who you are."

Selina's eyes popped open, and she handed the bracelet back to Kyla, who scowled. "Chained to a throne?"

Selina nodded. "In wolf form."

"Which throne?"

"The owner of the throne was hidden from me."

I blew out a breath. "Well, there are really only three options. Four if you count the merfolk's throne, but I'm assuming you didn't see water in her future?"

Selina shook her head.

"Samael would never do anything like that if he took his throne back, but for now, we know it would either be Lucifer's throne, Finvarra's throne, or the seelie king's throne."

"But… what do you mean by sitting on one?"

"The visions are not always literal," Selina smiled at her. "Sometimes, they must be interpreted in various ways, and sometimes the meaning won't become clear until closer to the time."

Relief coursed through me. "So being chained to a throne or sitting on a throne could mean figuratively. For example, she could be responsible for someone else sitting on the throne, or have enough political power that she's influencing the person who *is* on the throne."

Or, be kept in servitude to someone who was sitting on a throne. The thought made my gut clench.

Selina nodded. "Exactly. The visions can be interpreted in hundreds of ways."

Kyla still looked perturbed, and Selina reached over and squeezed her hand. "Fretting over the future will only make you second-guess yourself when the time comes. If there's one thing I can tell you, it's that you must stay true to yourself."

I swallowed. "If she needs to return the sword to its rightful owner, but she also has to fulfill her bargain with Finvarra, does that mean she needs to steal it twice?"

Selina sighed. "Yes. That part was clear. Finvarra may hold the sword for a short time, but if he keeps it for more than a few months, the worlds burn."

"No pressure," Kyla muttered.

I got to my feet and carried the dishes to the sink while they spoke in quiet voices. If I was still alive when Kyla went after the sword, I'd help her in any way I could. But that didn't stop the guilt that twisted in my stomach. I should never have taken her with me to Finvarra.

"Hey," Kyla elbowed me, and I jumped. I'd rinsed

the dishes and now I was staring into the sink as if it held the answers to the universe.

"Sorry, daydreaming."

"You were wallowing in guilt is what you were doing." Kyla leaned back on the counter and turned to Selina. "I'm assuming that I was probably supposed to return the sword to its rightful owner regardless of my little bargain with Finvarra, right?"

Selina nodded. "There are extra steps now, different… threads that might be torn, snipped, or woven into your future. But that thread was as unbreakable as the strongest rope."

Kyla leveled me with a hard stare. "So Danica blaming herself is a waste of time and energy?"

Selina grinned. "Exactly. If not that bargain, something else would have happened to ensure you learned of the importance of stealing the sword. Leave the rest of the dishes and go give the sword to the seelie king," she said. "I need to get ready for a date."

I opened my mouth, warring with the urge to interrogate Selina all about this date. But I snapped my mouth shut at the thought of how much time we'd spent here. It hadn't been wasted, but I needed to get the sword to the king and get the counter spell before it was too late.

CHAPTER TWENTY

Danica

"He's not here," one *of* the guards told us when we arrived at Taraghlan's castle.

"I'm sorry, what?"

"He will be returning soon. But for now, you'll need to wait."

Son of a bitch. I didn't have *time* to wait.

"This is a power play," I muttered as the guard showed us where to wait—a padded bench outside of the throne room. "I bet he *is* here, and he's just proving a point."

Kyla growled. The guards standing by the throne room door both stiffened, watching her with narrowed, assessing eyes.

We waited for hours. I paced back and forth, slowly growing more and more incensed. Next to me, Kyla's eyes were all wolf. The guards were as tense as we were, and two more had joined their ranks while we'd been waiting.

Finally, a look of concentration came across one of their faces, and he nodded at us, clearly listening to his king. "You may wait in the throne room."

The guards opened the door to the throne

room—empty except for two more guards positioned on either side of the throne.

I ignored them and paced some more.

Finally, the scent of ozone drifted through the air. We both froze. The hair on my arms stood at attention, and a *CRACK* sounded.

My hand tightened around the golden sword.

The seelie king had appeared. Cellen stood beside him, panting.

"Now that's a dramatic entrance," I said. "Should I clap?"

Cellen narrowed his eyes at me. Meanwhile, the seelie king's gaze was glued to the sword in my hand.

To say that I'd shocked him was an understatement.

"You did it," he breathed. Next to him, Cellen's mouth dropped open as he realized what I held. I was pretty sure the smile I shot him was dripping with smug satisfaction.

The king turned and strode to his throne. Cellen took up his place next to him, and one of the guards stepped forward, his hands outstretched for the sword. Kyla stepped in front of me and bared her teeth at him.

"The counter spell," I said. Cellen leaned over and whispered something in the seelie king's ear, and I had a pretty good feeling he was encouraging him to have his guards take the sword from me.

I smiled at both men.

"The merfolk told me something interesting about this sword," I murmured, my voice light. The seelie king narrowed his eyes at my tone and I continued. "It turns out, the whole blade-melting thing was built into the spell that created the sword. It wasn't the blood of Grendel's mother that made it melt. In fact, it can be melted with nothing more than the will of the sword's current owner. Honestly, I'd be lying if I didn't admit I was impressed with that level of pettiness."

My smile widened as the king leaned forward on his throne. "You wouldn't."

"Try me," I invited. "Or go ahead and watch me destroy this sword. Oh, don't worry, the blade will grow back in a few hundred years. But I'm not so sure you've got that amount of time to waste."

Kyla nodded. "Turns out, the unseelie king hates you. It was practically dripping from him. And while Finvarra may be a bastard, I know who I'd put my money on if it came down to it."

"Ooh," I said. "We should start a pool. The demons would get in on that."

Cellen hissed something at Taraghlan once more, and he held up his hand, clearly pissed. "Are you insinuating that I would break my vow?"

Oh, I'm sure you would if you thought you could get away with it, you prick.

"Merely making it clear that if I don't walk out of here with what I want, you don't get what you want either."

Taraghlan stared at me in silence, clearly debating with himself. Finally, he nodded at one of his guards, who moved toward a small chest near the throne. He took a key from his pocket and opened the chest, revealing a gold ring. I peered at it. Every part of the band was heavily engraved, and something about it pricked at my memory.

Another guard stepped closer to me, holding out his hand for the sword. I held out my other hand, waiting for the ring. From the amusement that flickered across the seelie king's face, he found us all endlessly entertaining. Goodie.

The guard placed the spelled ring in my right hand, and I opened my left hand, giving them the sword in return.

A weight slowly floated off my shoulders. The moment Samael killed Ben, a ball of dread had formed in my gut, and I'd carried it around ever since. This didn't remove it, but it felt lighter, tempered by hope.

"Not long now, Samael."

He didn't reply. I didn't think he could.

Taraghlan nodded at the ring in my hands. "The spell must be used at the witching hour." I mentally translated that. Midnight.

This was why he'd kept us waiting. By the time we got back tonight, it would be too late. That meant I'd have to wait an entire day. My hands were fisted so tight, my nails were cutting into my palms.

The bastard had given us the counter spell, but he'd wasted enough time that Samael could die anyway—something that would work out well for him

The king was still talking, and I glanced up at him.

"What was that?"

Irritation twisted his lips as he stared at me, likely unused to repeating himself. "Exactly three days after you use the counter spell, the ring must be returned to me."

I scowled. "That wasn't part of the deal."

He ignored that. "Cellen will find you and you will give it to him."

I stiffened. "You'll be able to use the counter spell to the Spell of Three again, won't you?"

Taraghlan stared at me silently. Son of a bitch. I'd assumed it was a one-and-done kinda thing. He smiled, obviously following my train of thought. His expression was so smug, my fist ached with the need to slam into his face.

"The counter spell may be used three times. I have used it once. You will use it once, and I will be able to use it once more. After that use, there will be no counter spell left in any of the realms."

"Fine." I glanced at the golden sword in his guard's hand. "Nice doing business with you."

Taraghlan's gaze dropped to the sword and lit up with a combination of pleasure and hope. I shook my head and turned to leave. The guy was planning to use the sword to kill the unseelie king, and he gazed at it as if it was his lover.

Kyla was tense, both of us silent as we left the seelie realm. I was convinced someone was going to come and steal the counter spell at any moment, and from the low growls that occasionally left her throat, and the suspicious look in her eyes whenever we passed the seelie, I was guessing she felt the same.

Finally, we were driving back through the portal.

"Was that true?" Kyla asked.

"Was what true?"

"The whole blade-melting thing."

I snorted. "Nope."

Her mouth dropped open, and I grinned at her. "But the king couldn't risk it. The fae can't lie, so they're unused to dealing with creatures who can. But a seelie as old as Taraghlan would have plenty of ways to get around their oaths and vows. I had to make him think I'd destroy the sword rather than walk out of there empty-handed."

"You're a sneaky bitch."

My grin widened. "Thank you."

Kyla reached over and squeezed my hand. "You did it Danica. No one thought you could, but you did it."

My eyes were hot, and for a single moment, I let myself revel in all that we'd managed to do. "I couldn't have done it without you. So thank you."

She grinned at me, but her face grew somber as she studied me. "You're welcome. You looked surprised when you saw the ring—why?"

Kyla missed nothing.

"I could be wrong, but there's something about it that seems familiar. I've seen it somewhere. I need to do a little research, but I think it might be Angelica's ring."

Her head angled, her eyes sharpened, and I couldn't help but grin.

"You've heard the story."

"Yeah. Joel was into history, and mythology and shit like that." Her face darkened, and then turned blank, curiosity lighting her eyes. "It was an Italian epic poem, right?"

"Yeah. Orlando Innamorato. To sum it up, Angelica is the daughter of the king, and all the men fall in love with her. A bunch of them fight each other—blah blah. The original poem was never finished, but another poet stepped in with the Orlando Furioso."

"How do you know all this?"

"Edward–the man who trained me–was obsessed with the epics. All of them. His theory was that there were elements of truth within many of the myths, and that some of them were retellings of history and interactions with paranormals. From what we've learned about Beowulf, I would say his theory holds."

"It sure does. So what did the poem say?"

I took a left onto Chapel Hill Road, scowling at the line of traffic. Some asshole behind me began laying on his horn. As if that would help.

I tuned the sound out and frowned, attempting to remember the key details. "This knight, Orlando, was scarily obsessed with Angelica. She went off and had adventures around the world, while he basically stalked her. Eventually, she ended up chained to a rock, about to be sacrificed to a sea monster.

"Luckily, this other knight had her back. His name was Ruggiero, and he gave her a ring." Edward had been obsessed with the idea of Angelica's ring, spending two years, and a solid chunk of cash, researching everything he could about it. If he had any inkling that it had ended up in *my* hands, he'd lose his mind.

But thanks to all that research, I had a pretty good idea of what that ring could do.

"The ring removes enchantments. That much, Edward was sure of. According to the poem, it also contains a spell of invisibility when you put it in your mouth. That's how Angelica escaped the sea monster. And now we know that its resistance to enchantment means it's a key part of the Spell of Three."

"No wonder Taraghlan wants it back."

"Yeah."

A howl announced we were driving into wolf territory and Kyla sighed. "It's good to be home."

We parked outside Nathaniel's and walked past his house, down the dirt path and toward the clearing that held Samael's cabin.

Nathaniel had obviously decided the griffin could stay, because he was sniffing at the forest near Liam, who was in human form. Liam nodded at me, and I waved back. Several demons were gathered outside the cabin, all of them watching the griffin incredulously.

I hid my smile.

"I wish you could see this. The demons don't know what to make of the griffin. Meanwhile, the wolves are mostly ignoring him."

No reply. My hands wanted to shake, but I forced myself to take several deep breaths. He was fine.

The demons parted, allowing me to walk into the cabin. I went straight to Samael's room, Kyla trailing behind me.

Samael was little more than a husk. I turned and rushed for the bathroom, vomiting up what little I'd eaten. Kyla found a washcloth and wet it, rung it out, and handed it to me. I wiped my mouth.

"Thanks."

"He's still alive, Danica. He just has to last until midnight tomorrow."

"I know. I just don't see how the counter spell can possibly fix that much damage."

"It will. Taraghlan wouldn't guard it that fiercely if it didn't work."

I let out a shuddering breath. "Okay."

Kyla wandered into the living room, giving me a moment with Samael. All of his limbs were gone, as were his ears and nose. No wonder he wasn't able to communicate with me.

I tamped down the urge to sit next to his bed. That wasn't exactly going to be the best for my mental health. Instead, I stepped into the living room. Vas was murmuring to Kyla, and he glanced at me when I walked in, his eyes dark with grief. He opened his arms and I walked into them.

The hug steadied me. I wasn't alone. I stepped back, and we were all silent as I moved outside into the cool air. It was close to 2am, and most of the demons had cleared out when I'd arrived. I was pretty sure they'd be circling overhead, but for now, my attention was on the griffin who was curled up on the porch.

I sat down next to him. "Are you sure you want to hang out here?" I asked him. "If you want to find your… pack, I can help you, just as soon as Samael's no longer on death's door."

The griffin leaned his face closer to me. My heartrate sped up. I didn't think he would hurt me—he'd had plenty of opportunities for that. But his teeth were very long, and they looked very sharp.

He stared into my eyes. It wasn't like when I'd spoken to Nuri, and she'd sent images into my mind.

No, communicating with the griffin was different. The knowledge he wanted to share simply appeared in my mind, as if it had always been there.

It wasn't a violation. He was gentle, but it still weirded me out.

The griffin had been wounded while fighting vicious unseelie creatures who were lethal, both in the air and on the ground. He had no name for them, but they seemed similar to harpies, only deadlier, if that were possible.

The griffin had leapt in front of his pack's leader, taking the brunt of one of the creature's attacks. He'd been so consumed with protecting the other griffin, he'd been off balance, and the creature had ripped at his wing, almost tearing it from his body.

The pain had been unspeakable.

I took a shaky breath as the griffin nuzzled my shoulder. His pack had killed the remaining creatures, and he'd been left wounded on the ground while his pack moved to a safer location. For days, he'd lain there, slowly dying of thirst, until the rain had saved his life.

When he was strong enough to stagger to his feet, he'd known he would never fly again.

My throat tightened at the desolation that had swept through him at that realization.

He'd tracked his pack, following them by instinct, and they'd ignored him when he finally arrived, half-starved and wounded.

Rage swept through me.

"They treated you like an outcast. Why?"

His eyes glittered. Was that amusement? It hit me then.

"You were seen as a weakness. Like the runt of the litter."

And so, he'd followed his family, loyal as ever, but ignored. He was the last to eat, and the pack made no allowances for the fact that he had to travel by land to meet them. Sometimes, he would arrive, exhausted, in pain, and half-starved, and the pack would already be preparing to leave.

"They threw you away," I ground out. "You saved their leader, and they treated you like trash."

And then I'd arrived with the order to kill him. The griffin had watched me, coolly interested, almost accepting.

"I'm sorry. They didn't deserve you. I'll talk to Nathaniel. Maybe he'll let you stay here. Otherwise, you can come with me. We'll figure something out."

He butted me with his head, in the exact same way Lia did. I laughed and ran my hand over his soft fur, marveling at his wings. They were even silkier than Samael's.

I stroked his twisted wing. "If you want, I can have a healer look at this."

He gazed at me steadily, giving no indication of a preference either way. I shrugged.

A low voice sounded behind me. "I've told him he can stay."

I jumped about a foot in the air. Goddamn werewolves. Nathaniel smiled at me, then shifted his attention to the griffin, who bowed his head. Nathaniel nodded back.

"You'll let him stay here?"

"Loyalty should be rewarded."

I frowned at that. I didn't want the griffin to be used just because he was honorable. Nathaniel shook his head at me.

"My pack is nothing like the pack he left," he said. The griffin must have shared his history with the Alpha. "All of us are only as strong as our weakest member, but we don't excise our weakness, we work to make it stronger."

I let out a shaky breath and turned to the griffin. "Do you have a name?"

Nothing. I chewed on my lower lip. I didn't love calling him 'the griffin.' "Would you like one?"

Curiosity sparked in those kind eyes. I smiled.

"Hmm, how about… Bob," I teased. The griffin blinked.

"No? Frank?"

He stared solemnly at me. Nathaniel tutted and sat on the porch next to me.

"How about Virtus?" he asked. "It has several meanings. Among them are valor, courage, and excellence."

The griffin's eyes shone. Then he let out a low growl.

I grinned. "I think he likes it."

Virtus put his head on his paws and sighed, closing his eyes. Everything else might be falling apart, but at least I'd done something right.

"Thank you," I said to Nathaniel. "I know the demons signed an alliance with you, but I still appreciate everything your people have done."

He smiled. "I would be a fool to miss the opportunity to ally with the future demon queen." His smile widened at whatever he saw on my face. "I have no intention of being on the wrong side of history for this, even disregarding your sister."

I went still. "What about my sister?"

The tension in his body told me he would take his words back if he could, but he was an Alpha, so he continued.

"Evelyn is my mate."

I gaped at him. My sister, who loathed all authority, who'd been spelled her whole life, and was only now discovering who she really was…

"You're wrong."

Nathaniel's laugh was bitter. "If only."

His eyes met mine, and for the first time in a while, he Alpha-stared me. Holding his gaze took everything I had.

"No one will tell her," he said.

I narrowed my eyes at him. "You think I'm going to lie to my sister?"

"Werewolves are more than just our beasts. That one truth allowed me to tame even the most feral of my people when the portals opened. Tell me, Danica, how do you think your sister will react to learn that, even in this, her choices would be removed? That she would be destined to be mine?"

Bile crawled up my throat.

"She would run," I said through numb lips. "And she'd never return." I took a deep breath and let it out. Next to me, Virtus nudged my shoulder as if in silent support. I petted him. "Explain how this... mate business works."

The corner of Nathaniel's mouth lifted, but his eyes remained serious. "Werewolves are a unique pairing of man and wolf. When the portals first opened, the wolf suddenly awoke in those who had been shut off from their wolves their entire lives. Some went insane. Most had no experience negotiating with their wolves and were forced to... watch as they rampaged through this realm."

He sighed, running his hand through his hair. It wasn't often that Nathaniel looked tired, but his face seemed to have acquired new lines, etched deep. "Most wolves mate with the woman their human selves choose. The wolf must accept the mating, but most understand that a mate is a key part of a long and happy life. However... there are some wolves–most consider them blessed by whatever gods watch over us–whose wolf recognizes the mate of its heart. And the man recognizes the same."

I swallowed. "So, your wolf recognized Evie first?"

He nodded.

"When?"

"The first time we met her. I had no understanding of what was happening, or why my wolf raged when she feared us. It explains why I was able to scent the chip in her neck. But I didn't fully understand until the funeral. I caught her scent, no longer clouded by the chip… and my wolf showed me the truth."

I didn't know what to say. Nathaniel's gaze was steady on my face. "Your sister is many things, but she's not a witch. Or at least, not just a witch. She's going to need to be protected, and yet, if she learns I am her mate, she will leave. She knows we're watching over her right now, but if she wanted, she could take steps to end that. I have no doubt that if your sister put her mind to it, she could leave without a trace."

I took a deep, shuddering breath. "And what about Liam?"

He shrugged, not at all worried about the threat the other wolf could present. "Evelyn left him a note. Likely similar to the one she left you."

I was curious despite myself. "Your wolf doesn't want to kill Liam?"

"He doesn't enjoy seeing him touch our mate. But there is a reason I am Alpha. A reason I was able to gain control of my wolf before any other. I struck a partnership with my wolf, and if there is one thing we are both good at, it is patience. We can wait for Evelyn to realize she is ours, but we can't protect her if she leaves for good. And that enrages my wolf to the point where I may be unable to control him."

"If I don't tell Evie, she may never forgive me."

"If you tell her and she leaves, and whoever is hunting her finds her, you will never forgive yourself either."

Nathaniel got to his feet, cast one last affectionate look at the griffin, and prowled back into the forest.

CHAPTER TWENTY-ONE

Danica

My neck ached as I blinked open my eyes. The scent of caffeine wafted toward me, and I struggled to sit up. I'd fallen asleep on the sofa, unwilling to risk lying next to Samael.

He hadn't been in my dreams.

My eyes were heavy as I stared into space. Today, I'd make sure I had a representative from every faction ready to help with the spell.

Vas emerged from the small kitchen, silently handing me a cup of coffee.

"Thanks."

"Did you get much sleep last night?"

I shrugged, glancing at my phone. It was 8am.

"A few hours."

He took a seat in the recliner opposite me, and we both sat and sipped our coffee in exhausted silence.

A representative from every faction.

I obviously had the demons, and while Kyla had offered to represent the werewolves, Nathaniel had stepped in, claiming that it was a good move politically. I had a feeling it was his Alpha need to protect at work, his wolf unwilling to allow one of his pack members to risk themselves when he could do it instead.

Meredith would be my witch representation, since Evie was still nowhere to be seen. I was also planning to ask Aubrey to represent the seelie. If he told me he couldn't, thanks to his loyalty to Taraghlan, I would ask Eldan, who would be there in his capacity as healer anyway.

That left the unseelie… and the mages.

I'd managed to alienate every single mage in the Triangle. Not only had I left the Council to work for Samael, but I'd then killed a handful of mages. Not to mention, I'd destroyed their facility. Keigan was my only hope.

I chewed on my lower lip. Disappointment had been written all over his face when I blew up the facility. Who knew if he'd help me save Samael's life?

He would be my first stop. I glanced at Vas. "I need an unseelie for the counter spell. Any ideas?"

He nodded. "Leave it to me." He frowned at my silence. "You've done enough. You get everything else you need, and I'll figure out the unseelie."

"Thanks."

I showered, collected my weapons, and avoided looking in Samael's direction. The silence in my head was excruciatingly loud.

Kyla met me out by her car. "Where to?"

I frowned. I'd never been to Keigan's house, although I was pretty sure I had the address in my phone somewhere. He sure wouldn't be at the mage facility. Guilt burrowed deep in my chest, and I tamped it down as I pulled out my phone.

"Stonehouse Court," I said, and Kyla took the wheel. I glanced around at the empty street. "Have you seen Virtus this morning?"

"Virtus?"

"The griffin. He liked the name."

Kyla grinned, then shrugged, and I gaped as her cheeks heated. "You took him home with you, didn't you?"

She cast me a defiant look. "He was going to be cold in the forest."

"Try again. You'd know better than me just how warm all that fur would keep him."

"He was lonely."

That wasn't entirely impossible, given that Virtus had been part of his own pack, even if he'd been largely ignored. I'd left him snoring on the porch, the front door of the cabin open a few inches in case he wanted to come inside.

"Fine," Kyla glowered at me as if I'd spoken. "*I* was lonely."

"I'm sorry."

She sighed. "Don't be. It was probably all that shit with my brother. I saw the griffin–Virtus–lying on the porch and I told him he could stay with me. He slept on my sofa."

I grinned at the mental image that popped into my head, and her expression lightenesd.

"Yeah, it was pretty funny." We pulled up outside of Keigan's house—a large, two-storied brick home with a double garage. Along the steps leading to the screened porch, small immaculately trimmed shrubs were spaced apart so precisely that I could picture Keigan measuring the distance with a ruler.

The sight made my heart hurt.

Kyla glanced at me as we got out of the car. "What kind of approach do you want to take?"

I sighed. "Honesty, with a large side of regret."

Keigan's car was in the driveway. He didn't keep us waiting, but his expression was guarded as he opened the door. "Come in," he said with a wave of his hand. He didn't offer us a seat, didn't lead us out of his entranceway. I swallowed around the lump in my throat. Keigan had been my longest friendship. It looked like that friendship was dead.

I took a deep breath and explained what I needed. He pondered it for a long moment, his eyes turning thoughtful.

"This would save Samael's life, and he would wage war against Lucifer."

"Yes."

He sighed. "I'm sorry, Danica, but I can't step in here."

The world must have kept spinning, but for me, it came to a grinding halt.

"Excuse me?"

If I wasn't struggling against pure, unrelenting grief, I might've been pleased with the look of anguish on his face.

"The man I love will die. You understand that, right?"

"Yes." He swallowed. "It's very sad, and I wish it didn't have to be this way. But I can't, in good conscience, allow Samael to live when he is the mages' biggest threat."

I stared at him. "You said you were thinking of leaving the Council. You said Albert was a bigot!"

"I was. And he is. But after what happened the night you were kidnapped, I was convinced to stay."

Had someone drugged me when I wasn't paying attention? I couldn't understand this for the life of me. I glanced at Kyla, but her face was pale, her expression cold as she studied Keigan like she was wondering what his insides looked like.

"There is a sickness within the Council," Keigan said. His lips firmed. "And when I learned about the events of that night, I realized I needed to remain part of it in order to drive that sickness out. If I help you with this, I will be excised from the Council, and I truly believe I can do some good in the Council, and ultimately the world, by staying."

"The Council is rotten at its core," I snapped. "You don't try to cure rot, you cut it out."

"I don't expect you to understand. Don't even expect you to ever forgive me. But I believe this is the right call."

"You're damn right I'll never forgive you." I raked my eyes over him coldly. "Enjoy being Albert's lackey for the rest of your life."

I turned to stalk out the door, and Kyla let out a snarl that raised the hair on the back of my neck.

Uh-oh.

I whirled, but she was already holding Keigan up against the wall.

"That life will be mighty short, mage. Because when Samael dies, so does Danica, which means I'll come right back here and make you regret the day you were born." I clamped my hand on her shoulder, but she shrugged me off, sending Keigan a vicious smile. "Maybe we'll see if you have the werewolf gene. I think my Alpha would like that."

I gaped at her. To Keigan's credit, he didn't piss his pants. But I watched as the blood drained from his face, and he looked over Kyla's shoulder, his eyes meeting mine.

"You'll die?"

I sighed. "It's more than likely."

He wriggled in Kyla's hold, and I elbowed her. "Enough. Let him go."

Keigan brushed the wrinkles out of his shirt and turned to me, ignoring Kyla as if she wasn't there. Oh, she'd scared him alright. Obviously, he wasn't keen to see if he had the werewolf gene. I tucked that threat away for future use.

"I'll help you," Keigan said wearily. "Text me the details."

My mouth dropped open. "You will?"

"Yes." He looked like he'd agreed to poison himself, and he turned to climb his stairs, pushing past Kyla. "You can see yourselves out."

Danica

With Keigan onboard—however reluctantly—and Vas figuring out the unseelie representative, I texted Mere the details, receiving a dancing girl emoji back.

There was nothing else to do except talk to Aubrey.

I'd texted him earlier asking if he was in town, and he'd said I could stop by if I needed to talk to him. I had a feeling he knew what I was going to ask for.

Kyla gave the plants a suspicious look as we stepped up to his front door. "You think they're really alive?"

"Yes. Plants are alive. That's kind of how it works."

She elbowed me. "You know what I mean."

I shrugged. "Aubrey acts like they are. Who knows what he can sense that people without his affinity for plant life can't?"

The door opened at that moment and the fae himself beamed at us.

"Come in, come in. Coffee?"

I shook my head. "We don't have time. I'm just stopping by–"

"To ask if I can represent the seelie for your counter spell."

I nodded, studying his face. "Well, yeah."

"Yes, I can."

I raised one eyebrow and waited him out. Either he'd keep that on the down-low from Taraghlan, or it was some political move on the seelie court's part that was too sophisticated for me to understand.

Aubrey sighed. "There's another reason I asked you here. And I have a feeling it's important. I believe my king may not have disclosed everything you need for the counter spell."

My ears began to ring as the blood slowly drained from my face. Aubrey grabbed my arm and led me into a small sitting room, Kyla trailing behind us.

Within moments, I was sitting in a plush armchair.

Some of the dizziness left me, and Aubrey's concerned face came into view. "When was the last time you got some actual sleep?"

I shrugged. "What do you mean he didn't disclose everything?" My voice came out high and thready. "The counter spell has to be performed tonight."

Aubrey sighed. Across the room, Kyla took a wary step away from a vine which was hanging from the ceiling, slowly creeping toward her. Aubrey gave the vine a warning look and it stopped moving.

"By now, you're well aware of the hatred between the seelie and unseelie kings. I won't go into the reasons why, as that would take hours. But I will say that I believe my king isn't thinking as clearly as usual." He frowned, as if saying such a thing was blasphemous. "Taraghlan has been receiving advice from those who may not have his best intentions at heart."

I couldn't care less about that dipshit's personal problems. "What does that mean for Samael?"

A line appeared between Aubrey's eyebrows, and he squatted in front of me, his gaze intent. "My king is playing a dangerous game—giving you only some of the information so that if the counter spell does not work, no one can blame him, and yet he will benefit from Samael's death."

"Why are you telling me this? Isn't your loyalty to Taraghlan?"

His lips firmed. "Yes. And that's why I must protect him from himself. If you and Samael both died, and then your people learned of his deception after you risked your life to find the sword…"

"War," Kyla finished, and Aubrey nodded.

I pinched the bridge of my nose. "What do I need to do?"

"The counter spell requires one more element. And it's why the Spell of Three has been so successful in its evil over the centuries. It benefits the witches for the other factions to kill each other, you see."

I waited him out, barely resisting the urge to scream at him to get to the goldarned point. He gave me a faint, apologetic smile.

"A witch bone."

I got to my feet, fury making my hands shake. I wanted Taraghlan dead for this. But I didn't have time to rage about it. I needed to go negotiate with Gemma if I was going to save Samael's life.

The success of the counter spell would depend on my ability to convince her to help me.

"Thank you for telling me," I said. "Out of curiosity, how close are you to the throne?"

He smiled at me. "Not close enough for you to kill the seelie king and plant my rather exceptional arse on that throne. I think you have quite enough to do without playing kingmaker, Danica."

I gave him a slow smile. It was going on my list anyway.

Aubrey shook his head. "I'll see you tonight."

I appreciated that he clearly believed I'd get what I needed. I nodded and glanced at Kyla. "Let's go."

CHAPTER TWENTY-TWO

Danica

Gemma's coven had already moved out of the hotel they'd been staying in after the fire. Now they were living in a light gray triplex with brick columns on Lamond Avenue—just a couple of streets over from the home that had burned to the ground.

It didn't surprise me at all. Gemma would expect her coven to walk past their old home–where so many of them had died–without showing a hint of emotion.

Kyla parked beneath an oak tree and turned to me. "You want me to wait here?"

I pondered it. Gemma certainly wouldn't appreciate me bringing a wolf into witch territory. "She won't be in a good mood when she finds out what I want, but there's no need to piss her off even more."

"No worries." She opened her door, pushed her seat back, and closed her eyes. "I'm taking a nap."

I shook my head at her and got out of the car.

I rolled my shoulders, attempting to work out some of the tension, and then I put my game face on. If Gemma sniffed out a hint of weakness, it was all over.

She opened the door herself, eyeing me as I walked up the stairs to the wide porch.

"What are you doing here?"

"Hello to you too. I need to talk to you."

She sniffed and turned, leaving the door open. I rolled my eyes and strode after her, closing the door behind me.

It was quiet at this time of the day. Most of the witches had outside jobs, bringing money into the coven. Gemma hobbled into the small sunroom and sat in an armchair that looked remarkably similar to the one she'd loved in her old house. My chest ached and I shrugged it off.

No point dragging this out. "When I brought Caroline back to you, you said you owed me a debt."

Gemma sucked on a tooth, a scowl darkening her face. "And why am I not surprised that you're here to collect so soon?"

"I'm just resourceful that way." I sent her a sunny smile, and a hint of reluctant humor glittered in her eyes.

"What is it you want?"

"I want one of Caroline's bones. A fingerbone should do it."

All humor fled, and instant denial took its place. "Witch bones are sacred."

I sighed. "You owe me the debt, Gemma."

"Pick something else."

"This is what I want."

She stared at me. "You ask too much."

I waited her out. It wasn't too much—especially for

the discovery of the betrayal of one of their own. She knew it and I knew it.

"Give it to her," a hoarse voice said behind me. I turned, meeting Gail's eyes. She nodded at me, and her gaze drifted past me to Gemma. "It's only right."

Gemma's lips thinned, but she got to her feet. "Wait here," she told me.

Gail walked to the window, gazing out at the street. "We had a better view at the old house," she said.

I didn't know what to say to that, so I stayed silent. She let out a rough laugh.

"Have you finally learned to control that tongue of yours?"

"Nope. Just making allowances for your grief."

"It doesn't seem right to grieve for someone who caused so much pain. My grief is better spent on her victims."

I sighed. "If there's one thing I've learned, it's that grief doesn't care about logic. And the more you try to suppress it, the more it rises up at the worst possible moments. Until it would take over your entire fucking life if you let it. Feeling guilty because you miss the person you loved—even if you only loved a single part of them— that serves no one."

She turned back to me, and her eyes were filled with tears.

"Thank you. For that, and for what you did for our coven. Some of the others blame you, for discovering a truth that ripped us apart, but that truth was always there, waiting to be found."

I nodded, getting to my feet as Gemma appeared, a

small cloth bag in her hand. She held it out, and I took it before she could change her mind, shoving it into my back pocket.

"Where is your sister?"

I frowned. "She didn't tell you? She left to follow up on a lead…" I let my voice trail off. As her coven leader, Gemma would have needed to give Evie permission to leave Durham. The fact that she hadn't definitely did not bode well.

"You have no need to protect your sister from me," Gemma sighed. "She is no longer a member of this coven and is therefore free to do whatever she likes."

My body went hot with fury. "What?"

Gemma's face turned blank. "After our coven was slaughtered, there were some who blamed Evie. While it was not her fault, many did agree with Caroline—the coven would not have been targeted if Evie was not hunted."

I was glad I had the bone safely tucked away in my pocket, because I was about to erupt.

Evie had seen this coming. That's why she hadn't spent much time with the coven while I was searching for the killers. Why would she want to spend time with people she'd considered family, who were in the process of turning their backs on her?

"Evie agreed that this was the right choice. No witch wants to be a member of a coven that no longer trusts her."

"Evie had nothing to do with what Caroline *chose* to do. She's a victim as much as anyone else. And you know damn well we had the chip in her neck removed, so she can't be tracked."

Gemma sighed. "And you know that whoever was

tracking her knows her coven is here, in Durham. Do you think she would want to put them at risk?"

I shook my head and turned toward the door. "I think she grew up in this coven thinking you were a family. And at the first test to that family, you threw her out. That's what I think."

I met Gail's eyes. Tears were rolling down her cheeks. I whirled away and stalked out the door.

Kyla sat up, her eyes bleary as I slid into the car. Those eyes sharpened as she moved her seat back upright.

"What happened?"

"I got the bone."

"Ew. But I mean, why are you so pissed?"

"Gemma threw Evie out of the coven."

"That bitch."

I glanced at her. "You don't sound surprised."

"I mean, I didn't spend much time with the witches, but from the little I did see, it seems true to form. They're insular, paranoid, and suspicious of outsiders."

"That means a lot coming from a werewolf."

She grinned at me. "Look, if there's one thing I've learned about your sister, it's that she'll come back stronger. Now can you please explain why the hell that bone smells so bad? It's all I can do not to snatch it and throw it out the window."

I pulled the pouch from my pocket and opened it, peering inside. I couldn't smell whatever Kyla was scenting, but I could feel the magic deep within the bone, thick and deadly.

"When a witch betrays her coven, they kill her."

Kyla nodded. "Yup."

"They then take her bones."

Kyla grimaced. "Of course they do. Because why wouldn't they?"

In spite of my mood, I couldn't help but laugh. "They then perform a spell on those bones. It ensures that they retain some of the witch's power."

"So there's a little bit of Caroline in that bone?"

"Not anything that made her who she is. Her… soul, or whatever, has gone wherever souls go, and I have a pretty good feeling I know where hers ended up."

Kyla nodded sagely. "I've got that same feeling."

"But the bones retain the witch's power—larger amounts for the larger bones. They're then used in spells to make the coven stronger. It's seen as a way to balance the betrayal—the death of the traitor, and the addition of her magic to bolster the coven as a whole."

"Makes sense, I guess. It's gross, but it makes sense."

I shrugged. "Now, unless there's something else the seelie king *forgot* to tell me, we should be good to go."

Did you hear that, Samael? I've got everything I need, and we're going to save you. Tonight.

I glanced at Kyla. "Let's head back to the cabin and make sure everyone else knows every step of the plan."

Her lips twitched. "And by that, you mean micromanage the hell out of everyone. I can get behind that."

As soon as we parked outside Nathaniel's, the Alpha stepped outside, as if he'd been waiting for us.

There was an expression I couldn't quite place on his face, and I mentally prepared for more bad news.

He stepped to the side, and there was my sister.

I shot out of the car, grinning at Evie. Her curly blonde hair looked longer, which was likely impossible. Huge blue-green eyes gleamed with tears as she flew down the path and threw herself into my arms.

"I'm sorry," she said, sobs wracking her body.

She was okay. A weight I hadn't realized I'd been holding was suddenly lifted off my shoulders. I eased back from her, gaping at her wet face. Evie wasn't a crier. Especially in public.

"What's going on?"

"I never should've left. I'm so sorry I wasn't here to help."

"Hey," Kyla remarked as she walked past. "You got here just in time for the best part."

Evie let out a tight laugh, and I shot Kyla a grateful look. She winked at me and wandered into Nathaniel's house, likely planning to find some coffee.

"Come with me," I told Evie.

I led her down the path to the cabin. We both stopped dead at the scene in the clearing. Bael and Vas were playing catch, Virtus between them. He leapt several feet into the air as we watched, snatching the ball out of the air. Then he jerked his head and threw the ball back at Vas.

Evie rubbed at her eyes. "Is that what I think it is?"

"It sure is. Long story. I want to hear all about you first."

She stepped into the cabin, striding straight to the bedroom. I frowned and then it hit me. She knew this cabin because she'd spent time here with Liam before the coven was murdered. That felt like years ago.

I forced myself to follow her, carefully keeping my

gaze away from the bed. Was I dealing with this situation in a healthy way? No. Did I have time to examine my emotions? Also no.

Evie took a deep breath as she stared at Samael.

"I didn't manage to find the dark fae guy. I had an address for him, but he recently moved. I did find a woman named Ainfean, who was his lover during that time period. She said his name is Eachann. His brother, Lorcan, disappeared one day with no warning. Apparently, he was skilled, powerful, and old enough that he had exceptional instincts. Most of his friends thought he'd met a woman and gotten a little distracted—the fae have different ideas about time than we do."

I nodded. When you were that long-lived, a few months probably felt like a few days. "I'm guessing that's not what happened."

Evie opened her mouth. Then she turned and walked out of the room. I gave her a few minutes, and then found her sitting on the sofa with her head in her hands.

"Ainfean had a picture of both brothers together," she mumbled into her hands as I sat down next to her.

I wrapped my arm around her shoulders, and she lifted her head. "I look like him. Lorcan. My father. Only a little, but I could see it in small things—the arch of our eyebrows. The shape of our earlobes."

I didn't know what to say. Evie seemed content to just get it all out, and she leaned back on the sofa, her eyes distant.

"Ainfean said Eachann blamed himself. Apparently it took him a while to realize Lorcan wasn't off with his hand up some woman's skirt. He said he should've known his brother was missing. Should've felt that he was in trouble. He left Ainfean and went looking for Lorcan."

I ran it over in my mind. "Somehow, Lorcan ended up on the radar of whoever was running that fucking lab."

Evie nodded. "They took him. And likely tortured him. Eachann disappeared as well, hunting for his brother. Ainfean said, at one point, Eachann thought Lorcan was in the Middleground. But she also met Mom."

My mouth dropped open. "I'm sorry, what?"

"I'm getting this all mixed up." Evie jolted to her feet and began to pace back and forth across the living room.

"After Mom realized Lucifer would be hunting you, she decided to find the Black Books. I guess she was desperate, Dani, and she'd probably heard that they were the only way to take down Lucifer.

"From what Ainfean said, Mom found one of the books. And she hid it here in Durham. Then she left you with someone she trusted and went looking for another one. But it was a trap."

I closed my eyes for a long moment. Of course it was. I tried to put myself in Mom's shoes. I'd been born when she was only nineteen, which meant she'd been in her early twenties when she'd been alone with a toddler to protect—a toddler the Underking wanted. So she'd decided she'd hunt for the books.

Of course, Samael had been collecting them for years. Mom hadn't stood a chance of beating him to them.

I took a deep breath and slowly blew it out, watching Evie as she paced. "So," I said slowly, "someone lured Mom into thinking she could get her hands on another book, and she ended up in the lab."

Evie nodded. "And in the lab, she must have met Lorcan. My… father. She told Ainfean that he was tortured so badly he was barely sane by the end of it, but he held onto enough of himself to help her plan an escape." Her eyes gleamed with tears, and I jumped to my feet, wrapping my arms around her.

"Oh, Evie."

She sniffed, her shoulders trembled, and she pulled away, refusing to break down. "According to Ainfean, Lorcan got Mom out. He tried to get in touch with Eachann, but he was in another realm, so he sent mom to Ainfean. And he stayed behind to try to break some of the others out. That's the last she ever heard of him."

Evie's face was so pale, she looked like she was about to pass out. I pulled her toward the sofa and pulled her down with me.

We both sat in silence for a long moment.

She turned and looked at me. "Do you remember anything from right before you turned three?"

I shrugged, wishing I did. Who had Mom left me with?

"Not really. My earliest memory is of mom telling me I had to share my toys with you." I gave her a pissy look and was rewarded with a hiccup that might have been distantly related to a laugh.

I'd take it.

"There's no record of you being anywhere near the lab. Mom gave you to someone to look after. Someone she must have trusted implicitly."

I frowned. "Harriette?"

"I don't think so. But I think Harriette knew who it

was, and that's why they killed her."

My stomach swam at the memory of Harriette's body. It hadn't been an easy death. No matter what I'd thought of the light fae woman, no one deserved to go out that way.

Unless…

"What are you thinking?" Evie asked.

"I'm thinking Mom trusted Harriette—maybe not with me, but with the original black book she found."

Evie's eyes widened and I shrugged. "Think about it. Every time I saw Harriette, she practically stunk of guilt. Especially the first few times I met her. She was powerful enough that she could probably have protected the book. Plus, she would've known exactly how valuable it was."

It hit me and I shot to my feet. "The attic."

"Huh?"

"I saw Mom."

Evie grabbed my arm. "What?"

"Long story. But I died for a few moments."

"You died?"

I waved that away. "She told me what I needed was in the attic. Oh, and she loves you."

Evie looked torn between laughing, crying, and scowling. It wasn't the most attractive expression she'd ever made. "You think the black book is in Harriette's attic? And it's been in Durham the whole time?"

I shrugged. "I think I want to check. We can't perform the counter spell until midnight, anyway. Are you coming with me?"

"You bet your ass."

CHAPTER TWENTY-THREE

Danica

I filled Evie in on everything Mom had said while I drove. Then I told her about the hunt for the sword.

She let out a low whistle. "I know you died, but is it weird that I'm a little jealous? I would've loved to see her. Did she look… angelic?"

I shrugged. "She looked normal. Honestly, it could've been a hallucination brought on by oxygen starvation."

"I guess we'll find out."

"Unless she *was* talking about the attic in the coven's house."

"If you really did talk to her, she must've known what happened to the coven."

"I guess." We were both silent as I drove toward Hope Valley. I glanced at Evie and cleared my throat. "I talked to Gemma."

"Oh?" Her voice was carefully neutral, and I explained my deal with Gemma, and the witch bone she'd given me.

She nodded, her face blank. I stopped at a traffic light on Hope Valley Road and narrowed my eyes at her.

"You didn't tell me she kicked you out of the coven."

Evie stiffened. "She didn't kick me out… she just suggested I leave."

I gave her a look, and she reached out, squeezing my arm. "Don't, Danica. It's for the best, really."

"In what realm could that possibly be the best?"

Someone laid on their horn behind me, and I accelerated through the intersection. A woman in a white Toyota ran the red and stuck her middle finger in the air as she passed us. I ignored her, turning right onto Dover Road as Evie sighed.

"You know I'm not fully a witch."

"So what?"

"Even though Caroline was ultimately responsible for killing so many of us, the fact remains that she wouldn't have been approached if they weren't looking for me. Gemma felt it would be a good idea for me to give the others some space. She said I was a constant reminder of what had happened and why."

Evie threw up her hands at my expression. "I agreed, Dani. I can't be around the others without being swamped with guilt. And I know it's something I need to work through, but for now… I just need you to support me."

I blew out a breath, forcing myself to let it go. "You know I will."

She didn't want to talk about it, so I'd give her some time. I parked outside the stately home of the woman who had been my mother's friend. We both eyed the ward.

Since Harriette had been high fae, there was an investigation into her murder. Mariam had refused to give me any information, and I had a pretty good feeling that was because the seelie didn't *have* any information. But someone powerful had created that ward, and they'd know the moment we broke it.

"We need to haul-ass," Evie said.

"Yup. You ready?"

She nodded, and we got out of the car, both of us stepping up to the ward, which shone silver. I sliced into my forearm with a throwing knife, and we both held up our hands at the same time, slapping them into the ward.

Even with both of us aiming our power at the ward, it fought back, and I instinctively knew it was alerting its owner that we were here. Three seconds later, the ward fell, and we sprinted for the front door.

The seelie had left it unlocked, obviously relying on the ward to keep out anyone who might be overly interested. I shook my head and pushed the door open, and we both carefully stepped inside, neither of us speaking as we crossed the entrance where we'd found her body.

We took the stairs at a run.

The attic was warded as well, but it was one of Harriette's wards, and her magic was no match for Evie's.

Sunlight poured in from skylights on either side of the triangular ceiling, highlighting the dust motes floating through the air. Evie let out a cough behind me, and I nodded.

"No one has been up here for a while. You go through those boxes. I'm going to check this chest."

I reached into my utility belt and pulled out my lock picks, getting to work on the padlock which held the chest tightly closed. Sweat dripped down the back of my neck as the seconds ticked by, each of them bringing the seelie who'd warded the house closer.

I popped the lock open and pulled it free, letting out a grunt as I hauled the lid of the chest up. Old blankets, towels, moth-eaten sheets, a gown made of lace so delicate, I held my breath as I gently handled it… but no grimoire.

There was another smaller chest nearby, but all it held was old photo albums and an antique jewelry box which had been carefully wrapped in bubble wrap.

I glanced at Evie. She'd pulled every book out of the boxes and stacked them in piles around her. Nothing.

We both got to our feet, and I surveyed the attic. Panic warred with disappointment in my gut.

"You've seen the books before, right?" Evie asked.

"Yeah." I stepped toward the window and peered down. The street was empty, but I could *feel* the seelie who created the ward, and I knew without a doubt that they were on their way.

"Close your eyes."

I frowned over my shoulder at Evie and she gave me a look. "I'm serious."

I sighed, but did as she asked. "Good. Now picture the books you saw. You must've felt their power—or at least a hint of it. Drop your shields and see if you can feel something similar."

I opened one eye. "Where did you learn—never mind." I closed my eyes again and rolled my shoulders.

I'd seen the grimoires a few times. One was when the McCormick descendants had attempted to kill Samael and take his power. I focused on it, but my body went straight into fight-or-flight mode at the memory. My hands fisted and I blew out a breath.

Gloria had used a spell from one of the black books when she interrogated Cassie. But the thought of Gloria made my gut twist with rage, so that was out.

I focused on the last black book I'd seen—the one Bel had handed me. I channeled the feel of it, the power which had bitten at me.

Frustration made my neck muscles tighten. "I'm not getting anything."

"Keep trying. You've got this."

I took a deep breath. I'd seen Samael reading a grimoire once. I'd woken in his bed and found him sitting next to me, the black book in his lap. He'd used his power to send me to sleep that day, and I'd been furious. Not furious in the same way I was when I thought of Gloria, though. No, this had been a fury tinged with frustration, because I wanted the demon so badly, and he'd once again overridden my choices.

And after I'd bitterly told him exactly how much it made me *loathe* him, he'd shown me the memory of his family's slaughter. He'd bared a piece of his soul, and I'd understood him a little more. All he'd ever wanted was to keep me safe.

My eyes filled with tears, but I embraced the pain, taking my mind back to the feeling of waking up in his bed with the demon watching over me. I'd woken angry, but beneath it, I'd wondered what would happen if Samael had lain down next to me. Had dropped the book from his lap and…

I focused on the book. He'd had it open on the first page, but I'd known even then that he hadn't been reading.

No, he'd been watching me. Likely preparing himself for my hostile words.

"I can feel it," I said, and my eyes popped open. As soon as I let the memory go, I could no longer feel one of the books with us, though. I slammed my eyes closed and pulled up the memory again, focusing on the hint of power I'd felt even though I'd been lying several feet from the book.

With my eyes closed, I pointed. Evie's steps sounded on the wooden floor, and then she sighed. "You're pointing at the wall, Dani."

"It's there. I know it is." And the more I talked, the less I sensed the book. I ground my teeth and focused again.

Then I slowly began to walk toward where I could feel the book. Evie grabbed my arm, steering me around the boxes on the floor. I ran my hands over the smooth wall. Then I paused. "It's right here."

I opened my eyes. Evie glanced between me and the wall. "I believe you." She contemplated the wall some more. Then she took a deep breath and lifted one hand. Gold light shot from her hand like a blast of water from a firehose, cutting into the wall. Her jaw clenched at the effort as she directed the light until she'd cut out a hole large enough for me to reach in and grab the book.

"Samael's going to lose his mind when he finds out this has been in Durham the whole time."

Evie shot me a grin. "Let's go."

We ran back down the stairs and through the ward. It felt like pushing through glue—a clear sign that whoever created it was close.

But not close enough. We climbed into the car, and I

passed Evie the grimoire. "Can you keep this safe?"

She nodded, lifting her hand to finger wave at the fae who appeared on the street in front of us. She shoved the book down the side of the seat and wound down her window.

"Can we help you?"

The seelie stared at us with narrowed eyes the color of sapphires. "State your business."

"Just out for a drive. You're going to want to get out of our way before the demons arrive, though."

The seelie glanced at me, recognition tightening the muscles in his cheeks. He knew we were up to no good, but he also didn't want to piss off the demons. He stepped aside, stalking toward the house. I had no doubt that he'd find the mess we'd left in the attic, including the hole in the wall, but by then we'd be long gone.

Tension made my muscles ache, and I let out a long, slow breath as we finally left Hope Valley.

"I wish Harriette were alive." Evie's expression was pure wrath, and it was obvious she mostly wanted her alive so she could interrogate her. Right now, I was feeling the same.

But the sun was going down, which meant it was time to make the final preparations for the counter spell that was Samael's only hope. Evie seemed to realize where my thoughts had gone, because she reached out and squeezed my hand where it was clenched around the steering wheel. "We'll figure this all out later," she said. "Now it's time to save your demon."

"I'm glad you're here."

"I am too."

CHAPTER TWENTY-FOUR

Danica

Time crawled.

I paced, wrung my hands, checked in with every single person who would be part of the plan—multiple times—and generally made a nuisance of myself. By the time we needed to leave, I was ready to crawl out of my own skin.

The atmosphere was grim as the demons strode into Samael's room and picked up the mattress, carrying it out through the open sliding doors.

Sathanas refused to look at me. I had a feeling he blamed me for Samael's current condition. But he'd shown up.

Asmodeus nodded at me, then quickly glanced away. We all knew this was our one shot. I was banking everything on this.

My eyes met Bael's, and he gave me a reassuring nod as he stepped out of the cabin, holding his corner of the mattress steady.

"You've got this," he told me. I took a deep breath and attempted a smile. Vas stepped up next to me.

"You ready?"

He had me in the air a moment later. Azazyel was carrying Evie, who had her eyes squeezed tight. Kyla and the wolves would meet us there.

I pretended not to see the ash that drifted from the mattress, dispersed by the breeze. It was as if Samael had already been cremated and we were all attempting to hold him together by sheer willpower.

Several demons entered the portal first, scouting the conditions on the other side before the group carrying Samael's mattress followed them.

Vas and I left them waiting near the portal and kept flying, until Vas slowly lowered us to the ground outside Scylla's cave. I could feel the tension in Vas's body, and he eyed the cave as if expecting the dragons to fry us to a crisp.

"You're sure Scylla will help with this?" Vas kept his arms around me, ready to launch into the air at a moment's notice. I wiggled until he reluctantly released me, eyes narrowed on the cave's entrance.

"Yes. I'm pretty sure she understands that she'll die, too, if Samael doesn't make it. And she won't want to leave Nuri alone."

I let my voice carry—a nice little reminder for Scylla that she needed to cooperate.

I didn't need to enter the cave. A shadow darkened the ground in front of us as she stuck her head out, the sun dancing off indigo scales.

She stared at me for one long moment.

"He's by the portal," I said. I nodded to Vas, and he

gathered me in his arms once more, rising into the air.

Scylla walked out of the cave. Nuri let out a shriek but from the look Scylla shot her daughter, she wasn't invited to this little party.

I couldn't blame her.

The portal came into view below us. Vas landed, and I surveyed the crowd. Kyla moseyed over to me, casting a suspicious look at the dragon as she landed.

Keigan stood next to Meredith, who brushed shoulders with Aubrey. My mouth dropped open as I spotted the unseelie Vas had chosen.

"Finvarra?" I muttered, and Kyla stiffened next to me.

Vas merely shrugged. "I went to him and asked him to send a representative to help, mentioning the alliance he signed. He said he had a few words to say to Samael when he awoke, and he may as well be part of this foolishness."

I nodded at Finvarra. "Your Majesty."

He sent me a sharp smile back. "It's a little too late for that, don't you think?" His gaze lingered on Kyla, and then he scrutinized the rest of my band of misfits. "I believe we are ready."

Evie stepped forward and smiled at Mere. "Do you mind if I take over? Samael's basically my brother-in-law."

Mere grinned back. "Of course."

I laid the artifact on the mattress next to Samael. Then I took a deep breath.

"I need everyone who is standing for their factions to cut their right palm and allow three drops of blood to fall onto Samael."

Nathaniel went first. I could see why he was an Alpha. Throughout this entire experience, he'd never once exuded anything other than calm confidence. Except, of course, when he happened to glance at my sister.

Evie was up next, followed by Keigan. He refused to look at me and I swallowed, my mouth dry, but I pushed the pain down. He didn't have to like me, as long as he helped me save Samael's life.

Aubrey smiled at me. The smile was sad in a way that told me he wasn't expecting this to work. That was fine. I had enough hope for all of us. He squeezed the cut over his palm and stepped aside for Finvarra.

The king nodded at me, slicing deep into his hand. He healed so quickly that he had to cut himself open twice more before three drops had fallen onto the husk of Samael's body.

I turned to Scylla. "I need some blood," I said.

She must have cut her mouth with one of her teeth, because she leaned over the mattress and dripped blood onto Samael.

"Thank you."

I went last.

"Please Samael," I whispered. "Fight for us."

I'd made sure everyone had the words to the spell. I nodded, and we began to chant.

The wind picked up, throwing my hair around my face. Our voices simply rose louder. I clutched at Kyla and Evie's hands, and even those who weren't here to represent their factions… their voices joined ours, rising louder and louder.

The air was charged, as if lightning was about to

strike in this exact spot.

Tears burned the back of my eyes. All of these people, representing every faction, all of them fighting for Samael's life.

Please. I begged whoever was listening. *Please.*

I'd asked everyone to think of Samael as they'd last seen him before this, strong and whole. And I did the same. I pictured him, burning with wrath as he found me, broken and chained by that portal.

His fury had been glorious, but the look in his eyes when he'd realized what was happening to him… it was pure, unwavering love.

At least we'd had that. If this didn't work… at least we'd both had that.

Lightning struck and I jumped. Evie's hand tightened around mine and she gathered her power, pouring more into the spell. I did the same, for once allowing my power to take over, to roar through me.

Thunder rumbled, although the day was still clear and sunny. Pain ripped into me, and I fell to my knees, conscious of everyone else doing the same. Gasps and screams sounded, but were quickly cut off as the chanting continued.

The pain shifted to agony, which crawled up my spine. Black dots danced in front of my eyes. I was on the edge of flaming out, and if that happened, I wouldn't be able to help.

Something shifted. The wind died down. The thunder ended. The world grew still, the quiet broken only by our voices.

Evie's hand tightened around mine to the point of

pain, and I glanced at her. She'd given herself a nosebleed, but her gaze was fixed to the mattress, eyes wide and stunned.

Ash was drifting toward the mattress. It came slowly at first, just a little at a time, and then it was carried through a new breeze, a gentle breeze, which came from all directions.

A sob left my throat, but I managed to keep chanting. It was working. The ground trembled beneath my feet, but I barely noticed as Samael's body slowly rebuilt, the rest of his torso first, followed by his ears, then his arms and legs. Within a few moments he was whole.

But he was still ash.

The chanting quieted. "Why isn't it working?"

A voice came behind us, and everyone tensed. All these parnanormals and none of us had heard her approaching.

"You were to include *all* factions, halfling. You forgot the black witch."

Of course. How could I have been so stupid?

Hannah hobbled toward us, glowering at me. "My invitation must have been lost in the mail."

Sitri grinned at me from behind her, his pretty face glowing with good humor. "She showed up at the edge of werewolf territory. Insisted I fly her here."

"Enough chatter," Hannah snapped. "Chant!"

I launched back into the chant, and voices slowly joined me as Hannah walked toward the mattress. She cut her hand, allowing the three drops to fall on Samael. Why wasn't I surprised that she knew exactly how the counter spell worked?

Her voice joined ours as she took a step back, and a golden glow streamed from Samael's body.

The glow shone brighter, brighter, brighter, until I had to slam my eyes closed or be blinded. And then the glow disappeared.

I opened my eyes, and they met exultant silver.

"Hello, little witch."

At the sound of his voice, every ounce of the stubborn willpower, the false confidence, the sheer *grit*… it all drained away until I had nothing left.

Nothing but exhausted hope that this wasn't a dream. That I'd done it.

That he was alive.

I let out a sound, somewhere between a whimper and a sob, and Evie and Kyla each grabbed my arms, holding onto me. I ignored the relieved laughter surrounding me as I ugly cried.

And then he was there, holding me tight, his arms wrapped around me like he'd never let me go.

"Am I dreaming?" I managed to croak out, and Samael drew back far enough that he could smile down at me, but his eyes were serious.

"You were so brave," he murmured, dropping kisses over every inch of my face. "You saved us both, Danica."

Danica

Things wrapped up quickly after that. Samael greeted everyone there, thanking each one personally. He'd refused to let me go, which I was just fine with, basking in the feel of his arm clamped around me.

Vas leaned close. "I've arranged for a new mattress for Samael's bed in his penthouse. I figured you guys would need it." He gave me a lewd wink, but the relief was obvious on his face.

"Thanks. Can you make sure Lia gets back to the apartment?"

"I'll have to fight Bael for that little task. Consider it done."

Hannah stepped up next to me and I turned to her. "There aren't enough words–"

She snorted. "I didn't do it for you, girl, I did it for myself. If Samael dies, the mages will immediately turn their attention to the black witches."

I grinned. "Uh-huh. Well, I'm glad you're so self-serving."

Her mouth trembled with a hint of a smile, and then she turned to Sitri. "Well? What are you waiting for? I have things to do."

She nodded at Samael, who nodded back, and then she was gone.

I socialized for as long as I could, drinking in the relief and elation. But my muscles began to ache, a steady tremble warning me that I'd pushed my body as far as it could go.

Samael's arm tightened around me. "To bed, I think."

I groaned as everyone started up with wolf whistles and lewd comments, and Vas sent me another filthy wink. Samael grinned at me, and then we were shooting into the sky, faster than he'd ever flown.

"Is it just me or are you–?"

"Stronger than I've been for some time? Yes. And I have plans…" he laughed, and I forced my eyes open, unaware I'd closed them.

His expression was tender. "Close your eyes, witchling. Rest."

I nuzzled into him, burying my face in his neck. His arms tightened around me, and I breathed him in as we flew home.

Samael

Danica did it. When others told her to move on, that there was no hope, she ignored them and traveled the realms to save my life.

If I hadn't been sickeningly in love with her before this, I would have lost my heart to her the moment I saw her exhausted face and understood—truly understood—what she'd been through without me.

She would never be without me again.

I watched her, the color slowly returning to her pale cheeks as she shoved pasta into her mouth. "You've lost a few pounds."

"Yeah." She shrugged, clearly unconcerned. Most of the women I'd known would worry about becoming too thin, or maybe celebrate the accidental weight loss and vow to keep it off. Danica took another huge bite, and I had a feeling she'd be training again tomorrow, ensuring her body was fit and strong for whatever she would go up against next.

She raised her champagne. "I better not drink too much of this or I'll be too boozed to roll around naked with you. But here's to you and your fine ass, and the fact that we're both alive."

I couldn't help but laugh. "From the sound of you, you're a little impaired already."

She shrugged and took a large gulp, sending me a flirtatious wink.

And something stronger than grief, deeper than shock, burrowed deep in my gut.

I'd gone centuries feeling like something was missing, and that something was *her*. Danica. My little witch. I'd been waiting my whole life for her to be born, without even knowing it, and if not for her search for her mother's killer, I might never have met her.

"You're so tired," I said. She smiled, but I could see the dark circles beneath glassy eyes, the pale skin that spoke of too much stress and not enough sleep. And yet she glowed with satisfaction of a job well done. With relief, and with love.

My witchling. My bondmate.

"The nap helped. And if you'd told me a few days ago that I'd fall asleep while flying between realms, I would've called you a dirty liar."

She was too far away. I'd forced my hands to open, forced myself to let her go when we arrived, knowing she needed to eat. But I was almost shaking with the effort it took to hold myself back.

Danica's smile dropped as she studied me. She dropped her fork and got to her feet.

"Come here."

My mouth twitched. No one had ordered me to do anything before this woman. No one would have even dared.

I cleared my throat. "You need to eat."

She gave me a look and then turned, stripping off her t-shirt.

"I'm taking a bath. You're welcome to join me. Or not. But in a few moments, I'm going to be hot and wet and–"

She squealed as I launched myself at her, and I knew, just as no one else would dare order me to do anything, she would never allow anyone else to hear her make that exact sound.

Her laughter was the best thing I'd ever heard as she bolted for the bathroom. I followed her, arriving just in time to find her bent over and struggling out of her jeans.

"Now that's a view I've been waiting for."

She cast me a look over her shoulder and I took a mental snapshot. I wanted to remember this moment for the rest of our lives.

The tub was already filling with hot, scented water, and I stripped off my clothes. A handful of ash dropped from them, and she bit down on her lower lip.

I caught her chin in my hand. "I'll never allow such a thing to happen again."

She gave me a look. "You didn't know it was going to happen this time."

"And now I know how few people can be trusted." I burned to tear Gloria apart with my power, but from the vengeance in Danica's eyes, she would prefer to have that pleasure.

"I'm sorry, Samael. I should have known–"

I laughed at her. As I'd hoped, it pissed her off. Her eyes narrowed, her nose wrinkled, and she attempted to jerk free of my hold. I shook my head, keeping her chin firmly caught.

"I hadn't realized you were a seer," I mused, and she scowled. I released her, my point made, and used my claw to cut through her underwear. Her panties fell to the ground and then I lifted her, stepping into the huge tub and placing her on my lap so I could keep her close.

"Show me," she demanded, and I revealed my waterlogged wings. She marveled at them, stroking the feathers lightly.

We were both silent for a long moment. I'd missed this. Just touching her, having her close. Knowing that she was right *there*.

"What's wrong?" I knew her moods better than my own. She shook her head lightly, as if shaking off something unpleasant.

"Nothing."

I merely raised one eyebrow and waited her out. She poked me in the stomach, her hand immediately giving my abs one long stroke.

I caught her hand before she could distract me. "You will tell me."

Annoyance flared in her eyes, immediately followed by amusement. "You're just trying to piss me off now."

I grinned at her. "It's remarkably easy. Tell me, little witch."

She blew out a breath, then wrapped her arms around

my neck. Her breasts were almost at my mouth level, the perfect place for me to–

I glowered at her.

She let out a low laugh. "Fine. Look, it's not a huge deal, but the Dearg Due… she took a memory from me. A memory of us. Something important. I can feel the hole, like a missing tooth. And I want it back, Samael."

Fury clawed through me, but I kept my voice even. Danica didn't need my anger. She needed solutions.

"Do you know which memory?"

She shook her head, and I tucked her hair behind one delicate ear. I couldn't resist pressing a kiss to the shell of that ear, and she shivered.

"Then I will just have to share my favorite memories with you until we find which one she took."

She smiled, and I wanted to be responsible for that expression every day for the rest of my life.

"Well then," she said, "In the meantime, we should get to creating some new, very dirty memories." Her grin turned wicked, and she clamped her hand around me, until all of the blood seemed to rush from my head.

We'd been together in dreams, of course, but nothing compared to actually having her in my arms, to feeling her soft skin, to knowing she was *safe* and I was now here to protect her.

"If you're thinking that hard, I'm obviously not doing a good enough job distracting you," my little witch murmured. She moved her hand, leaned close, and nuzzled my neck, before biting down in a way that made me curse, my hips lifting and thrusting into her hand of my own accord.

A low laugh.

I opened my eyes to find her looking extremely pleased with herself.

Time for the tables to turn. Since her breasts were still at mouth level, I took full advantage, lowering my head and kissing every inch of them, carefully avoiding her nipples, which had already hardened enticingly.

"Tease," Danica growled, and I laughed. She shivered as my breath caressed her damp skin, so I blew against her, groaning as she shivered in pleasure.

I wanted to take my time with her. Wanted to inhale her. Wanted to cut myself open and tuck her under my skin where I could keep her safe. Knowing she was risking her life to save mine had driven me slowly crazy, and now I was barely teetering on the edge of self-control.

And I was relatively sure she'd be concerned about the direction my thoughts were taking if she knew what I was thinking.

"You have your psycho face on," she said.

Obviously, she'd determined the direction of my thoughts herself.

I nipped at her chin, and she laughed, batting me away.

I reached for the scented soap and ran it over her arms, shoulders, and finally, her breasts. She shivered as I replaced it with my hands, caressing every inch of her.

Her soft moans drove me on, until I couldn't take it any longer. I lifted her from the tub, grabbing a thick, fluffy towel so I could pat her dry.

That lasted for approximately three seconds, and then I was pushing her against the door, holding her in place for my kiss.

I couldn't get enough of the feel of her, the taste of her, the knowledge that she was alive. I'd *never* get enough of her, and I'd accepted that the witch I'd bound to me, out of ego and retaliation, had become more necessary to me than oxygen.

I thrust my tongue into her mouth, growling against her lips as she gave as good as she got. She pushed her body against mine, writhing in the way that made my mind go blank.

I tore my lips from hers to make my way down her neck, kissing, biting, driven wild by her desperate moans.

I lifted her into my arms once more, pulling the door open and stalking toward my bedroom. She let out a low laugh and licked at a spot beneath my ear, her nails scratching at my back.

Then she was moving in my arms, positioning my cock at her entrance.

She laughed some more as I almost stumbled.

That was it.

We weren't making it to the bedroom. I pushed her against the nearest wall, sliding my thumb down to her clit. The noise she made almost made me come right there. Her hips twisted as she ground against my hand, and I angled her where I needed her and slowly pushed inside her, inch by inch. She panted, eyes closed as she tightened her legs around my hips.

"Look at me."

Her eyes slid open to slits, emerald green and burning with lust. I pulled back and thrust deeper, fisting my hand in her hair and holding her still for me as I took her mouth.

"More," she demanded. So I stopped holding back, driving deep as I flicked her clit, enjoying the way she tightened around me. The way her eyes grew blurry, and her mouth dropped open as a low moan spilled from her.

Her breath caught, and she trembled against me, tightening around me until I had no choice but to follow her over as pleasure engulfed us both.

CHAPTER TWENTY-FIVE

Danica

I woke to something cool wrapping around my wrist. My eyes cracked open, and I stared into Samael's amused eyes.

"Caught," he murmured ruefully.

I glanced down at the bracelet encircling my wrist. The stones shone with an internal fire, the unworldly sparkle putting diamonds to shame.

The bracelet was once Samael's mother's. It had been her favorite, and I'd found a human attempting to sell it at an illegal auction.

I'd stolen it back, and now Samael was stroking my wrist, gaze admiring as he watched the stones glitter.

"This was your mom's."

"I know."

"I can't take this, Samael."

He merely dropped a kiss to my lips. "You will."

He said it as if the subject were closed, and I merely raised one eyebrow. I knew him well enough by now to know he'd planned for me to get in a snit at his order, distracted enough that I'd end up forgetting about the bracelet entirely.

"It belongs somewhere safe."

"I won't have it locked up, out of sight. Seeing it reminds me of my mother, and seeing it wrapped around your wrist reminds me that you're mine."

I didn't bother arguing with that. I *was* his, and we both knew it. Just as he was mine.

"It's too precious. I can't wear it every day."

He nodded. "So wear it on special occasions. And when you're not working."

He wasn't budging. Despite myself, I stroked the bracelet, marveling at its beauty. Samael smiled. He knew he had me.

I hooked my legs around his waist and rolled us, pleased by his surprised laugh. It warmed something deep within me to hear him relaxed enough to laugh and play. When I first met the cold, remote demon, I hadn't imagined he *could* laugh, unless he was enjoying someone's torture.

"Now it's your turn to do something for me," I purred.

His eyes lit up, his hand sliding down to find me already wet for him.

"Oh, little witch, I'd be happy to."

I shook my head. "I want you to feed from me."

His eyes widened slightly. I'd told him I wanted to feed him before, and he'd argued that he wanted to wait until I was absolutely sure.

I was more than sure.

"The spell you performed restored me to full strength.

I won't need to feed for several weeks."

I grinned. "Are you telling me you never snack between meals?"

Interest flared in his eyes. "Are you sure about this?"

I was more than sure. "I thought about it when you were lying in that bed, slowly turning to ash. I wished I'd had the chance to do this with you, just once."

His eyes glittered, and then we were rolling once more, my demon positioned above me. "This won't be a just-once kind of thing, witchling. I have a feeling that once I feed from you, I'll never wish to feed from anyone else again."

"Good." Pure possessiveness roared through me. I blinked at the feral edge that felt sharp enough to cut.

"Ah," Samael murmured. "Your demon half is coming out to play. This will be… interesting."

He caressed my clit, the movement entirely possessive. I sighed as pleasure made my body tighten, and then he was moving down, kissing and licking his way down to my thighs, before pushing them open.

I watched him, entranced at the sight of him as he paused—just long enough to send me a wicked grin—and then gave me a single lick that made every muscle in my body tense.

He groaned against me and then he was holding me down, circling my clit, using his tongue and his mouth and the edge of his teeth. I writhed, aching to get closer, and he pushed one finger inside me while he sucked…

I reared off the bed, shuddering with my climax, and then he was above me, pushing inside me, his silver eyes wild.

I moaned at the feel of him, so deep within me. I closed my eyes, and he caught my chin. I knew what he wanted, so I opened them again, watching him watch me.

Coming that close to death, and being forced to allow me to take care of the whole situation, had made the control freak demon even more domineering than usual. I'd give him a little leeway for now, since he was also doing that thing with his hips that drove me–

"Oh God."

He grinned down at me. But it was a strained grin, his hips slapping against mine as he drove deeper. I gasped, and he leaned down to press an achingly gentle kiss to my cheek, so at odds with the way he was plowing into me.

"Are you ready?" he murmured.

"Yes."

His eyes began to *glow*, and, as I stared up at him, something ancient and alien stared back. For a fraction of a second, true fear slammed into me, but in the next moment he lowered his mouth to mine, and my entire body began to tingle.

"Is this it?" I murmured against his mouth, almost disappointed.

His low, amused laugh was my only response, and the tingle kicked up a notch as he drove into me, caressing my g-spot with each thrust. I let out a whimper of such *want* that it would've embarrassed me if my body hadn't chosen that moment to spontaneously combust.

Fireworks behind my eyes. Ringing in my ears. The taste of sunshine on my tongue. I was transported somewhere *else* for the briefest of moments and then I slammed back into my body, pleasure ripping through me—and through our bond.

I could practically see it in my mind, lit up like a shooting star, and I felt him, at the other end, hopelessly in love with me in a way he'd never anticipated.

The tingling sharpened along my skin, turning into tiny bursts of pleasure that made my eyes roll back.

Samael deepened our kiss, pounding into me as release swept along my every nerve ending, deeper than anything I'd felt before.

"We're not done," he breathed against me, and I opened my eyes, gaping at him.

He was still thick and hard inside me, and I was limp, worn out with pleasure.

He flipped me over, thrusting back inside me in a way that made me clench around him. I lifted one hand from where I'd buried it in the pillow and waved it lazily in the air.

"I guess I'll just lie here and take it."

Teeth scraped my neck, and I shivered, a laugh bubbling from my chest. He slowly pulled out, then plunged back in, lifting my hips to hit the spot that made me gasp.

He slid his hand beneath my hips, sliding down to the wet heat of me, and I climaxed, a shocked groan ripped from my throat.

His arms tightened around me as he thrust a few more times, then gasped my name against the side of my neck as he pulled me even closer.

I collapsed onto my stomach. He followed, lying next to me, one hand lazily trailing up and down my spine.

"Don't even think about it," I warned him. "You

wore me out."

"I'm sure, over the next several centuries, we can work on your stamina."

I lifted my head, just enough to give him a filthy look, and he pulled me into his arms. "You were delicious."

"I meant what I said. No feeding from anyone else." The thought made me want to get violent.

"Deal."

I nuzzled into him, exhausted again. Tomorrow, we'd get back to work. We'd plan our revenge, put together our strategy to finally kill Lucifer. But for tonight, all I wanted was to fall asleep here, in his arms.

Samael kissed my forehead. "Go back to sleep, little witch."

I yawned and closed my eyes, something that felt a lot like contentment radiating back at me from the other end of our bond.

Samael

We slept on and off all day, until I reluctantly pulled myself from my bed the next morning, moving slowly and quietly enough that I hoped Danica would continue sleeping.

There was work to do, and then I planned to wake Danica myself, indulge in a late dinner, and fly with her over our city. For now, I wanted her to rest.

She wouldn't be pleased if she learned I was concerned for her health. But a few days of sleep and food and she'd be back to her usual self.

I showered in one of the guest bathrooms, well aware that, if Danica woke, I'd be unable to resist dragging her under the warm water with me.

My mind was still in bed with Danica while I shook out a small portion of food for the cat. Vas had fed her when he dropped her off, but if I ensured she had a full belly, she wouldn't wake Danica up with her yowling. Lia wound her way around my legs in a way that made it clear that *I* was her favorite, regardless of what Bael and Vas liked to think.

By the time I got downstairs to the main conference room, Ag had gathered everyone I needed, including my inner circle and the demons who remained bonded to me.

Everyone went silent as I walked in.

And then, as one, they dropped to one knee, bowing their heads.

"Rise," I said. "We have much to talk about."

Awareness tickled at my mind, and I turned. Danica stood in the doorway. She was dressed in jeans and a sweater, a sleep crease on one cheek and a scowl on her face. She carried a canvas bag, and she'd armed herself with her blades.

She'd never looked more beautiful.

"Is there a reason you decided to hold this meeting without me?" Her voice was cold, but I caught the tiniest spark of hurt down the bond.

I was standing in front of her before I realized I'd moved.

"I hoped you'd get more sleep." I told her. *"I had planned on filling you in…"*

Her scowl deepened. *"I don't need more sleep, Samael. I need a seat at the table. I kept this shit running while you were taking your little nap, and don't you forget it."*

She stalked past me, striding toward the table with a nod at the demons gathered and waiting.

I caught Ag's mouth twitch and barely suppressed my own smile. I'd never imagined that I would have a queen who would rule beside me, who would be more than just a sounding board to my problems and strategies.

Elation speared through me, until I thought my heart would burst with it. I barely resisted the urge to haul my little witch into my arms and carry her back to our rooms, where I would demonstrate my appreciation.

She glanced over her shoulder at me, and from the amusement in her eyes, she could feel the emotions roaring through me.

Danica took my seat, and, across the table, Lilith winked at her. I stepped behind my witchling and pressed a kiss to her hair, inhaling the sweet scent.

"I apologize."

"Forgiven."

I placed my hand briefly on her shoulder and then surveyed the room, addressing my people.

"It's difficult for me to truly explain what it was like, knowing I was separated from you all. But even in my darkest moments, I knew I could trust each and every one of you. I knew you would pull together to do what you could for me, but most importantly, you would protect the woman who gave my life meaning."

I felt Danica's shoulder hunch beneath my hand, and

I squeezed her lightly. "I'm in awe of the way this family guarded our territory and worked together to bring me back from the brink of death. Thank you all. Now, I would like to know what has happened in my absence."

Some of it I knew, but the more my people talked, the more they seemed to relax, until the previous formality left the room.

"We're now allied with the wolves," Vas said, and a quick glance told me that not everyone was happy with that decision.

Danica tensed beneath my hand, and I noted the faces of those who didn't agree with the choice.

"Having the wolves willing to fight with us is a good thing," I said.

Bael nodded. "I've never known a wolf to back down from a fight," he said, and several demons grinned, a few of them reluctantly.

"Not to mention the griffin," Sitri mused, taking a sip of coffee. "Aren't they meant to be good luck?"

Danica murmured something that sounded like 'pain in my ass,' and I suppressed a smile.

Bel waited until the table went silent once more, and then he reached beneath his seat and placed a grimoire on the table.

"Found it," he said. "We now have eight of them."

Danica had told me, of course, but I rounded the table and slapped him on the shoulder. "Good work. While we will plan our attack based on the assumption that we won't have time to find the last of the black books–"

"Ahem."

A delicate female cough sounded. I glanced at Lilith,

but she was smirking at Danica, the look on her face telling me she found her exceptionally entertaining today. My little witch colored slightly as all eyes landed on her, and then she reached into her canvas bag and laid another book on the table.

"Turns out we have all nine of them," she said.

The room exploded into sound. Bael jolted to his feet, his mouth dropped open, and he rounded the table, pulling Danica out of her seat. He dropped a kiss onto her forehead, and I tamped down the possessive instinct that told me to hurt him, choosing to focus on the joy that swept through the room.

"It was right under your noses," Danica said, sending me a smug look. "Harriette had it the whole time."

The seelie woman who'd placed the suppression spell. I wished I could bring her back to life just so I could kill her once more. From the agreement on my witchling's face, she felt the same way.

"Just wait until you hear the rest of it," she told me. *"But for now, I need to go meet Kyla,"* she said.

I scowled. "You need to rest."

As expected, Danica ignored that. *"Cellen will be returning for Angelica's ring, and then I'm all yours. Wrap up your business and I'll meet you after we're both free."*

I had to tamp down all of my instincts in order to let Danica out of my sight. I had no doubt she could feel the dark possessiveness taking hold of me, but she chose not to comment as she pressed a kiss to my chin and sailed out of the room. Bael took one look at my face and grinned.

"You look like Danica's cat when she smells another

creature on her," he mused.

I shot him a look. "If there's nothing else, I have a meeting," I said to the room at large. "Of course, I'm available for any questions or concerns, but I want everyone to take some downtime. Work out a schedule that allows for some rest."

CHAPTER TWENTY-SIX

Danica

I met Kyla at my office. She'd said she had something to talk to me about, and I arched one eyebrow as I took in her jeans, which were covered in white fur. "Been hanging with the griffin, have you?"

"He's peaceful to be around," she said defensively.

"Hey, I'm not judging. You two were pretty cute together, all curled up and sleeping."

She narrowed her eyes at me, and I chuckled, pleased to have gotten the reaction I was hoping for. A girl had to get her kicks where she could find them.

I unlocked the door and stepped into my office. Next to me, Kyla let out a low whistle.

"What the hell?" I glanced at Kyla. From the pleased look on her face, she'd been in on this.

The office was immaculate. No boxes, no files, and no dust. Instead, it had been fully furnished.

The walls had been painted a cool gray, so light it was almost white. Tasteful paintings hung on those walls, along with a framed newspaper cutout which detailed how I'd solved the case involving the human hate group who had been killing demons.

A small gray couch occupied the spot next to the door. It looked like the kind of couch you'd sink into for a few hours with a good book. On the coffee table in front of the couch, there were a few magazines and a copy of the most recent Durham Denizens. It was a space that would function as both a waiting area and a spot to take a break during the workday.

One corner held a plant, which I was guaranteed to kill, but there was a small chance Kyla had a green thumb.

Past the plant, a desk waited, large and majestic. Probably too large for the space, but I didn't care. Tears filled my eyes.

Only one person had been there when I'd admired that desk. Evie had convinced me to go shopping with her weeks ago, before Keigan had given me this office. She'd obviously taken note as I stroked my hand across the top of it, longing for it in a way I rarely longed for any material things.

I still didn't know what kind of wood it was, only that it was so dark it was almost black. I hadn't tormented myself enough to check the price tag, because I'd known damn well that it was hideously expensive.

My sister had bought it anyway. My sister, who'd only ever worked part-time jobs, because the spell tying her to her home had swallowed up any ambition for more.

The lump in my throat felt like it might choke me as I stared at the desk, and I forced myself to move on to the comfortable, supportive-looking chair behind it, and the guest chair where clients would describe their problems and needs.

A rug covered most of the floor in subtle whites and greys, picking up the color from the walls but not being too flashy about it. If there was one thing Evie had always had, it was taste.

My chest clenched as my gaze found the smaller desk across the room, a brand-new laptop sitting on it, ready to go. For Kyla.

The wolf was staring at it, eyes wide. Obviously, she hadn't known about that little part of the surprise. My chest tightened. Evie had somehow known how much this would mean to Kyla, how much she loved being a part of something. And she'd given Kyla a space that represented just how important she was to my business.

When the hell had Evie found the time? She'd just returned.

I grinned at the picture on the desk. It was the two of us at Meredith's. Evie had insisted on the selfie a few weeks before the coven had been murdered.

Kyla turned toward the small kitchenette on the other side of the office. "You can come out now, Evie."

My sister strolled out, looking mighty pleased with herself. I launched myself at her, and she laughed as I wrapped my arms around her and rocked.

"You didn't have to do this."

"I know. I wanted to. Do you like it?"

I drew back and gaped at her. "Are you kidding me?"

Relief flickered in her eyes. "Good."

Both of my offices had been furnished by the people I loved. I was a lucky duck.

Evie stepped back and Kyla cleared her throat. "The laptop, it's too much."

Evie's chin stuck out and I grinned at Kyla. "I know that expression. Just say thank you and be done with it."

An elbow jabbed into my ribs and Evie stepped toward Kyla, her face serious. "You've been here for my sister while I wasn't. I know it's your job and all, but I also know I wouldn't have wanted anyone else at her back. So this is just a small way for me to say thank you."

"It's not small to me," Kyla said. "But thank you right back."

We all turned at a knock on the door. I strolled over and opened it. Keigan's eyes widened when he glanced over my shoulder. Evie strode across the room and planted her butt in the chair behind my new desk. I had a feeling someone had filled her in about my newly strained relationship with Keigan, and she'd clearly decided she wasn't going anywhere.

"Hi," I said as the silence stretched awkwardly. "Uh, do you want to come in?"

I opened the door wider and gave Kyla a warning look. She had her claws out and was examining them as if she'd recently chipped her manicure. Meanwhile, Evie was studying Keigan the way a cat would study a mouse.

I sighed, but Keigan didn't look worried. He was too busy glancing around at my new office. I strode toward Kyla and leaned against her desk. Tomorrow was a full moon. Out of all of us, she had the shortest fuse.

A sudden thought occurred to me, and I tensed. "Are you here to tell me I can't rent this office anymore?"

Keigan's eyes widened, and I knew him well enough

to recognize the flicker of hurt before he shuttered his gaze.

"No," he said tightly. "I'd never do that."

I was making things worse. "I'm sorry. It's just… I know you're disappointed in me."

Keigan merely shook his head with a sigh. "I never expected you to be anything other than what you are, Dani."

My heart twisted, both at the weariness in his voice, and the fact that he'd called me Dani again.

"And what am I?"

"You react without thinking when those you love are threatened. Sometimes, the choices you make have consequences that you don't think about until after the fact."

Kyla slid me a look. "I mean, he's not wrong."

I scowled at her, then at Keigan. His lips twitched.

"But, you have a big heart. And as difficult as it's been to lose you to the demons, your life is better for it. When I first met you, you were antisocial, closed-off, and obsessive."

I angled my head. "Please, don't hold back."

He smiled. "And now you're in love, you've repaired your relationship with your sister, you have a new business, and your life is full of people you care about. In spite of my disappointment over some of your actions, I'm still proud of you."

My throat tightened. "Well, thanks."

He took a few steps closer, opening his mouth.

The smell of ozone made me tense.

CRACK

Cellen stood in the middle of my office, unannounced.

Evie shot to her feet, her power flaring through the

room warningly.

"Relax," I said. "He's just here for the counter spell." I'd lost track of time, but I'd been expecting him at some point tonight. Was it midnight already?

Keigan had positioned himself next to me, and he eyed the seelie with what looked like interest. It was easy to forget how little interaction most of the mages had with the other factions—until I saw the wonder in Keigan's eyes.

Cellen merely glanced around my office, then turned back to me dismissively.

"The counter spell," he said.

Kyla reached into her pocket and handed it to him. His nose wrinkled at her as if he'd smelled something filthy and shoved it in his own pocket.

Then he looked at me, and there was nothing but death in his gaze. Keigan lay his hand on my lower back, a silent support, and I stared back at the seelie.

"What is your problem?"

"Simply wondering what all the fuss is about. Why Lucifer would be so desperate to get hold of you that he would kidnap my sister."

I froze. The sister that was missing. If Lucifer had her…

Cellen snapped his mouth shut, but I'd already pulled my Nim Cub.

Kyla lunged in front of me, teeth bared.

Evie jumped onto my desk and launched herself at Cellen, her hands raised as she screamed a spell.

But it was too late.

CRACK.

The world disappeared.

CHAPTER TWENTY-SEVEN

Danica

I slowly got to my feet, dread a ball of poison in my stomach. Kyla was crumpled, unconscious on the ground next to me, while Keigan trembled on my other side.

My gaze found polished leather shoes, traveled up tailored black pants, past a white shirt, and locked onto eyes the exact same shade of green as my own.

All of the spit disappeared from my mouth. I didn't bother attempting to run. Even if I could make it, I'd never leave Keigan and Kyla behind.

The Underking smiled, a vicious, satisfied smile that cut right to the bone, and my heart skipped a beat. There was a hint of my own smile in there, too.

"Hello, granddaughter."

CHAPTER TWENTY-EIGHT

Danica

I took a bite of my dessert. I wasn't sure what it was, but it was rich and sweet.

"More wine, my love?"

I glanced up. Pischiel was watching me with his dark, inscrutable eyes. I smiled at him. "No, thank you."

He reached out and took my hand, playing with the bone bracelet on my wrist.

"This doesn't suit you."

I narrowed my eyes at him. "I like it."

He sent me a slow smile. "I bet I can convince you to remove it."

My cheeks heated and butterflies danced in my stomach at the promise in that smile.

Wrong. This is wrong.

I frowned.

Pischiel squeezed my hand. "Are you okay?"

"Yes. Just… Déjà vu, I guess."

Pischiel glanced at my grandfather, who was deep in discussion with Daimonion. I barely refrained from sneering. I couldn't remember a time when I *hadn't* hated Daimonion. Ever since I was a little girl…

Pain stabbed into my temple and my hand tightened around my spoon. I slowly laid it on the table next to my plate and reached for my water goblet.

My grandfather's concubine sat on his right, her own bracelet gleaming in the candlelight. My chest ached with a strange kind of *want* at the sight of it. Hera smirked at me, and I forced myself to pull my gaze away from the gems, which sparkled with internal fire.

I'd never been particularly avaricious before. I felt like I was losing my mind.

Then I got to my feet. "I think I'll take a walk in the gardens," I said.

"I will walk with you," Pischiel said.

What I wanted was some time alone. My grandfather looked up and met my eyes, sending me an encouraging smile. My lips trembled as I shook my head at him. He'd long hoped that I'd fall in love with Pischiel—was already planning our bondmate ceremony.

The long, midnight blue gown I wore trailed across the ground as I rounded the table. I leaned down and brushed grandfather's cheek with my lips on my way out the door.

"I know what you're doing, you romantic fool," I whispered.

His eyes sparkled as he grinned at me. "Enjoy your walk."

I ignored Daimonion's sneer and nodded at grandfather's other advisors before taking the arm Pischiel held out to me.

We strolled out of the dining room and toward the royal gardens.

I'd placed my hand in the crook of Pischiel's arm and he covered it with his.

"It's a nice night," he said.

"Yes," I smiled, shaking off my weird mood and surveying the beauty of the night-blooming garden. "It is."

The End

Thanks for reading Luck of the Demon! Danica and Samael's story continues in *Demon's Advocate*.
If you'd like to hang out with a fun group of like-minded fans, come check out my reader group on Facebook-Stark Society.

Want to go along for the ride as Danica hunts for the Mistilteinn Dagger? Visit staciastark.com for your free copy of Fool the Demon.

ALSO BY STACIA STARK

The Deals with Demons Series

Speak of the Demon
Dance with the Demon
Inner Demons
Luck of the Demon
Demon's Advocate
Play the Demon

The Bargains with Beasts Series

Unnatural Magic
Unbroken Magic
Unending Magic

The Kingdom of Lies Serie

A Court This Cruel and Lovely
A Kingdom This Cursed and Empty
A Crown This Cold and Heavy
A Queen This Fierce and Deadly